As hard as Alex tried to see, he could not make out anyone among the trees; the Indians blended into the background. Suddenly he felt firm hands on his arms, and when he looked around, he saw that Nadia and he were surrounded.

"Ah-ee-ah," he said tentatively in greeting.

A hand clamped over his mouth, and before he could realize what was happening, he felt himself lifted off the ground by his ankles and upper arms. He started to twist and kick, but the hands did not let go. He felt a sharp blow to his head, whether a fist or a rock he couldn't tell. He thought about Nadia and wondered if she, too, had been taken by force. He seemed to hear his grandmother's voice in the distance, calling him, as the Indians—and he—vanished into the darkness like spirits of the night.

ALSO BY ISABEL ALLENDE

Isabel Allende

City of the Beasts

Translated from the Spanish by
Margaret Sayers Peden

rayo

HarperTrophy®
An Imprint of HarperCollins*Publishers*

Rayo is an imprint of HarperCollins Publishers Inc.

Harper Trophy® is a registered trademark of
HarperCollins Publishers Inc.

City of the Beasts
Library of Congress Cataloging-in-Publication Data
Allende, Isabel.
City of the beasts / by Isabel Allende;
translated from the Spanish by Margaret Sayers Peden.
p. cm.
Summary: When fifteen-year-old Alexander Cold accompanies his indi-
vidualistic grandmother on an expedition to find a beast in the Amazon,
he experiences ancient wonders and a supernatural world as he tries to
avert disaster for the Indians.
ISBN 0-06-050918-X — ISBN 0-06-050917-1 (lib. bdg.)
ISBN 0-06-051195-8 (large print: pbk.)
ISBN 0-06-053503-2 (pbk.) — ISBN 0-06-077645-5 (pbk.)
[1. Adventure and adventurers—Fiction. 2. Supernatural—Fiction. 3.
Amazon River Valley—Fiction. 4. Indians of South America—Amazon
River Valley—Fiction. 5. Grandmothers—Fiction.]
I. Peden, Margaret Sayers. II. Title.
PZ7.A43912 Ci 2002   2002022338
[Fic]—dc21   CIP
                                                                    AC
Typography by Larissa Lawrynenko
❖
First Harper Trophy edition, 2004
Visit us on the World Wide Web!

www.harperchildrens.com

To Alejandro, Andrea, and Nicole,
who asked me for this story

Contents

CHAPTER ONE

The Nightmare

ALEXANDER COLD AWAKENED at dawn, startled by a nightmare. He had been dreaming that an enormous black bird had crashed against the window with a clatter of shattered glass, flown into the house, and carried off his mother. In the dream, he watched helplessly as the gigantic vulture clasped Lisa Cold's clothing in its yellow claws, flew out the same broken window, and disappeared into a sky heavy with dark clouds. What had awakened him was the noise from the storm: wind lashing the trees, rain on the rooftop, and thunder.

He turned on the light with the sensation of being adrift in a boat, and pushed closer to the bulk of the large dog sleeping beside him. He pictured the roaring Pacific Ocean a few blocks from his house, spilling in furious waves against the cliffs. He lay listening to the storm and thinking about the black bird and about his mother, waiting for the pounding in his chest to die down. He was still tangled in the images of his bad dream.

Alexander looked at the clock: six-thirty, time to get up. Outside, it was beginning to get light. He decided that this was going to be a terrible day, one of those days when it's best to stay in bed because everything is going to turn out bad. There had been a lot of days like that since his mother got sick; sometimes the air in the house felt heavy, like being at the bottom of the sea. On those days, the only relief was to escape, to run along the beach with Poncho until he was out of breath. But it had been raining and raining for more than a week—a real deluge—and on top of that, Poncho had been bitten by a deer and didn't want to move. Alex was convinced that he had the dumbest dog in history, the only eighty-pound Labrador ever bitten by a deer. In the four years of his life, Poncho had been attacked by raccoons, the neighbor's cat, and now a deer—not counting the times he had been sprayed by the skunks and they'd had to bathe him in tomato juice to get rid of the smell.

2

Alex got out of bed without disturbing Poncho and got dressed, shivering; the heat came on at six, but it hadn't yet warmed his room, the one at the end of the hall.

At breakfast Alex was not in the mood to applaud his father's efforts at making pancakes. John Cold was not exactly a good cook; the only thing he knew how to do was pancakes, and they always turned out like rubber-tire tortillas. His children didn't want to hurt his feelings, so they pretended to eat them, but anytime he wasn't looking, they spit them out into the garbage pail. They had tried in vain to train Poncho to eat them: the dog was stupid, but not that stupid.

"When's Momma going to get better?" Nicole asked, trying to spear a rubbery pancake with her fork.

"Shut up, Nicole!" Alex replied, tired of hearing his younger sister ask the same question several times a week.

"Momma's going to die," Andrea added.

"Liar! She's not going to die!" shrieked Nicole.

"You two are just kids. You don't know what you're talking about!" Alex exclaimed.

3

"Here, girls. Quiet now. Momma is going to get better," John interrupted, without much conviction.

Alex was angry with his father, his sisters, Poncho, life in general—even with his mother for getting sick. He rushed out of the kitchen, ready to leave without breakfast, but he tripped over the dog in the hallway and sprawled flat.

"Get out of my way, you stupid dog!" he yelled, and Poncho, delighted, gave him a loud slobbery kiss that left Alex's glasses spattered with saliva.

Yes, it was definitely one of those really bad days. Minutes later, his father discovered he had a flat tire on the van, and Alex had to help change it. They lost precious minutes and the three children were late getting to class. In the haste of leaving, Alex forgot his math homework. That did nothing to help his relationship with his teacher, whom Alex considered to be a pathetic little worm whose goal was to make his life miserable. As the last straw, he had also left his flute, and that afternoon he had orchestra practice; he was the soloist and couldn't miss the rehearsal.

★ ★ ★

The flute was the reason Alex had to leave during lunch to go back to the house. The storm had blown over but the sea was still rough and he couldn't take the short way along the beach road because the waves were crashing over the lip of the cliff and flooding the street. He took the long way, running, because he had only forty minutes.

For the last few weeks, ever since his mother got sick, a woman had come to clean, but that morning she had called to say that because of the storm she wouldn't be there. It didn't matter, she wasn't much help and the house was always dirty anyway. Even from outside, you could see the signs; it was as if the whole place was sad. The air of neglect began with the garden and spread through every room of the house, to the farthest corners.

Alex could feel his family coming apart. His sister Andrea, who had always been different from the other girls, was now more Andrea than ever; she was always dressing in costumes, and she wandered lost for hours in her fantasy world, where she imagined witches lurking in the mirrors and aliens swimming in her soup. She was too old for that. At twelve, Alex thought, she should be interested in boys, or piercing her ears. As for Nicole, the youngest in the family, she was collecting a zoo full of animals, as if she wanted to make up for the attention her mother couldn't give her. She was feeding several of the raccoons and skunks that roamed outside the house; she had adopted six orphaned kittens and was keeping them hidden in the garage; she had saved the life of a large bird with a broken wing; and she had a three-foot snake in a box in her room. If her mother found that snake, she would drop dead on the spot, although that wasn't likely, because when she wasn't in the hospital, Lisa spent the day in bed.

Except for their father's pancakes and an occasional tuna-and-mayonnaise sandwich, Andrea's specialty, no one in the family had cooked for months. There was nothing in the refrigerator but orange juice, milk, and ice cream; at night they ordered in pizza or Chinese food. At first it was almost like a party, because each of them ate whenever and what-ever they pleased, mainly sweets, but by now everyone missed the balanced diet of normal times.

Alex had realized during those months how enormous their mother's presence had been and how painful her absence was now. He missed her easy laughter and her affection, even her discipline. She was stricter than his father, and sharper. It was impossible to fool her; she had a third eye and could see the unseeable. They didn't hear her singing in Italian now; he missed her music, her flowers, the once-familiar fragrance of fresh-baked cookies, and the smell of paint. It used to be that his mother could work several hours in her studio, keep the house immaculate, and still welcome her children after school with cookies. Now she barely got out of bed to walk through the rooms with a confused air, as if she didn't recognize anything; she was too thin, and her sunken eyes were circled with shadows. Her canvases, which once were explosions of color, sat forgotten on their easels, and her oils dried in their tubes. Lisa seemed to have shrunk; she was little more than a silent ghost.

Now Alex didn't have anyone to scratch his back, or brighten his spirits when he got up feeling depressed. His father wasn't one for spoiling children. Besides, John had changed, like everyone else in the family. He wasn't the calm person he once had been. He was often cross, not only with his children but with his wife, too. Sometimes he shouted at Lisa because she wasn't eating enough or taking her medicine, but immediately he would feel terrible about his outburst and ask her to forgive him. Those scenes left Alex trembling; he couldn't bear to see his mother so weak and his father with tears in his eyes.

When Alex got home that noontime, he was surprised to see his father's van; at this hour he was usually at the clinic. He went in through the kitchen door, which was always unlocked, intending to get something to eat, pick up his flute, and shoot back to school. He looked around, but all he found were the fossilized remains of last night's pizza. Resigned to going hungry, he went to the refrigerator to get a glass of milk. That was when he heard the crying. At first he thought it was Nicole's kittens in the garage, but then he realized that the sound was coming from his parents' bedroom. Not meaning to spy, almost without thinking, he walked down the hall to their room and gently pushed the partly opened door. He was petrified by what he saw.

In the center of the room was his mother, barefoot and in her nightgown, sitting on a small stool with her face in her hands, crying. His father, standing behind her, was holding an old straight razor that had belonged to Alex's grandfather. Long clumps of black hair littered the floor and clung to his mother's fragile shoulders, and her naked skull gleamed like marble in the pale light filtering through the window.

For a few seconds, Alex stood frozen, stupefied, not taking in what he saw: the hair on the floor, the shaved head, the knife in his father's hand only inches from his mother's neck. When he came to his senses, a terrible cry rose up from his very toes and a wave of madness washed over him. He threw himself on John, pushing him to the floor. The razor traced an arc through the air, brushed past Alex's forehead, and landed point first in the floorboards. His mother began to call Alex's name, tugging at his clothing to pull him away as he blindly pounded on his father, not seeing where the blows landed.

"It's all right, son! Calm down, it's nothing," Lisa begged, weakly trying to hold Alex as his father protected his head with his arms.

Finally his mother's voice penetrated Alex's consciousness and his anger dissolved in a flash, giving way to confusion and horror at what he had done. He got to his feet and staggered back, then ran out as fast as he could and locked himself in his room. He dragged his desk in front of the door to block it, and covered his ears to keep from hearing his parents calling him. For a long time, he leaned against the wall with his eyes closed, trying to control the hurricane of feelings that shook him to his marrow. Then, systematically, he set about destroying everything in his room. He pulled the posters from the walls and tore them to bits; he swung his baseball bat at pictures and videos; he crushed his collection of antique automobiles, and airplanes from World War I; he ripped pages from his books; he gutted his mattress and pillows with his Swiss Army knife; he slashed all his clothes and bedding; and as a final touch he kicked and stomped on his lamp until it was in pieces. He carried out this destruction deliberately, methodically, in silence, like someone performing a necessary task, and stopped only when his strength was spent and there was nothing else to break. The floor was covered with feathers and mattress stuffing, broken glass, papers, rags, and pieces of toys. Weak from emotion and effort, he threw himself down in the midst of that devastation, curled up like a snail, his head touching his knees, and cried until he fell asleep.

Alexander woke up hours later to the voices of his sisters. It was a few minutes before he remembered what had happened. He wanted to turn on his light, but he had wrecked the lamp. He felt his way to the door, tripped, and cursed when he fell on some pieces of glass and cut his hand. He didn't remember that he had to move his desk so he could open the door. The light from the hall fell on the battlefield that had been his room, and on the astonished faces of his sisters in the open doorway.

"Are you redecorating your room, Alex?" his sister Andrea joked, while Nicole clamped her hand over her mouth to choke back her laughter.

Alex slammed the door in their faces and sat

11

down on the floor to think, pressing hard on his cut hand. The idea of bleeding to death seemed tempting; at least that would save him from having to face his parents about what he'd done, but he soon changed his mind. He needed to wash the cut before it got infected, he decided. Besides, it was beginning to hurt; it must be pretty deep, he might get tetanus . . . He fumbled his way out into the hall. He could barely see because he had lost his glasses in the disaster area and, on top of that, his eyes were swollen from crying. He went into the kitchen, where all his family was gathered, including his mother, who had a kerchief tied around her head that made her look like a refugee.

"I'm sorry," Alex blurted out, his eyes on the floor.

Lisa stifled a cry when she saw her son's bloodstained T-shirt, but when her husband gave her a sign, she took her two girls by the hand and led them away without a word. John went over to Alex to check his injured hand.

"I don't know what came over me, Dad," he murmured, not daring to look up.

"I'm really afraid, too, son."

"Is Mom going to die?" asked Alex, in a voice as thin as a thread.

"I don't know, Alexander. Here, let this cold water run over your hand," his father directed.

John washed off the blood, examined the cut, and decided to inject an anesthetic so he could pick out the glass fragments and stitch the wound. Alex, who felt weak just at the sight of blood, bore the procedure without a word, grateful for having a doctor in the family. Then his father applied a disinfectant cream, and bandaged his hand.

"Mom's hair was going to fall out anyway, wasn't it?" Alex asked.

"Yes, because of the chemotherapy. It's better to cut it all at once than watch it come out by the handful. That's the least of it, son. It will grow back. Sit down, we need to talk."

"I'm sorry, Dad. I'll work hard to replace everything I broke."

"It's all right. I suppose you had to get it out of your system. We won't mention this again. There are other things, more important things, I need to tell you. I have to take Lisa to a hospital in Texas, where she's going to undergo a long and complicated treatment. It's the only

13

place it can be done."

"And will that make her well?" Alex asked anxiously.

"I hope so, Alexander. I will go with her, of course. We'll have to close this house for a while."

"What will happen to the girls and me?"

"Andrea and Nicole will go live with their grandmother Carla. You are going to go to my mother," his father explained.

"Kate? I don't want to go to her, Dad! Why can't I go with my sisters? At least grand-mother Carla knows how to cook."

"Three children would be too much for her."

"I'm fifteen, Dad, and that's plenty old for you to at least ask my opinion. It isn't fair for you to ship me off to Kate as if I were some package or something. That's always how it is. You make the decisions and I have to follow them. I'm not a baby anymore!" Alex protested. He was furious.

"Well, sometimes you act like one." John smiled and pointed to the injured hand.

"It was an accident, it could have happened to anyone. I'll behave at Carla's, I promise."

"I know your intentions are good, son, but sometimes you act without thinking."

"I told you, I'll pay for everything I broke," yelled Alex, banging a fist on the table.

"You see how you can't control your temper? In any case, Alex, this has nothing to do with what you did to your room. Things were already arranged with Lisa's mother and mine. The three of you will have to go stay with your grandmothers; there's no other solution. You'll be leaving for New York in a couple of days," his father said.

"Alone?"

"Alone. I'm afraid that from here on you will have to do a lot of things alone. Take your passport, because I think you're going on an adventure with my mother."

"Where?"

"To the Amazon."

"The Amazon!" Alex exclaimed, horrified. "I saw a documentary about the Amazon. That place is crawling with mosquitoes and caimans and bandits. There are a zillion diseases there—even leprosy!"

"I expect that my mother knows what she's doing; she wouldn't take you anywhere you'd

15

be in danger, Alexander."

"Kate is quite capable of pushing me into a river filled with piranhas," Alex blurted out. "With a grandmother like mine, I don't need enemies."

"I'm sorry, but you will have to go, son."

"And what about school? It's exam time. And besides, I can't just walk out on the orchestra—"

"You're going to have to be flexible, Alexander. Our family is going through a real crisis. In the Chinese language, do you know what the characters for 'crisis' are? 'Danger' plus 'opportunity.' Maybe your mother's illness will offer you an extraordinary opportunity. You'd better go pack your things."

"What's to pack? I don't *have* anything much," Alex muttered.

"Then take what you have. Now go give your mother a kiss. She's very shaken by all she's going through. It's much more difficult for Lisa than for any of us, Alexander. We have to be strong, the way she is," John said sadly.

Up until a couple of months ago, Alex had been happy. He had never felt any great curiosity to explore beyond the safe boundaries of his own existence; he believed that if he didn't do anything silly, everything would work out fine. He had simple plans for the future. He planned to be a famous musician, like his grandfather Joseph Cold, marry Cecilia Burns, if she would accept him, have two children, and live near the mountains. He was satisfied with his young life. He was a good student and, if not outstanding, he was good at sports; he was friendly, and he never got into serious trouble. He thought of himself as a pretty normal person, at least in comparison with the freaks you find in this world, like those kids who went into that school in Colorado and machine-gunned their classmates. He wouldn't have to look too far in his own school to find some scary types. But no, he wasn't like them. Truth was, the only thing he wanted was to go back to the kind of life he'd had a few months before, when his mother was well. He didn't want to go to the Amazon with Kate. He was a little afraid of his grandmother.

Two days later, Alex said good-bye to the place where he had spent the fifteen years of his life. He carried with him the image of his mother in the doorway of their home, a cap covering her shaved head, smiling and waving good-bye as tears ran down her cheeks. She looked small, vulnerable, and beautiful despite everything. He boarded the plane thinking about her and about the terrifying possibility of losing her. No! I won't think about that, I have to have positive thoughts. My mother will get well, he murmured over and over during the long flight.

CHAPTER TWO

The Eccentric Grandmother

ALEXANDER FOUND HIMSELF in a New York airport in the midst of a crowd with suitcases and bundles, pushing by him, shoving and stepping on his heels. They looked like robots, half of them with a cell phone clamped to one ear and talking into the air like crazy people. He was alone, his backpack slung over his shoulder and a wrinkled twenty-dollar bill in his hand. He had another three folded and stuck down in his boots. His father had cautioned him to be careful; in that huge city, things were not the way they were in the small town on the California coast where they lived, where nothing ever happened. The three Cold children had grown up playing outside with the other kids; they knew everyone, and went in and out of their neighbors' homes as if they were their own.

Alex had traveled six hours, crossing the continent from one end to the other, seated beside a large, sweaty man whose girth spilled outside his seat, cutting Alex's space in half. Every other minute, the man reached down, with difficulty, fished something out of a bag of treats, and proceeded to chomp away, ending any chance for Alex to sleep or watch the movie in peace. Alex was very tired, and he kept counting how many hours were left of that torture, until finally they landed and he could stretch his legs. He got off the plane with relief, looking for his grandmother, but he didn't find her at the gate as he had expected.

One hour later, Kate still hadn't arrived, and Alex was beginning to worry for real. He had his grandmother paged twice, with no response, and now he was forced to get change in order to make a telephone call. He was grateful for his good memory; he remembered the number, just as he remembered her address. He had never been to Kate's house, but he had written her postcards from time to time. His grandmother's telephone rang and rang as he sent a mental plea for someone to answer. What do I do now? he wondered with confusion. It occurred to him to call his father long distance and get instructions about what to do, but that could be expensive. Besides, he didn't want to act like a big baby. What could his father do from so far away? No, Alex decided, he couldn't lose his head just because his grandmother was a little late; maybe she was tied up in traffic, or was wandering around the airport looking for him and they had passed each other without noticing.

Another thirty minutes passed, and by then Alex was so angry with Kate that if she had been standing in front of him, he would surely have said something rude. He remembered all the heavy-handed jokes she had played on him over the years, like the box of chocolates filled with hot-pepper sauce she had sent him one birthday. No normal grandmother would have taken the trouble to remove the fillings of each piece of candy with a syringe and replace it with Tabasco, wrap the chocolates back in silver paper, and arrange them in the box—just to play a joke on her grandchildren.

He also remembered the scary stories she had terrified them with when she came to visit, and how she insisted on telling them with the lights off. Her stories wouldn't have the same effect now, but when they were young, they had almost died of fright. His sisters still had nightmares about the vampires and zombies that escaped from their tombs when the children's wicked grandmother summoned them in the dark. He had to admit, though, that they were all addicted to her bloodcurdling tales. They never got tired of hearing her tell about the real—or imaginary—dangers she had confronted on her travels around the world. His favorite was the twenty-four-foot python in Malaysia that had swallowed her camera. "Too bad it didn't swallow you, Grandmother," Alex had commented the first time he'd heard the tale, but she wasn't offended. This same woman had taught him to swim in less than five minutes by pushing him into a pool when he was four years old. He swam to the other side out of pure desperation, but he could have drowned. His mother, with good reason, got very nervous when her mother-in-law came to visit; she had to watch closely to keep her children safe.

After another hour and a half had gone by,

Alex really did not know what to do. He could imagine how pleased Kate would be to see him so worried, and decided not to give her that satisfaction. He must act like a man. He put on his jacket, slung on his backpack, and went outside. The contrast between the heat, the racket, and the bright light inside the building, and the cold, the silence, and the darkness outside shocked him. He had no idea that wintertime in New York was so unpleasant. It was damp and smelled of gasoline; there was filthy snow on the sidewalk and an icy wind that stung his face like needles. He realized that in the emotion of telling his family good-bye, he had forgotten to bring his gloves and cap, which he had no use for in California and kept in a trunk in the garage with the rest of his ski equipment. The wound in his left hand was throbbing, though up until then it hadn't bothered him, and he told himself he would have to change the bandage as soon as he got to his grandmother's. He had no way to estimate how far her apartment was or how much it would cost to get there by taxi. He needed a map but didn't know where to get one. With his ears like ice and his hands jammed into his pockets, he walked to a bus stop.

"Hello. Are you by yourself?" a girl walked up to him and asked.

She had a canvas bag over her shoulder and was wearing a hat pulled down to her eyebrows, blue fingernail polish, and a silver ring in her nostril. Alex stared at her in wonder; she was almost as pretty as his secret love, Cecilia Burns, despite looking half starved and more than a little dirty in her ragged jeans and combat boots. Her only wrap was a short jacket of orange artificial fur that barely came to her waist. She didn't have gloves. Alex mumbled some vague reply. His father had warned him not to talk to strangers, but this girl couldn't be dangerous, she was only a couple of years older than he was, at the most, and almost as thin and short as his mother. To tell the truth, standing beside her, Alex felt strong.

"Where're you going?" the stranger pressed on, lighting a cigarette.

"To my grandmother's. She lives at Fourteenth Street and Second Avenue. Do you know how I can get there?" Alex inquired.

"Sure. I'm going the same way. We can take

24

the bus. My name's Morgana," the girl informed Alex.

"I've never heard that name," said Alex.

"I chose it myself. My stupid mother gave me a name as obnoxious as she is. And what's yours?" she asked, blowing smoke in his face.

"Alexander Cold. They call me Alex," he replied, a little shocked to hear her talk about her family that way.

They waited by the curb, stamping their feet in the snow to keep warm. Morgana used that ten minutes to give Alex a brief rundown of her life: she hadn't gone to school in years—school was for jerks—and she had run away from home because she couldn't stand her stepfather, who was a disgusting pig.

"I'm going to play in a rock band, that's my dream," she added. "All I need is an electric guitar. What's in that case you have tied to your backpack?"

"A flute."

"Electric?"

"No, it runs on batteries," Alex joked.

Just when his ears were turning to ice cubes, a bus drove up and they got on. Alex paid his fare and took his ticket, while Morgana dug through one pocket of her orange jacket, and then the other one.

"My wallet! I think s-someone took it," she stammered.

"Sorry, kid. You'll have to get off," the driver ordered.

"It isn't my fault someone robbed me!" she said, almost shouting, to the mortification of Alex, who hated scenes.

"And it's not my fault either. Go tell the police," the driver said coldly.

The girl opened her canvas bag and dumped everything on the floor of the aisle: clothing, cosmetics, French fries, assorted boxes and packets, and some high-heeled shoes that must have belonged to someone else—it was difficult to imagine her in them. She checked every article of clothing with maddening slowness, turning clothes upside down, opening every box and every wrapping, shaking out her underwear in front of everyone. Alex looked the other way, more and more upset. He didn't want people to think he and this girl were together.

"I can't wait all night, kid. You'll have to get

26

off," the driver repeated, and this time his tone was threatening.

Morgana ignored him. By then she had taken off the orange jacket and was feeling around the lining, while the other passengers on the bus began to complain about the delay.

"Lend me some money," she demanded finally, turning to Alex.

Alex felt the ice melt from his ears, and imagined them turning red; that always happened in moments of high emotion. The ears were his cross; they always betrayed him, especially when he was with Cecilia Burns, the girl he had loved since kindergarten without the slightest hope of its being returned. Alex had concluded that there was no reason for Cecilia to notice him, since she could have her pick of the best athletes in the school. There was nothing special about him; his only talents were climbing mountains and playing the flute, but no girl with an ounce of sense was going to be interested in hills and flutes. He was condemned to love her in silence for the rest of his life, unless some miracle occurred.

"Lend me the money for my fare," Morgana repeated.

Under normal circumstances, Alex didn't mind losing money, but, at that moment, he wasn't in any position to be generous. On the other hand, he decided, no man can abandon a woman in a jam. He had enough to help her without having to fall back on the money in his boots. He paid for the second ticket. Morgana blew him a mocking kiss, stuck out her tongue at the driver, who gave her a dirty look, quickly scooped up her belongings, and followed Alex to the last row in the bus, where they sat down together.

"You saved my butt. As soon as I can, I'll pay you back," she assured him.

Alex didn't answer. He had a principle: if you lend money and never see the person again, that's money well spent. Morgana aroused mixed feelings of fascination and repulsion in him; she was completely different from any of the girls in his school, even the most daring. To keep from staring at her with his jaw hanging open like a ninny, he spent most of the long ride in silence, his eyes fixed on the dark window where Morgana's face was reflected beside his: black hair like his mother's, thin face, round eyeglasses. When would he ever start shaving? He hadn't developed like some of his friends; he was still just a beardless kid, one of the shortest in his class. Even Cecilia Burns was taller than he was. His one advantage was that, unlike the other adolescents in his school, he had good skin, because as soon as a zit appeared, his father injected it with cortisone. His mother kept telling him not to worry, that some grow early and some later. All the men in the Cold family were tall, but he knew that it's a matter of luck what genes you inherit, and he might very well favor his mother's family instead. Lisa was short even for a woman; seen from behind she could pass for a girl of fourteen, especially since her illness had turned her into a skeleton. When he thought about his mother, he felt as if something was squeezing his chest and cutting off his air, as if a gigantic fist had him by the throat.

Morgana had taken off her orange jacket. Beneath it, she was wearing a short black-lace blouse that left her midriff bare, and a leather necklace with metal studs, something like a dog collar. "I'm dying for a joint," she said. Alex pointed to the sign that said smoking was prohibited on the bus. She looked all around her. No one was paying any attention. There were several empty seats around them and the other passengers were reading or dozing. When she saw that no one was looking at them, she put her hand in her blouse and pulled out a filthy pouch. She elbowed Alex in the ribs and waved the pouch in his face.

"Grass," she murmured.

Alex shook his head. He didn't think of himself as a puritan, not at all. He had tried marijuana and alcohol several times, like almost all his high-school classmates, but he couldn't understand their attraction—except for the fact that they were forbidden. He didn't like to lose control. In mountain climbing, he had developed a taste for the thrill of controlling his body and mind. He was exhausted when he got home from those excursions with his father, hurting all over, and hungry, but absolutely happy, filled with energy, proud of having once again conquered his fear and the obstacles of the mountain. He felt electrified, powerful, almost invincible. On those occasions, his father would give him a friendly clap on the back as a kind of prize for his accomplishments, but he never said anything that would feed Alex's pride. John wasn't a person for flattery. It took a lot to win a word of praise from him, but his son never expected it. That manly clap on the back was enough.

Imitating his father, Alex had learned to do his best to fulfill his obligations without bragging, but secretly he took pride in the three virtues he thought he possessed: the courage to climb mountains, a talent for the flute, and a clear head for thinking. It was more difficult to analyze his defects, although he realized he had at least two he should try to improve, things his mother had pointed out to him more than once: his skepticism, which made him question almost everything, and his bad temper, which caused him to explode when least expected. That was something new because only a few months earlier he had been easygoing and always in a good humor. In any case, Morgana's offer held no charm for him. The times he had tried pot he hadn't felt as if he were flying to paradise, as some of his friends said they did, but that his head was filled with smoke and his legs as weak as cotton wool. For him there was no greater stimulation than swinging on a rope at three hundred feet, knowing exactly the next move to take. No, drugs weren't for him. Cigarettes either, because he needed healthy lungs for climbing and for his flute. He couldn't help smiling when he thought of how his grandmother Kate had short-circuited any temptation to use tobacco when he was eleven years old. Even though his father had given him the sermon about lung cancer and the other consequences of nicotine, he had sneaked smokes with his friends behind the gym. Kate had come to spend Christmas with them, and her bloodhound nose had quickly sniffed out the telltale odor, despite the chewing gum and cologne Alex used to disguise it.

"Smoking so young, Alexander?" Kate asked pleasantly. He tried to deny it, but she didn't give him a chance. "Come on, we're going for a little drive," she said.

Alexander got into the car, fastened his seat belt tight, and muttered a good-luck prayer, because his grandmother was a terrorist at the wheel. Using the excuse that no one had a car in New York, she drove as if carjackers were on her tail. She took Alex, lurching and braking, to the supermarket, where she bought four large cigars of black tobacco, then drove to a quiet street, parked far away from prying eyes, and proceeded to light one stogie after another. They puffed and puffed, with doors and windows closed, until the smoke was too thick to see through the windows. Alex's head was spinning and his stomach doing flip-flops. After a while he couldn't take it anymore; he opened the car door and dropped into the street like a sack of flour, deathly sick. Smiling, his grandmother waited as he vomited his guts out—not offering to hold his forehead and console him as his mother would have done—and then lighted another cigar and handed it to him.

"Come on, Alexander, prove to me that you're a man, smoke this one," she challenged him, highly entertained.

He had to stay in bed for the next two days, as green as a lizard and convinced that he would die of nausea and the pain in his head. His father thought he had a virus, and his mother immediately suspected her mother-in-law but didn't dare accuse her of poisoning her only grandson. From then on, the idea of smoking, so popular among his friends, turned Alex's stomach.

"This is the very best weed," Morgana insisted, referring to the contents of her little pouch. "I have this, too, if you prefer," she added, displaying two small white tablets in the palm of her hand.

Again Alex concentrated his gaze on the bus window, not answering. He knew from experience that the best choice was either to say nothing or change the subject. Anything he said was going to sound stupid, and the girl would think he was a baby, or some kind of religious fundamentalist. Morgana shrugged and put her treasures away for a more appropriate time. They were approaching the midtown bus station, and would have to get off there.

At that hour, the traffic and the number of people in the street still hadn't thinned, and although offices and businesses had closed, the bars, theaters, coffee shops, and restaurants were open. Alex could not see the faces of the people he met, just hunched-over figures bundled in overcoats and walking fast. He saw

34

shapeless lumps beside sidewalk grates billowing columns of steam. He realized that those "lumps" were homeless people huddled together beside the heat ducts from the buildings, their only source of warmth in that wintry night.

The harsh neon signs and car headlights made the wet, dirty streets look unreal. There were mounds of black plastic bags on the street corners, some torn, with garbage spilling out. A beggar wrapped in a ragged overcoat was poking through the bags with a stick as she muttered some endless litany in an invented language. Alex had to jump aside to avoid stepping on a rat with a bloody, bitten tail; it had planted itself in the middle of the sidewalk and refused to move as the people went by. Horns, police sirens, and the occasional wail of an ambulance filled the air. A very tall and ungainly young man went past shouting that the world was coming to an end; he thrust a wrinkled sheet of paper into their hands that featured a half-naked, pouty-lipped blonde advertising massages. Someone on skates, with a Walkman plugged in his ears, ran into Alex, slamming him against a wall. "Look where you're going, moron!" the aggressor shouted.

Alex could feel the wound in his hand beginning to throb again. He felt as if he were trapped in a sci-fi nightmare, in a terrifying megalopolis of cement, steel, glass, pollution, and loneliness. A wave of nostalgia washed over him for the town beside the sea where he had spent his lifetime. That tranquil, boring place he had so often wanted to escape from now looked wonderful. Morgana interrupted his mournful musings.

"I'm starving. Could we get a bite to eat?" she asked.

Alex tried to excuse himself. "It's really late, I need to get to my grandmother's."

"Chill, man. I'm going to get you to your grandmother's. We're almost there, but it would do us good to get something in our stomachs," she insisted.

Without giving him a chance to protest, she dragged him by the arm into a noisy hole-in-the-wall that reeked of beer, rancid coffee, and fried food. Behind a long Formica counter, a couple of Asian waiters were handing out plates of greasy noodles. Morgana climbed onto a stool at the counter and studied the chalkboard menu on the wall. Alex realized that he was going to have to pay for the meal, so he went to the men's room to get out the money he had hidden in his boots.

The walls of the rest room were covered with four-letter words and obscene drawings. There were crumpled paper towels on the floor and puddles of water that had dripped from the rusted pipes. He went into a stall, shot the bolt, set his backpack on the floor, and, overcoming his distaste, sat on the toilet to take off his boots, a task that was none too easy with a bandaged hand in that cramped space. He thought about germs, and all the diseases his father had told him he could contract in a public rest room. And he had to watch what he spent.

He counted his money with a sigh. He wouldn't order anything, and he hoped Morgana would be happy with something that didn't cost very much; she didn't look like she ate a lot. Until he was safe in Kate's apartment, those three folded and refolded bills were all the money he had in the world; they represented the difference between salvation and dying of hunger and cold, in the street, like the beggars he'd seen a few minutes before. If he couldn't find his grandmother's address, he could always go back to the airport, curl up in a corner for the night, and fly back home the next day—at least he had a return ticket. He put his boots back on, stuck the money in a compartment in his pack, and left the stall. There was no one else in the bathroom. As he passed the washbasin, he set his backpack on the floor, adjusted the bandage on his left hand, and meticulously washed his right hand with soap. He splashed enough water on his face to pep him up a little, and then dried it with a paper towel. As he bent down to pick up his backpack, he realized with horror that it was gone.

He ran out of the men's room like a shot, his heart galloping. The theft had happened in less than a minute, the thief could not be far; if he hurried, he might catch him before he lost him in the crowded street. Nothing had changed in the restaurant: the same sweating employees behind the counter, the same indifferent customers, the same greasy food, the same sounds of dishes and rock music at full volume. No one noticed his alarm, no one turned to look when he yelled that he had been robbed. The only difference was that Morgana was not at the counter where he had left her. There was no trace of her.

Alex guessed in an instant who had quietly followed him, who had waited just outside the door, calculating her opportunity, who had grabbed his backpack in the blink of an eye. He clapped a hand to his forehead. How could he have been so naive! Morgana had foxed him as easily as if he were a two-year-old, making off with everything he had except the clothes on his back. He had lost his money, his return plane ticket, even his precious flute. The only thing he had left was his passport, which by chance he had put in his jacket pocket. It took all his strength not to bawl like a baby.

CHAPTER THREE

The Abominable Jungleman

KATE LIKED TO SAY, "Where there's a will, there's a way." Her work obliged her to travel to remote places where she surely had put that saying into practice many times. Alex was rather shy; it was hard for him to go up to a stranger to ask anything, but there was no other way. As soon as he had calmed down a little and could talk, he went over to a man chewing a hamburger and asked him how to get to Fourteenth Street and Second Avenue. The man shrugged his shoulders without answering. Feeling insulted, Alex could tell he was turning red. He hesitated a few minutes but finally went up to one of the waiters behind the counter. The man pointed his carving knife in some vague direction, and shouted instructions over the roar in the restaurant, in an accent so thick that Alex didn't understand a word. He decided to use logic: he needed to find out what direction Second Avenue was and then count the streets. Simple. But it didn't seem quite so simple when he found out that he was on Forty-Second Street at Eighth Avenue and figured how far he had to go in that icy cold. He was grateful for his training in mountain climbing; if he could rock climb for six hours, like a fly, he could certainly walk a few blocks on level ground. He zipped up his jacket, tucked his head down between his shoulders, put his hands in his pockets, and started walking.

It was after midnight and beginning to snow when Alex reached the street his grandmother lived on. The neighborhood looked run-down, dirty, and ugly; there wasn't a tree in sight and it had been some time since he had seen a human being. He thought only someone as desperate as he was would be walking through the dangerous streets of New York City at that hour. The only thing that had saved him from being mugged was that no criminal in his right mind would want to be out in this cold. His grandmother's building was a gray tower in the middle of many other identical towers surrounded by security fences. He rang the bell and immediately the harsh, hoarse voice of Kate answered, asking who it was who had the nerve to bother her at that hour of the night. Alex could tell she had been waiting for him, although of course she would never admit it. He was frozen through and through, and never in his life had he needed so much to throw himself into someone's arms, but when the elevator door finally opened onto the eleventh floor and he was standing before his grandmother, he was determined not to let her see his weakness.

"Hello, Grandmother," he said as clearly as he could, given the way his teeth were chattering.

"I've told you not to call me Grandmother!" she scolded.

"Hi, Kate."

"You took your time getting here, Alexander."

"I thought we agreed that you were going to pick me up at the airport," he replied, struggling to hold back the tears.

"We didn't agree to anything. If you're not capable of getting from the airport to my house, you certainly aren't capable of going into the jungle with me," said Kate. "Take off your jacket and boots. I'll give you a cup of hot chocolate and draw a warm bath for you, but you can be sure I'm doing it only to keep you from getting pneumonia. You have to be healthy for the trip. Don't expect me to pamper you in the future. Understand?"

"I have never expected you to pamper me," Alex replied.

"What did you do to your hand?" Kate asked when she saw the soaked bandage.

"That's a long story."

Kate's small apartment was dark, crowded, and chaotic. Two windows—the panes were filthy—looked out on a light shaft, and a third faced a brick wall and a fire escape. He saw suitcases, knapsacks, bundles, and boxes in all the corners. Books, newspapers, and magazines were piled on tables. There were human skulls she had brought from Tibet, bows and arrows from African pygmies, funeral vessels from the Atacama Desert, petrified scarabs from Egypt, and a thousand other objects. A long snakeskin stretched the length of one wall. It had belonged to the famous python that had swallowed Kate's camera in Malaysia.

Until that moment, Alex had never seen his grandmother in her own surroundings, and he had to admit that now, seeing her among her things, she was much more interesting. Kate was sixty-four years old, thin and muscular—pure fiber, and skin like leather from spending so much time outdoors. Her blue eyes, which had seen a lot of the world, were as sharp as daggers' points. Her gray hair, which she herself cut without looking in the mirror, stood out in every direction, as if it had never been combed. She was proud of her teeth, large and strong enough to crack walnuts and pop bottle caps. She was also proud that she had never broken a bone, never seen a doctor, and had survived everything from malaria to scorpion bites. She drank straight vodka and smoked black tobacco in a sailor's pipe. Winter and summer she wore the same baggy trousers and a sleeveless jacket covered with pockets in which she carried everything she needed to survive in case of a disaster. On the rare occasions when she needed to get dressed up, she took off the vest and put on a necklace of bear's teeth, the gift of an Apache chieftain.

Lisa, Alex's mother, was afraid of Kate, but

the children eagerly awaited her visits. This outlandish grandmother, the protagonist of incredible adventures, brought them word of places so exotic it was hard to imagine them. The three grandchildren collected the stories of her journeys that had been published in various magazines and newspapers, and the postcards and photographs she sent them from the four corners of the globe. Although her grandchildren were sometimes embarrassed to introduce her to their friends, deep down they were proud that a member of their family was almost a celebrity.

A half hour later, Alex had warmed up with his hot bath and, swaddled in a bathrobe and wool socks, was devouring meatballs and mashed potatoes, one of the few things he liked to eat and the only thing Kate knew how to cook. "These are leftovers from yesterday," she said, but Alex suspected she had prepared them especially for him. He did not want to tell about his adventure with Morgana and look like a yokel, but he had to admit that everything he had brought with him had been stolen.

"I suppose you're going to tell me to learn

not to trust anyone," he mumbled, blushing.

"On the contrary, I was going to tell you to learn to trust yourself. You see, Alexander, in spite of everything, you got here to my apartment without problems."

"Without problems? I almost froze to death on the way. They could have discovered my corpse in the spring thaw," he replied.

"'A journey of a thousand miles begins with a single step.' What about your passport?" Kate inquired.

"It's safe because I had it in my pocket."

"Tape it to your chest with adhesive, because if you lose that, you've had it."

"What I hate most is that I lost my flute," Alex commented.

"Well, I will have to give you your grandfather's flute. I meant to keep it until you showed some talent, but I suppose it's better in your hands than just lying around here."

She searched through the shelves that covered the walls of her apartment from floor to ceiling, and handed him a case covered with thick black dust.

"Here, Alexander. Your grandfather played this for forty years. Take care of it."

The case held the flute of Joseph Cold, "the most celebrated flutist of the century," as the critics had written when he died. "It would have been better if they'd said that while poor Joseph was alive," was Kate's comment when she read the notices in the newspaper. They had been divorced for thirty years, but in his will Joseph left half of everything he had to his ex-wife, including his best flute, which his grandson now held in his hands. Alex opened the worn leather case with reverence, and stroked the flute; it was beautiful. He picked it up and delicately placed it to his lips. When he blew, the notes escaped from the instrument with such beauty that he himself was surprised. It sounded very different from the flute Morgana had stolen from him.

Kate gave her grandson time to inspect the instrument and to thank her profusely, as she expected, then handed him a big yellow book with a loose binding: *Health Tips for the Adventurous Traveler*. Alex opened it at random and read the symptoms of a deadly illness acquired by eating the brain of one's ancestors.

"I don't eat organ meats," he said.

"You never know what people put in meatballs," was his grandmother's response.

Startled, Alex looked suspiciously at the last bites on his plate. With Kate, you had to be very cautious. It was dangerous having an ancestor like her.

"Tomorrow you will have to be vaccinated against half a dozen tropical diseases. Let me see that hand; you can't travel with an infection."

She examined it roughly, decided that her son John had done a good job, poured half a bottle of disinfectant over the wound—just in case—and announced that tomorrow she herself would remove the stitches. It was easy, she said, anyone could do it. Alex shuddered. His grandmother was nearsighted and used scratched glasses she'd bought secondhand in a market in Guatemala. While she put on a new bandage, Kate explained that the *International Geographic* had financed an expedition to the heart of the Amazon jungle, on the border between Brazil and Venezuela, to look for a gigantic, possibly humanoid, creature that had been seen a number of times in that area.

Enormous tracks had been found, and people who had sighted it said that this animal—or primitive human being—was taller than a bear, had very long arms, and was covered with black hair—like the Yeti of the Himalayas, except that this one lived in the middle of the jungle.

"Maybe it's a monkey—" Alex suggested.

"Did it occur to you that someone might have thought of that possibility?" his grandmother said, cutting him off.

"But they don't have proof that it actually exists," Alex ventured.

"We don't have a birth certificate for the Beast, Alexander. Oh. An important detail. They say it leaves an odor so strong that animals and people in the vicinity faint or are paralyzed."

"If people faint, then no one's seen it."

"Exactly, but by its tracks they know it walks on two feet. And doesn't wear shoes, in case that's your next question."

"No, Kate. My next question is whether it wears a hat!" her grandson exploded.

"I don't think so."

"Is it dangerous?"

"No, Alexander. It's extremely mellow. It doesn't steal, doesn't kidnap children, and never destroys private property. It just kills. And kills cleanly, without any noise. It breaks the bones of its victims, and then guts them with true elegance, like a professional," his grandmother joked.

"How many people has it killed?" Alex inquired, feeling more and more uneasy.

"Not many, when you take into account how overpopulated the world is."

"How *many*, Kate!"

"Several gold prospectors, a couple of soldiers, a salesman here and there. The exact number isn't known."

"Has it killed any Indians? How many?" Alex persisted.

"They don't know, really. The Indians don't count past two. Besides, to them death is relative. If they thought someone had stolen their soul, or walked over their tracks, or taken control of their dreams, for example, that would be worse than being dead. Someone who is dead, however, can go on living in spirit."

"That's complicated," said Alexander, who did not believe in spirits.

"Whoever told you life is simple?"

Kate explained that the expedition was being led by a famous anthropologist, Professor Ludovic Leblanc, who had spent years investigating the trail of the so-called Yeti, or Abominable Snowman, on the border between China and Tibet, without finding him. He had also worked among a tribe of Indians in the Amazon, and made the claim that they were the most savage on the planet; when least expected, they ate their prisoners. This information was not soothing, Kate admitted. Their guide would be a Brazilian by the name of César Santos, who had spent his life in that region and had good relations with the Indians. He owned an airplane that was pretty beat up but still operating, and he planned to use it to fly them into Indian territory.

"In school we studied the Amazon in an ecology class," commented Alex, whose eyes were getting very heavy.

"Well! No doubt that one class will suffice!" Kate said sarcastically. And added, "I suppose you're tired. You can sleep on the sofa and tomorrow, early, start working for me."

"What do I have to do?"

"Whatever I tell you. For right now, I'm telling you to go to bed."

"Good night, Kate," murmured Alex, curling up on the sofa cushions.

"Bah!" his grandmother grumbled. But she waited until he fell asleep and then pulled a couple of blankets over him.

CHAPTER FOUR

The Amazon River

KATE AND ALEXANDER WERE flying across
northern Brazil in a commercial airplane. For
hours and hours, they had been seeing an endless expanse of forest, all the same intense
green, cut through by rivers like shining serpents. The most formidable of all was the color
of coffee with cream.

"The Amazon River is the widest and longest
on earth; five times greater than any other,"
Alex read in the guidebook his grandmother
had bought him in Rio de Janeiro. "Only the
astronauts on their way to the moon have ever
seen it in its entirety." What the book didn't say
was that this vast area, the last paradise on the
planet, was being systematically destroyed by
the greed of entrepreneurs and adventurers, as
he had learned in school. They were building
a highway, a slash cut through the jungle, on

which settlers were coming in and tons of woods and minerals were going out.

Kate informed her grandson that they would go up the Río Negro to the Upper Orinoco, to an almost unexplored triangle in which most of the tribes they were interested in were concentrated. The Beast was supposed to live in that part of the Amazon.

"In this book it says that those Indians are still in the Stone Age. They haven't even invented the wheel," Alex commented.

"They don't need it. There is no use for it in this terrain; they don't have anything to transport and they're not in a hurry to get anywhere," replied Kate, who didn't like to be interrupted when she was writing. She had spent a good part of the flight taking notes in a tiny, spidery writing like fly tracks.

"'They don't know how to write,'" Alex added.

"I'm sure they have a good memory," said Kate.

"'There is no expression of art among them, only the tradition of painting their bodies and decorating themselves with feathers,'" Alex read.

"They don't care about posterity, or showing off. Most of our so-called *artists* would do well to follow their example," his grandmother answered.

They were on their way to Manaus, the most populous city of the Amazon region, which had prospered in the times of the rubber plantations at the end of the nineteenth century.

"You are going to see the most mysterious jungle in the world, Alexander. There are places there where spirits appear in broad daylight."

"Right. Like the Abominable Jungleman we're looking for." Alexander smiled sarcastically.

"It's called the Beast. It may not be the only one, there may be several, a family or a tribe of Beasts."

"You're very trusting for your age, Kate," her grandson commented, unable to suppress a hint of mockery when he saw that his grandmother believed such tales.

"With age, you acquire a certain humility, Alexander. The longer I live, the more uninformed I feel. Only the young have an explanation for everything. At your age, you can afford to commit the sin of arrogance, and it doesn't matter much if you look ridiculous," his grandmother lectured.

When they got off the airplane in Manaus, the humidity hit them like a towel soaked in warm water. There they met the other members of the *International Geographic* expedition. Besides Kate and her grandson, Alexander, there were Timothy Bruce, an English photographer with a long horse face and yellow nicotine-stained teeth, his assistant, Joel González, and the famous anthropologist Ludovic Leblanc. Alex had imagined Leblanc as a wise old man with a white beard and imposing appearance, but he turned out to be a short, thin, nervous fifty-year-old man with a permanent expression of either scorn or cruelty on his lips, and the squinty little eyes of a mouse. He was decked out like a movie version of a wild-game hunter, from the pistols at his waist to his heavy boots and Aussie hat decorated with bright feathers. Kate muttered quietly that all Leblanc needed was a dead tiger to put his foot on. In his youth, Leblanc had spent a brief time in the Amazon and then had written a voluminous study on the Indians that had caused a sensation in academic circles. Their Brazilian guide, César Santos, who was supposed to meet them in Manaus, could not get there because his plane had broken down, so he planned to wait for them in Santa María de la Lluvia, where the group was to transfer to a boat.

Alex found that Manaus, located at the confluence of the Amazon and the Río Negro, was a large, modern city with tall buildings and crushing traffic, though his grandmother assured him that nature could not be tamed there and in times of floods, caimans and snakes appeared in patios and elevator shafts. It was also a city of traffickers, where the law was fragile and easily broken: drugs, diamonds, gold, precious woods, weapons. Only two weeks before, authorities had intercepted a boatload of fish . . . each stuffed with cocaine! For the young American, who had been outside his country only once—that time to go to Italy, the land of his mother's family—it was a surprise to see the contrast between the wealth of some and the extreme poverty of others, all mixed together. The *campesinos* who had no land and the workers who had no jobs came to the city in droves, looking for new horizons, but many ended up living in shacks, with no income and no hope. That day a fiesta was being celebrated and people were happy, as they are at a circus or a carnival. Bands of musicians strolled through the streets, and everybody was dancing and drinking, many wearing costumes. Their group was put up in a modern hotel, but they couldn't sleep for the noise of the music and fireworks and rockets. The next day, Professor Leblanc got up in a very bad mood. He had not slept well and he demanded that they get started as soon as possible because he didn't want to spend a minute longer than necessary in that "godforsaken city," as he called it.

The *International Geographic* group started upriver on the Río Negro—called the "black river" because of the sediment it carried in its waters—toward Santa María de la Lluvia, a village in the heart of Indian territory. Their boat was quite large, with an ancient motor that emitted both noise and smoke and a roof improvised of plastic to protect them from the sun and the rain, which fell like a warm shower several times a day. The boat was stuffed with people, bundles, sacks, hands of bananas, and a few domesticated animals in cages or simply tied by the foot. There were a few tables, some long benches to sit on, and a series of hammocks strung from poles, one atop another.

The crew, and most of the passengers, were *caboclos*, as the people of the Amazon are called, a mixture of several races: White, Indian, and Black. There were a few soldiers, a pair of young Americans—Mormon missionaries—and Omayra Torres, a Venezuelan doctor who was along for the purpose of vaccinating the Indians. She was a beautiful mulatto, about thirty-five years old, with black hair, amber-colored skin, and the green almond-shaped eyes of a cat. She moved with grace, as if dancing to the sound of a secret rhythm. Men followed her with their eyes, but she seemed not to be aware of the reaction her beauty provoked.

"We must be prepared," said Leblanc, showing off his weapons. Everyone could hear him, but it was evident that he meant his comments for Dr. Torres alone. "Finding the Beast is the least of our worries. Worse will be the Indians. They are brutal warriors, cruel and treacherous. Just as I described in my book, they kill to prove their courage, and the more murders they commit, the higher their place in the hierarchy of the tribe."

"Can you explain why that is so, Professor?" asked Kate, not trying to hide her sarcasm.

"It is very simple, madame . . . what did you tell me your name was?"

"Kate," she clarified, for the third or fourth time. Apparently Professor Leblanc had a bad memory for women's names.

"I repeat: very simple. It has to do with the lethal competition that exists in nature. The most violent men dominate in primitive societies. I suppose you have heard of the term 'alpha male'? Among wolves, for example, the most aggressive male controls all the rest and claims the best females. It's the same among humans. The most violent men command; they obtain more women than other men, and pass their genes on to more offspring. The others must be content with what's left. Do you follow that? The survival of the fittest," Leblanc explained.

"You mean that brutality is natural?"

"Precisely. Compassion is a modern invention. Our civilization protects the weak, the poor, the sick. From the point of view of genetics, that is a terrible error. And that is why the human race is deteriorating."

"What would you do with the weak in society, Professor?" Kate asked.

"What nature does: leave them to perish. In that sense the Indians are wiser than we are," Leblanc replied.

Dr. Omayra Torres, who had been listening attentively to the conversation, could not help offering her opinion.

"With all due respect, Professor, it does not seem to me that the Indians here are as ferocious as you describe; on the contrary, for them war is more ceremony than anything, a rite to prove their courage. They paint their bodies, prepare their weapons, sing, dance, and go out to make a raid upon the *shabono* of another tribe. They threaten each other and exchange a few blows, but rarely are there more than one or two deaths. Our civilization is just the reverse: no ceremony, only massacres."

"I am going to give you one of my books,

61

señorita. Any serious scientist will tell you that Ludovic Leblanc is an authority on this subject," the professor cut in.

"I am not as learned as you." Dr. Torres smiled. "I am only a rural physician who has worked more than ten years in this area."

"Believe me, my esteemed doctor, these natives are the proof that man is no more than a murderous ape."

"And woman?" interrupted Kate.

"I regret to tell you that women count for nothing in primitive societies. Only as booty in warfare."

Dr. Torres and Kate exchanged a glance, and both smiled, amused.

The first part of the trip up the Río Negro turned out to be a true exercise in patience. They moved forward at the pace of a turtle, and stopped almost as soon as the sun set in order to avoid being rammed by unseen tree trunks carried by the current. The heat was intense, but it got cool at night, and a blanket felt good. Sometimes, when the river looked clean and calm, they seized the opportunity to fish or swim awhile. The first two days, they passed boats of all kinds, from motor launches and houseboats to simple canoes hollowed from the trunks of trees, but from then on they were alone in the immensity of that landscape. This was a planet of water; life sailed along slowly, at the rhythm of the river, tides, rains, and floods. Water, water, everywhere. Hundreds of families lived and died on their boats without ever spending a night on solid ground; others lived in houses on stilts along the riverbanks. Everything was transported by river, and the only way to send or receive a message was by radio. To the American, it seemed incredible that anyone could survive without a telephone. One radio station in Manaus transmitted personal messages continuously; that was how people kept in touch with the news, their business interests, and their families. Upriver, money wasn't used much at all; the economy was based on barter; fish was traded for sugar, or gasoline for hens, or services for a case of beer.

The jungle loomed threateningly on both banks of the river. The captain's orders were clear: do not wander off for any reason; once among the trees, you lose your sense of direction. There were stories of foreigners who though only a few yards from the river had died without ever finding it. At dawn, they would see rosy dolphins leaping through the water and hundreds of birds flocking. They also saw the large aquatic mammals called manatees; the females of that species gave rise to the legend of the sirens. At night, they would see red dots in the dense growth along the banks, the eyes of caimans peering through the dark. One *caboclo* taught Alex to calculate the size of the reptile by how far apart its eyes were. When it was just a small one, the *caboclo* would dazzle it with a strong light, then jump in the water and trap it, holding the tail in one hand and clamping its jaws shut with the other. If the eyes were wide set, he would avoid it like the plague.

Time went by slowly, hours dragging into eternity; even so, Alex was never bored. He would sit at the prow of the boat and observe nature, and read, and play his grandfather's flute. The jungle seemed to come alive and respond to the sound of the instrument; even the noisy crew and the passengers on the boat would fall silent and listen. Those were the only times that Kate paid any attention to

Alex. The writer was a woman of few words; she spent her day reading or writing in her notebooks, and in general ignored Alex or treated him like any other member of the expedition. It was pointless to go to her and present a problem directly related to survival, such as food, health, or safety. She would look him up and down with obvious scorn, and answer that there are two kinds of problems: those that solve themselves and those that have no solution . . . so please not to bother her with foolishness. It was good that his hand had healed rapidly, because otherwise she would be capable of solving the matter by suggesting he cut it off. (Kate was a woman of extreme measures.) She had loaned him maps and books about the Amazon so he could look things up for himself. If Alex commented on what he had read about the Indians, or out-lined his theories about the Beast, she would reply, without taking her eyes from the page before her, "Never lose an opportunity to keep your mouth shut, Alexander."

Everything about this trip was so different from the world Alex had grown up in that he felt like a visitor from another galaxy. Now he had to do without comforts he had always taken for granted, like a bed, a bathroom, running water, and electricity. He used his grandmother's camera to take snapshots, in order to have proof to show back in California. His friends would never believe that he had held a three-foot-long alligator!

His most serious problem was food. He had always been a picky eater, and now they were serving him things he couldn't even name. All he could identify on the boat were canned beans, dried beef, and coffee, none of which he had a taste for. One day the crew shot a couple of monkeys, and that night when the boat was tied up along the riverbank they were roasted. They looked like a couple of burned infants, and Alex felt queasy just seeing them. The next morning they caught a *pirarucú,* an enormous fish that everyone but Alex, who didn't even taste it, thought was delicious. He had decided when he was three years old that he didn't like fish. His mother, weary of struggling to make him eat it, had given up, and from then on served him only food he liked. Which wasn't much. That short list kept him hungry the whole trip; all he had were bananas, a can of condensed milk, and several packages of crackers. It didn't seem to matter to his grandmother that he was hungry. Or to anyone else. No one paid any attention to him.

Several times a day a brief but torrential rain fell and the humidity was horrendous. Alex had to get used to the fact that his clothing never really got dry and that after the sun went down, they were attacked by clouds of mosquitoes. The foreigners' defense was to douse themselves in insect repellent—especially Ludovic Leblanc, who never lost an opportunity to recite the list of diseases transmitted by insects, from typhus to malaria. He had rigged a heavy veil over the Aussie hat to protect his face, and he spent a large part of the day tucked beneath a mosquito net he had the crew hang at the stern of the boat. The *caboclos*, on the other hand, seemed immune to the bites.

On the third day, a radiant morning, they had to stop because there was a problem with the motor. While the captain tried to repair it, everyone else stretched out in the shade of the roof to rest. It was too hot to move, but Alex decided it was a perfect place to cool off. He jumped into the water, which looked as shallow as a bowl of soup, but he sank like a stone beneath the surface.

"Only an idiot tests the bottom with his feet," Alex's grandmother commented when he came to the surface streaming water from his ears.

Alex swam away from the boat—he had been told that caimans prefer to stay close to the banks—and floated on his back for a long time in the warm water, arms and legs outspread, gazing at the sky and thinking about the astronauts who had experienced that immensity. He felt so comfortable that when something quickly brushed by his hand he took an instant to react. Not having any idea what kind of danger lay in store—maybe caimans didn't hug the riverbanks, after all— he began to swim as fast as he could back toward the boat, but he stopped short when he heard his grandmother yelling not to move. He obeyed out of habit, even though his instinct was advising the opposite. He floated as quietly as possible and then saw a huge fish at his side. He thought it was a shark, and his heart stopped, but the fish made a quick turn and came back, curious, coming so close that Alex could see its smile. This time his heart leaped, and he had to force himself not to shout with joy. He was swimming with a dolphin!

The next twenty minutes, playing with the mammal the way he did with his dog, Poncho, were the happiest of his life. The magnificent creature would circle around him at great speed, leap over him, stop a few inches from his face, and observe him with a friendly expression. Sometimes it swam very close, and Alex could touch its skin, which was rough, not smooth as he had imagined. He wanted that moment to never end; he was ready to stay in the water forever, but suddenly the dolphin gave a flip of its tail and disappeared.

"Did you see, Kate? No one is going to believe this!" Alex yelled when he was back at the boat, so excited he could barely speak.

"Well, here's the proof." She smiled, pointing to her camera. The photographers for the expedition, Bruce and González, had captured the event, too.

★ ★ ★

As they went farther up the Río Negro, the vegetation became more voluptuous, the air heavier and more perfumed, time slower, and distances beyond measuring. They moved as if in a dream through a landscape of fantasy. From time to time, the boat emptied as passengers got off carrying their bundles and animals, heading for the huts or tiny villages along the riverbank. The radios onboard were no longer receiving personal messages from Manaus, or booming with popular songs; people grew silent as nature vibrated with an orchestra of birds and monkeys. Only the noise of the motor betrayed a human presence in the enormous solitude of the jungle. By the time they reached Santa María de la Lluvia, the only people left onboard were the crew, the group from the *International Geographic*, Dr. Omayra Torres, two soldiers, and the two young Mormons, who were still with them, but had been felled by some intestinal bacterium. Despite the antibiotics the doctor had given them, they were so ill they could scarcely open their eyes, and sometimes they confused the blazing jungle with the snowy mountaintops of Utah.

"Santa María de la Lluvia is the last outpost of civilization," the boat captain told them when they saw the village at a bend in the river.

"From here on, Alexander, it is a magical land," Kate notified her grandson.

"Are there still Indians who have never had contact with civilization?" he asked.

It was Dr. Omayra Torres who answered. "It's believed there may be two or three thousand, but in fact no one knows for sure."

Santa María de la Lluvia rose like a human mistake in the midst of an overwhelming natural world threatening to swallow it up at any moment. The settlement consisted of about twenty houses, a large shed that served as a hotel, a second, smaller shed that housed a hospital and was under the charge of two nuns, a couple of tiny stores, a Catholic church, and an army barracks. The soldiers monitored the border and traffic between Venezuela and Brazil. In accordance with the law, they were also supposed to protect native peoples against the abuses of settlers and adventurers, but in practice, they never did.

71

Foreigners were moving into the region and no one was stopping them as they pushed the Indians farther and farther toward impenetrable jungle, or killed them, with no fear of being punished.

A tall man stood waiting on the docks at Santa María de la Lluvia. He had the sharp profile of a bird, strong features, and an alert expression; his skin was tanned by outdoor life and his dark hair was gathered into a ponytail.

He introduced himself. "Welcome. I am César Santos, and this is my daughter, Nadia."

Alex guessed that the girl was about the age of his sister Andrea, maybe twelve or thirteen. Her curly hair was wild, bleached by the sun, and her eyes and skin were the color of honey. She was dressed in shorts, a T-shirt, and plastic sandals. Several colored ribbons were tied around her wrists, a yellow flower was tucked over one ear, and a long green feather pierced the lobe of the other ear. Alex thought that if Andrea could see those adornments, she would immediately copy them, and if Nicole, his younger sister, saw the little black monkey on her shoulder, she would die with envy.

★ ★ ★

While Dr. Torres, helped by the two nuns who had come to meet them, took the two Mormon missionaries to the tiny hospital, César Santos supervised the unloading of the numerous supplies for the expedition. He apologized for not having been in Manaus, as they had agreed. He explained that he had flown his plane to every corner of the Amazon, but now it was very old and in recent weeks several pieces of the motor had dropped off. In light of the fact that it was in danger of crashing, he had decided to order a new motor, which was supposed to arrive any day; he added with a smile that he did not want to make an orphan of his daughter, Nadia. Then he led them to the hotel, which turned out to be by the river, a wooden construction on stilts similar to the other rickety buildings in the village. Cases of beer were stacked everywhere and liquor bottles were lined up along the counter. Alex had noticed during their trip upriver that, despite the heat, the men drank gallons and gallons of alcohol, at every hour of the night and day. This primitive building would serve the visitors as their base of operations, lodging, restaurant, and bar. Kate and

Professor Ludovic Leblanc were assigned cubicles separated from the others by sheets strung on a rope. The rest of the party would sleep in hammocks protected by mosquito netting.

Santa María de la Lluvia was a sleepy little village, so remote that it rarely appeared on maps. A few settlers raised longhorn cattle; the rest dealt in the gold found in the sandy riverbed or wood and rubber from the forests. A few daring souls set out alone into the jungle to look for diamonds, but most just vegetated, waiting for opportunity to fall miraculously from the sky. Those were the visible activities. The secret ones consisted of trafficking in exotic birds, drugs, and weapons. Groups of soldiers, rifles slung over their shoulders and shirts soaked with sweat, lounged in the shade, playing cards or smoking. The little village was in the doldrums, dazed by heat and boredom. Alex saw several bald, toothless men, some half blind, some with open sores, waving their arms and talking to themselves. These were miners crazed by mercury and slowly dying. For too long, they had dived to the bottom of the river, hauling powerful tubes to suck up the sand saturated with gold dust. Some drowned; others died because their competitors cut their oxygen lines, but most died slowly, poisoned by the mercury used to separate gold from sand.

The children of the village, in contrast, played happily in the mud, accompanied by a few tame monkeys and gaunt dogs. There were a few adult Indians, some wearing a T-shirt or shorts, others as naked as the children. At first, Alex was embarrassed, not daring to look at the women's breasts, but he quickly became accustomed to the sight and after five minutes didn't even notice them. These Indians had been in contact with civilization for several years and had lost many of their traditions and customs, as César Santos explained. The guide's daughter, Nadia, spoke to the Indians in their own language, and they treated her as if she were from their tribe.

If these were the ferocious natives Leblanc had described, they were not very impressive. They were small, for one thing; the men were under five feet and the children looked like miniature humans. For the first time in his life, Alex felt tall. This tribe had bronze-colored skin and high cheekbones; the men wore their hair cut as round as bowls, stopping just above the ears, a fashion that accentuated their Asian features. They were descended from inhabitants of the north of China, and had come by way of Alaska some ten to twenty thousand years before. They had escaped being enslaved during the conquest of the sixteenth century because they were so isolated. The Spanish and Portuguese soldiers had been unable to conquer the swamps, mosquitoes, jungle vegetation, enormous rivers, and waterfalls of this Amazon region.

Once the group was settled in the hotel, César Santos began organizing supplies for the expedition, and planning the remainder of the trip with the help of Kate and the photographers. Professor Leblanc had decided to rest until it was a little cooler since he did not do well in the heat. In the meantime, Nadia invited Alex to go for a walk with her.

"Don't go beyond the boundaries of the village after sunset, it's dangerous," César Santos warned them.

Following the advice of Leblanc, who talked as if he were an expert on the dangers of the jungle, Alex stuffed his pants legs inside his socks to guard against the voracious leeches that would suck his blood. Nadia, who was almost barefoot, laughed.

"You'll get used to the bugs and the heat," she told him. She spoke very good English because her mother was Canadian.

"My mother left three years ago," the girl clarified.

"Why did she go?"

"She couldn't get used to it here. Her health was bad, and it got worse when the Beast started roaming around. She could smell it; she wanted to get away, she couldn't stand to be alone, she screamed. . . . Finally Dr. Torres took her away in a helicopter. She's back in Canada now," Nadia said.

"Your dad didn't go with her?"

"What would my dad do in Canada?"

"And why didn't she take you with her?" Alex persisted. He had never heard of a mother who would abandon her child.

"Because she's in a sanatorium. Besides, I want to be where my dad is."

"Aren't you afraid of the Beast?"

"Everyone's 'fraid of it. But if it comes,

Borobá will warn me in time," she answered, patting the little black monkey that was always with her.

Nadia took her new friend around the village, which, because there wasn't that much to see, took barely half an hour. Out of the blue came a burst of thunder and lightning that streaked across the sky in all directions, and it began to pour cats and dogs. The rain was as warm as soup, and it turned the narrow little streets into steaming mud pits. As a rule, people sought shelter beneath a nearby roof, but the children and the Indians went about what they were doing, completely indifferent to the downpour. Alex realized that his grandmother had been right to suggest that he change his blue jeans for the light cotton clothing she had bought him in Manaus; it was cooler and quicker to dry. To escape the rain, the two children ducked into the church, where they found a tall, husky man with white hair and the huge shoulders of a lumberjack. Nadia introduced him as Padre Valdomero. He wasn't at all what you expected in a priest; he was wearing sandals and no shirt, and was up on a ladder whitewashing the walls. A bottle of rum sat on the floor.

"Padre Valdomero has lived here since before the invasion of the ants," was Nadia's introduction.

"I came when this village was founded, about forty years ago, and I was here when the ants came. We had to abandon everything and escape downriver. They came like an enormous black blob, unstoppable, destroying everything in their path," the priest told them.

"What happened then?" Alex asked, who could not imagine a town victimized by insects.

"We set fire to the houses before we left. Because of the fire, the ants detoured, and a few months later, we were able to come back. None of the houses you see now is more than fifteen years old."

The priest had a strange mascot, an amphibious dog that, according to him, was native to the Amazon, but a breed that was now nearly extinct. It spent a good part of its life in the river, and could keep its head in a bucket of water for minutes at a time. It acknowledged Alex and Nadia from a prudent distance, suspicious. Its bark was like a birdcall; it seemed to be singing.

"The Indians kidnapped Padre Valdomero. What I wouldn't give to have that happen to me!" Nadia exclaimed with envy.

"They didn't kidnap me, child. I got lost in the jungle and they saved my life. I lived with them for several months. They're good people, and free; for them, freedom is more important than life itself. They can't live without it. An Indian who is a prisoner is a dead Indian. He turns inward, stops eating or breathing, and dies," Padre Valdomero told them.

"Some versions say that they're peaceful, but others describe them as savage and violent," said Alex.

"The most dangerous men I've seen around here aren't the Indians, they're the people who traffic in weapons and drugs and diamonds and rubber, the gold prospectors and soldiers and timbermen who pollute and exploit the region," the priest rebutted. And he added that the Indians were primitive in terms of material goods, but very advanced on the mental plane. They were connected to nature the way a child is to its mother.

"Tell us about the Beast. Is it true that you saw it with your own eyes, Padre?" Nadia asked.

"I think I saw it, but it was night and my eyes aren't as good as they used to be," Padre Valdomero answered, tossing down a long swallow of rum.

"When was that?" asked Alex, thinking that his grandmother would be grateful for the information.

"A couple of years ago . . ."

"What did you see, exactly?"

"What I have told many times: a giant more than nine feet tall, which moved very slowly and had a terrible odor. I was paralyzed with fear."

"It didn't attack you, Padre?"

"No. It said something, then turned and disappeared into the trees."

"It said something? I guess you mean that it made noises, like grunts. Is that what you mean?" Alex insisted.

"No, son. Clearly the creature spoke. I did not understand a single word, but I have no doubt it was a spoken language. I fainted . . . When I came to, I wasn't sure what had happened, but I had that strong smell clinging to my clothes and hair and skin. That was how I knew I hadn't dreamed it."

CHAPTER FIVE

The Shaman

THE STORM ENDED as quickly as it had begun, and the night sky was clear. Alex and Nadia returned to the hotel where the members of the expedition had gathered around César Santos and Dr. Omayra Torres, who were studying a map of the region and discussing preparations for the journey. Professor Leblanc, somewhat recovered from his exhaustion, was with them. He had covered himself from head to foot with insect repellent, and had hired an Indian named Karakawe to fan him constantly with a banana leaf. Leblanc demanded that the expedition set off for the Upper Orinoco the very next morning, because he could not waste time in this insignificant little village. He had only three weeks to trap the strange jungle creature, he said.

"For years now, no one has been able to do

that, Professor," César Santos pointed out.

"It will have to show up soon, because I am scheduled to give a series of lectures in Europe," Leblanc replied.

"I am sure the Beast will respect your timetable," said the guide, but the professor showed no sign of having caught the irony.

Kate had told her grandson that the Amazon was a dangerous place for anthropologists, because they tended to lose their reason. They invented contradictory theories and fought among themselves with guns and knives. Some of them tyrannized tribes and ended up believing they were gods. One of them, totally mad, had to be taken back to his country in a straightjacket.

"I suppose you have been told that I am a member of the expedition, too, Professor Leblanc," said Dr. Omayra Torres, whom the anthropologist kept glancing at out of the corner of his eye, impressed by her beauty.

"Nothing would please me more, mam'selle, but—"

"It's *Dr.* Torres," the physician interrupted.

"You may call me Ludovic," offered Leblanc flirtatiously.

"And you may call me Dr. Torres," was her curt reply.

"We will not be able to take you, my most esteemed doctor. There is barely enough space for those sponsored by *International Geographic*. Our budget is generous, but it has limits," Leblanc replied.

"Then your team will not be going either, Professor. I am an employee of the National Health Service. I am here to protect the Indians. No foreigner may come in contact with them unless the necessary preventive measures are taken. They are extremely vulnerable to disease, especially those carried by Whites," said the doctor.

"An ordinary cold can be deadly for them. One whole tribe was wiped out by a respiratory infection three years ago when journalists came to film a documentary. One of them had a cough. He gave a puff of his cigarette to an Indian and that infected the whole tribe," added César Santos.

At that moment, there were new arrivals, Captain Ariosto, the commander of the local barracks, and Mauro Carías, the wealthiest of the local entrepreneurs. Nadia whispered to

Alex that Carías was very powerful. He had business dealings with the presidents and generals of several South American countries. She added that the man didn't have a heart in his chest but carried it in a totebag, and pointed to the leather case Carías had in his hand. Ludovic Leblanc, however, was greatly impressed with Carías, because the expedition had been organized thanks to his international contacts. He was the one who had interested *International Geographic* in the legend of the Beast.

"This bizarre creature has all the good people of the Upper Orinoco terrified. No one wants to go into the triangle where it is thought to live," said Carías.

"I understand that the area has never been explored," said Kate.

"That is true."

"I suppose it must be very rich in minerals and precious stones," the writer added.

"The wealth of the Amazon is found principally in the soil and in its forests," he replied.

"And plants," Dr. Omayra Torres intervened. "We don't know even ten percent of the medicinal properties they contain. As the shamans and native healers disappear, we lose that knowledge forever."

"I imagine that the Beast interferes with your business interests in that area, Señor Carías, just as the tribes do," Kate continued, who, once she got her teeth into something, did not let go.

"The Beast is a problem for everyone. Even the soldiers are afraid of it," Mauro Carías admitted.

"If the Beast exists, I shall find it. The man—certainly not the animal—has yet to be born who can elude Ludovic Leblanc," proclaimed the professor, who was given to referring to himself in the third person.

"Count on my soldiers, Professor," Captain Ariosto hastened to offer. "Contrary to what my good friend Carías has said, they are brave men."

"And you can count on all my resources as well, my dear Professor Leblanc. I have motor launches and a good radio transmitter," Mauro Carías seconded.

"And count on *me* to help with any problems of illness or accidents that may arise," Dr. Omayra Torres added smoothly, as if she didn't recall Leblanc's wish to exclude her from the expedition.

"As I have told you, mam'selle—"

"Doctor!" she corrected once again.

"As I have told you, the budget for this expedition is limited; we cannot take tourists," Leblanc stated emphatically.

"I am not a tourist. The expedition cannot proceed without an authorized physician and without the necessary serum."

"The doctor is right. Captain Ariosto will explain the law to you," César Santos intervened. He knew the doctor and evidently was attracted to her.

"Ahem, well . . . It is true that . . . ," the captain stammered, looking toward Mauro Carías with confusion.

"There will be no problem if you include Omayra. I myself will pay her expenses." The entrepreneur smiled and put his arm around the young physician's shoulders.

"Thank you, Mauro, but that will not be necessary, my expenses are paid by the government," she said, gently freeing herself.

"I see. In that case there is nothing more to discuss. I hope we find the Beast. If not, the venture will be pointless," spoke up the photographer Timothy Bruce.

"Trust me, young man. I have experience

regarding this type of creature, and I myself have designed some infallible traps. You can see models of my traps in my study of the Abominable Snowman of the Himalayas." The professor shot him a smile of satisfaction, at the same time gesturing to Karakawe to fan a little faster.

"Were you able to trap it?" Alex asked with assumed innocence, because he knew the answer all too well.

"It does not exist, young man. The supposed creature of the Himalayas is a hoax. Perhaps this famous Beast will be as well."

"People have seen it," Nadia declared.

"Ignorant people, no doubt, child," the professor scolded.

"Padre Valdomero isn't ignorant," Nadia protested.

"Who?"

"A Catholic missionary who was kidnapped by the savages and has been as crazy as a loon ever since," Captain Ariosto intervened. He spoke English with a strong Spanish accent, and as he was always chomping on a cigar, he was not easy to understand.

"He wasn't kidnapped and he isn't crazy!"

Nadia exclaimed.

"Calm down, sweetie." Mauro Carías smiled and patted Nadia's head; she immediately slipped out of his reach.

"Padre Valdomero is actually a very wise man," César Santos interjected. "He speaks several Indian languages and he knows the flora and fauna of the Amazon better than anyone. He can set fractured bones, pull teeth, and once or twice, he has operated on cataracts with a scalpel he made himself."

"Yes, but he has had no success at all in cleaning up Santa María de la Lluvia, or in converting the Indians to Christianity. You've seen how they still go around stark naked," Mauro Carías mocked.

"I doubt that the Indians need to be converted," said César Santos.

He explained that the indigenous peoples were very spiritual. They believed that everything had a soul—trees, animals, rivers, clouds. For them, spirit and matter were one and the same. They could not understand the simplicity of the foreigners' religion; they said it was the same story over and over, while they had many stories of gods and demons, and spirits of sky and earth. Padre Valdomero had given up trying to explain that Christ died on the cross to save humankind from sin, because the idea of such a sacrifice left the Indians dumbfounded. They had no concept of guilt. Nor did they understand the need to wear clothing in this climate, or to accumulate wealth, since they couldn't take anything to the other world when they died.

"It's a shame they're condemned to disappear; they are an anthropologist's dream, don't you think, Professor Leblanc?" Mauro Carías's tone was mocking.

"That is true. Fortunately I have been here to write about them before they succumb to progress. Thanks to Ludovic Leblanc, they will live on in history," the professor replied, totally unaware of Carías's sarcasm.

That evening, dinner consisted of servings of broiled tapir, beans, and cassava tortillas, none of which Alex wanted to try, even though he was as hungry as a wolf.

After dinner, while his grandmother was drinking vodka and smoking her pipe in the company of the men, Alex went down to the river with Nadia. The moon was shining like a great yellow lamp in the sky. They were surrounded by the sounds of the jungle, like background music: bird cries, chattering monkeys, croaking toads, and crickets. Thousands of fireflies darted past them, brushing their faces. Nadia caught one in her hand and placed it in her curls, where it kept on blinking like a little light. She sat down on the dock and dabbled her feet in the dark water of the river. Alex asked her about piranhas; he had seen dried ones in the souvenir shops in Manaus, looking like miniature sharks. They were about eight inches long and provided with formidable jaws and teeth as sharp as knives.

"Piranhas are very useful; they clean dead animals and junk from the water. My father says that they only attack if they smell blood or if they're hungry," she explained.

She told Alex about the time she had watched as a caiman, badly wounded by a jaguar, dragged itself into the water, where piranhas ate into the wound and devoured the caiman from the inside in a matter of minutes, leaving its hide intact.

At that moment, Nadia sat up straight and

made a sign not to speak. Borobá, the little monkey, began to jump up and down and shriek, very agitated, but Nadia quickly calmed it by whispering in its ear. Alex had the impression that the monkey understood its owner's words perfectly. All he could see were the shadows of the vegetation and the black mirror of the water, but it was obvious that something had captured Nadia's attention, because she got to her feet. In the distance, he heard the sound of someone strumming a guitar in the village. If he turned, he could see lights in the houses behind him, but they were alone at the river.

Nadia gave a long, sharp cry that to Alex's ears sounded exactly like an owl, and an instant later, a similar cry answered from the other bank. She repeated the call twice, and both times got the same response. Then she took Alex by the arm and motioned him to follow. He remembered César Santos's warning to stay inside the boundaries of the village after dusk, as well as all the stories he had heard about snakes, wild beasts, bandits, and drunks with guns. And best not even think about the ferocious Indians described by

Leblanc . . . or the Beast. But he didn't want to look like a coward in the eyes of the girl, so he followed without a word, grasping his opened Swiss Army knife.

They left the last huts of the village behind and moved forward with caution, their only light the moon. The jungle was not as thick as Alex had imagined; the vegetation was dense along the banks of the river but then it grew more sparse and it was possible to walk without much difficulty. They had not gone far before the cry of the owl was repeated. They were in a clearing, and they could see the moon shining in the heavens. Nadia stopped and waited, not moving a muscle. Even Borobá was quiet, as if it knew what they were waiting for. Suddenly Alex jumped with surprise: less than ten feet away a figure had materialized from the night, suddenly and silently, like a ghost. He raised his knife, ready to defend himself, but Nadia's calm attitude stopped him in midair.

"Ah-ee-ah," the girl murmured in a low voice.

"Ah-ee-ah, ah-ee-ah," a voice replied that to Alex did not sound human but more like a breath of wind.

The figure stepped forward until it was very close to Nadia. By then, Alex's eyes had adjusted a little to the dark, and by the light of the moon he could see an incredibly ancient man. He looked as if he had lived for centuries, even though he stood very straight and he moved nimbly. He was very small. Alex calculated that he was shorter than his sister Nicole, who was only nine. The man was wearing a brief apron of some plant fiber, and a dozen necklaces of shells, seeds, and boars' teeth covered his chest. His skin, wrinkled like a thousand-year-old elephant, fell in folds over his fragile skeleton. He was carrying a short spear, a walking stick hung with a number of small leather pouches, and a quartz cylinder that clicked like a baby's rattle. Nadia reached up to her hair, pulled out the firefly, and offered it to the man. He accepted it, placing it among his necklaces. Nadia knelt down and signaled Alex to do the same, as a sign of respect. Immediately, the Indian also crouched down so the three were at the same level.

Borobá gave a leap and landed on the shoulders of the old man, tugging at his ears; his owner batted him away, and the ancient burst out with a happy laugh. As far as Alex could tell, Nadia's friend did not have a tooth in his head, but since there was so little light, he could not be sure. The man and the girl became involved in a long conversation with gestures and sounds in a language as gentle as the breeze, as water, as birds. He supposed they were talking about him, because they pointed to him. At one moment, the man stood and shook his spear, very angry, but she calmed him with long explanations. Finally, the ancient pulled an amulet on a cord from around his neck, a piece of carved bone, and held it to his lips and blew. The sound was that same owl's call they had heard earlier, which Alex recognized because there were many of those birds around his house in northern California. The amazing old man hung the amulet around Nadia's neck, placed his hands on her shoulders in farewell, and disappeared as silently as he had arrived. Alex could have sworn that he did not see him step back; he simply evaporated.

"That was Walimai," Nadia said quietly in his ear.

"Walimai?" he asked, impressed by that strange encounter.

"Shhhh! Don't say it aloud. You must never speak the true name of an Indian; it's taboo. It's even worse to name the dead; that is a much stronger taboo, a terrible insult," Nadia explained.

"Who is he?"

"He is a shaman, a very powerful witch man. He speaks through dreams and visions. He can travel to the world of the spirits anytime he wants. He is the only one who knows the road to El Dorado."

"El Dorado? The city of gold the conquistadors invented? That's a crazy legend!" Alex replied.

"Walimai has been there many times with his wife. She is always with him."

"I didn't see her," Alex admitted.

"She is a spirit. Not everyone can see her."

"Did you?"

"Yes. She is young and very beautiful."

"What did the witch man tell you? What were you two talking about?" Alex asked.

"He gave me this talisman. With it, I will always be safe. No one—no person, no animal, no ghost—can hurt me. I can also use it to call him; all I have to do is blow and he will come.

Up till now, I've not been able to call him, I've had to wait until he came. Walimai says that I am going to need him because there is much danger. Rahakanariwa is walking again; it is *so* creepy, a spirit cannibal-bird. Whenever it appears, there is death and destruction, but I will be protected by the talisman."

"You are a very weird girl . . ." Alex sighed. He didn't believe half of what she was saying.

"Walimai says that foreigners should not go looking for the Beast. He says that several will die. But you and I must go because we have been called, and that is because our souls are pure."

"Who has called us?"

"I don't know, but if Walimai says so, it's true."

"Do you really believe those things, Nadia? You believe in witch men and cannibal-birds, and El Dorado, and invisible wives . . . and the Beast?"

Without answering, the girl turned on her heel and began walking toward the village; Alex followed close behind to keep from getting lost.

CHAPTER SIX

The Plot

THAT NIGHT ALEXANDER slept restlessly. He felt as if he were out in the open, as if the fragile walls that separated him from the jungle had dissolved and he was exposed to all the dangers of that unknown world. The hotel—wood planks, zinc roof, glassless windows—was barely enough shelter to keep out the rain. The outdoor sounds of toads and other creatures were added to the snores of his sleeping companions. His hammock turned over once or twice, throwing him onto the floor, before he remembered how to use it and stretched diagonally across it to keep from spilling out. It wasn't hot, but he was sweating. He lay awake in the dark for a long while beneath his insect repellent–soaked netting, thinking about the Beast and tarantulas and scorpions and snakes and other dangers lurking in the shadows. He went over the strange scene he had witnessed between Nadia and the Indian. The shaman had predicted that several members of the expedition would die.

It seemed unbelievable to Alex that in a few days' time his life had taken such a spectacular turn that suddenly he found himself in a fantastic place where, just as his grandmother had announced, spirits walked among the living. Reality was twisted out of shape; he no longer knew what to believe. He felt very homesick; he missed his house and his family and his dog, Poncho. He was all alone, and light years from things he knew. If only he could find out how his mother was doing! But calling a hospital in Texas from this village would be like trying to communicate with Mars. Kate was not any company or comfort. As a grandmother, she left a lot to be desired; she didn't even make an effort to answer his questions, because it was her opinion that the only way you learned was to find out for yourself. She maintained that experience was what you learned just after you needed it.

He was tossing and turning in his hammock, unable to sleep, when he thought he heard the murmur of voices. It might simply have been the hum of the jungle, but he decided to investigate. Barefoot, and in his underwear, he crept to the other side of the dormitory, to the hammock where Nadia was sleeping beside her father. He put his hand over the girl's mouth and whispered her name in her ear, trying not to wake anyone else. She opened her eyes, frightened, but when she recognized him, she calmed down and hopped from her hammock light as a cat, making a crisp gesture to Borobá to stay still. The little monkey immediately obeyed, rolling up in the hammock, and Alex compared Nadia's companion to his dog, Poncho, to whom he had never been able to teach even the simplest command. The two tiptoed outside and slipped along the wall of the hotel to the terrace, where Alex had heard the voices. They hid in the angle of the door, plastered against the wall, and from there they could see Captain Ariosto and Mauro Carías sitting at a small table, smoking, drinking, and quietly talking. Their faces were fully visible in the glow of their cigarettes and the spiral from the citronella candle burning on the table. Alex congratulated himself for having called Nadia, because the men were speaking in Spanish.

"You know what you have to do, Ariosto," said Carías.

"It won't be easy."

"If it were easy I wouldn't need you, hombre, nor would I have to pay you," Mauro Carías remarked.

"I don't like those photographers, they could land us in a mess. As for the writer woman, she seems pretty sharp to me," said the captain.

"The anthropologist, the writer, and the photographers are indispensable to our plan. They will leave here telling the exact story we want them to tell. That way, no suspicion will fall on us, and we prevent Congress from sending a commission to investigate events, as they have before. This time a group from *International Geographic* will be witnesses," Carías explained.

"I don't understand why the government protects that handful of savages, anyway. They take up thousands of square miles that should be divided among settlers, which is the only way progress will come to this hellhole," the captain commented.

"All in good time, Ariosto. There are emeralds and diamonds in that territory. By the time settlers come to cut trees and breed cattle, you and I will be rich. I'm not ready for adventurers to come nosing around yet."

"Then they won't. That's why the army's here, my friend Carías, to see that the law is obeyed. We have to protect the Indians, don't we?" Captain Ariosto asked, and they both laughed.

"I have it all planned; a person I trust is going along on the expedition."

"Who is that?"

"For the moment, I prefer not to name names," said Carías, but then explained further. "The Beast is the excuse for having that idiot Leblanc and the journalists go exactly where we want them to, and be there to cover the news. They will contact Indians; that's inevitable. They can't travel into that triangle of the Upper Orinoco to look for the Beast without coming across Indians."

"Your plan seems very complicated to me. I have some very discreet men; we can do the work without anyone finding out," Captain Ariosto assured Carías, taking a sip of his drink.

"No, hombre! Haven't I told you that we must be patient?"

"Tell me the plan again," Ariosto requested.

"Don't you worry, I'll take care of the plan. Before three months have gone by, there won't be a living soul left in that area."

At that moment, Alex felt something on his foot, and choked back a scream: a snake was slithering over his bare skin! Nadia put a finger to her lips and motioned him not to move. Carías and Ariosto jumped up, alerted, and both drew their pistols. The captain turned on his flashlight and swept it all around, its beam passing only a few inches from where the two were hiding. Alex was so terrified that he would happily have confronted the guns if he could have shaken off the snake, which now was curled around his ankle, but Nadia was holding him by one arm and he realized that he could not risk her life, too.

"Who's there?" the captain asked quietly, not lifting his voice in order not to wake the people sleeping in the hotel.

Silence.

"Let's go, Ariosto," ordered Carías.

The soldier again swept his flashlight around the room, then both men retreated to the stairs that led to the street, still holding their guns. A couple of minutes went by before the two friends felt they could move without revealing their presence. By then, the snake was around Alex's calf; its head had reached the level of his knee and sweat was pouring down his torso. Nadia pulled off her T-shirt, wrapped it around her right hand, and very cautiously seized the snake just behind the head. Immediately Alex felt the serpent's coils tighten, and it whipped its tail furiously, but the girl held it firmly and unhurriedly started unwinding it from her new friend's leg until it was free and the snake was dangling from her hand. She swung her arm like the blade of a windmill, faster and faster, and launched the snake over the banister of the terrace, into the darkness. Then she put her shirt back on, all with great calm.

"Was it poisonous?" Alex asked as soon as he could get the words out.

"Yes, I think it was a *surucucú*, but it wasn't very big. Its mouth was still small and it couldn't open its jaws very far; it might have bitten a finger, but not a leg," Nadia replied. Then she translated what Carías and Ariosto had been saying.

"What do you think those awful men are up

to? What can we do?" the girl asked.

"I don't know. The only thing that occurs to me is to tell my grandmother, but I don't know whether she would believe me. She says that I'm paranoid, and that I see enemies and dangers everywhere."

"For the moment, Alex, we can only wait and watch," Nadia concluded.

The young people went back to their hammocks. Alex was drained and fell straight to sleep. He awakened at dawn to the deafening howls of the monkeys. He was so starved that he would gladly have eaten his father's pancakes, but there was nothing at hand and he had to wait two hours until his traveling companions were ready for breakfast. He was offered black coffee, warm beer, and the cold leftovers of the tapir from the previous night. He refused it all, repulsed. He had never seen a tapir, but he imagined that it looked something like a huge rat. He would get a surprise a few days later when he learned that a tapir is an animal that weighs more than two hundred pounds and resembles a pig, and is greatly prized for its meat. He tried a *plátano*, but it was very bitter and left a harsh taste on his tongue; he found out later that though it looked like a banana, it had to be cooked to be eaten. Nadia, who had gone out early to swim in the river with the other girls, came back with a fresh flower over one ear and the same green feather in the lobe of the other. Borobá's arms were around her neck and she was carrying half a pineapple in her hand. Alex had read that the only safe fruit in tropical countries is something you peel yourself, but he decided that the risk of contracting typhus was preferable to malnutrition. Grateful, he devoured the pineapple she offered him.

César Santos appeared moments later, as clean and fresh as his daughter, inviting the sweaty members of the expedition to take a dip in the river. Everyone followed except Professor Leblanc, who ordered Karakawe to bring several buckets of water so he could bathe on the terrace; he was not attracted to the idea of swimming in the company of manta rays. Some were the size of a carpet, and their powerful tails not only cut like saws but also injected venom. Alex considered that after his experience with the snake the night before, he would not be daunted by the risk of bumping into a fish, no matter how bad its reputation. He dove headfirst into the water.

"If you're attacked by a manta ray, it means that these waters aren't for you," was the only comment from his grandmother, who went off with the women to bathe in a different area.

"Mantas are shy, and live on the bed of the river. Usually they scurry away when they see something moving in the water, but it's best to drag your feet as you walk in order not to step on them," César Santos instructed.

The swim was delicious, and left Alex feeling cool and clean.

CHAPTER SEVEN

The Black Jaguar

BEFORE SETTING OUT, the members of the expedition were invited to the camp of Mauro Carías. Dr. Omayra Torres excused herself, saying that she had to send the young Mormons back to Manaus on an army helicopter because they were sicker than before. The camp consisted of several trailers that had been transported by helicopter and set up in a circle in a clearing about a mile from Santa María de la Lluvia. The units were luxurious compared to the zinc-roofed huts in the village. The compound was equipped with an electric generator, a radio tower, and solar energy panels.

Carías had similar retreats at strategic points along the Amazon, from which he could oversee his many business dealings, from timber harvesting to gold mining, but he lived some distance away. It was said that he had princely mansions in Caracas, Rio de Janeiro, and Miami, and that he kept a wife in each city. He traveled in his own jet and a small plane, and he also had access to army vehicles, which certain friendly generals placed at his disposal. In Santa María de la Lluvia there was no airstrip large enough to land his jet, so he used his biplane, which, compared to the one César Santos flew, a rusty little tin can, looked supersonic. Kate noticed that the camp was surrounded by electric fences and by numerous guards.

"What can this man own that requires such heavy guards?" she commented to her grandson.

Mauro Carías was one of the few adventurers who had become rich in the Amazon. Thousands and thousands of *garimpeiros* went deep into the jungle, on foot and by canoe, to look for gold mines and beds of diamonds, slashing their way through the vegetation with machetes, devoured by ants, leeches, and mosquitoes. Many died of malaria, some from gunshots, still others from hunger and loneliness. Their bodies rotted in unmarked graves or were eaten by scavengers.

It was said that Carías had made his start with chickens, that he set them loose in the jungle and then split open their craws to retrieve the nuggets of gold the wretched fowls had swallowed. That story, however, like so much of the gossip about the man's past, must have been an exaggeration, because in truth gold was not scattered across the soil of the Amazon like kernels of corn. In any case, Carías never had to risk his health like the miserable *garimpeiros*, because he had good connections and a nose for business. He knew how to give orders and command respect; what he didn't get through legal means, he obtained by force. Many people whispered behind his back that he was a criminal, but no one dared say that to his face, and it was never proved that he had blood on his hands. There was nothing threatening or suspicious about his looks; he was a pleasant, good-looking, tan-skinned man with well-kept hands and flashing white teeth, always dressed in expensive sports clothes. His voice was melodious, and he looked you straight in the eye when he spoke, as if he wanted to prove his openness with every word.

This Amazon entrepreneur received the members of the *International Geographic* expedition in one of his trailers, decorated as a living room, with comforts that didn't exist in the village. Two attractive young women served drinks and lighted cigars, but never said a word. Alex supposed they didn't speak English. They reminded him of Morgana, the girl who had stolen his backpack in New York, because they had the same insolent attitude. He blushed when he thought about Morgana, and asked himself again how he could have been so foolish. The two girls were the only women he saw in Carías's camp; the other employees were men armed to the teeth. Their host offered them a delicious lunch of cheeses, cold meats, shellfish, fruit, ice cream, and other luxuries flown in from Caracas. For the first time since he had left his own country, Alex was able to eat to his liking.

"It appears that you know this region very well, Santos," Mauro Carías said to their guide. "How long have you lived here?"

"All my life. I couldn't live anywhere else," he replied.

"I've been told that your wife fell ill here.

I'm very sorry to hear that. . . . It doesn't surprise me; not many foreigners can survive in this isolation and this climate. And your little girl? She doesn't go to school?" Carías reached out to pat Nadia, but Borobá bared his teeth.

"I don't have to go to school. I know how to read and write," Nadia said emphatically.

"And that's all you need to know, sweetie." Carías smiled.

"Nadia knows the natural world, and she speaks English, Spanish, Portuguese, and several of the Indian tongues," her father added.

"What is that you're wearing around your neck, sweetie?" Carías asked in an affectionate tone.

"My name is Nadia," she said.

"Show me your necklace, Nadia." The entrepreneur host smiled, showing his perfect teeth.

"It's magic, I can't take it off."

"Would you like to sell it? I'll buy it," Mauro Carías said teasingly.

"No!" Nadia said, stepping back.

César Santos interrupted to apologize for the prickly behavior of his daughter. He was surprised that this very important man would waste time joking with a little girl. In the past, no one had ever noticed Nadia, but in recent months, his daughter was beginning to attract attention, and that did not please him at all. Mauro Carías commented that if the girl had lived her whole life in the Amazon, she was not prepared for society, and what did her future hold? She seemed very bright, he said, and with a proper education she could go far. He even offered to take her back with him to the city, where he could send her to school and make a little lady of her, which was as it should be.

"I can't give up my daughter, but I thank you, anyway," Santos replied.

"Think it over, hombre. I'd be like her god-father," Carías added.

"I can talk with animals, too," Nadia interrupted. Most of those present laughed at what she had said. The only ones who didn't were her father, Alex, and Kate.

"If you can talk with the animals, maybe you can act as my interpreter with one of my pets," the entrepreneur said, and in mellow tones invited them all to come along with him.

★ ★ ★

They followed Mauro Carías to the patio formed by the circle of trailers; in the center was an improvised cage constructed of poles and chicken wire. In the cage, a large cat was pacing with the crazed agitation of a wild beast in captivity. It was a black jaguar with a lustrous pelt and hypnotic topaz-colored eyes, one of the most handsome examples ever seen in the area. The minute Borobá glimpsed the jaguar, he screeched, leaped from Nadia's shoulder, and loped off at top speed with the girl close behind, calling him in vain. Alex was surprised, because it was the first time he had seen the monkey part from its owner voluntarily. The photographers immediately focused their lenses on the cat, and even Kate pulled her small automatic camera from her bag. Professor Leblanc stood back at a prudent distance.

"Black jaguars are the most feared animals in South America. They do not back off from anything; they have great courage," said Carías.

"If you admire it so, why don't you set it free?" César Santos asked. "This poor cat would be better dead than captive."

"Free it? No, hombre! Not a chance. I have

a small zoo at my home in Rio de Janeiro. I'm just waiting for a proper cage to send the cat there."

Alex had moved up close, as if in a trance, fascinated by the sight of that great feline. His grandmother called a warning that he didn't hear, and he kept going closer, until both hands were touching the wire that separated him from the animal. The jaguar stopped pacing, emitted a deep growl, and fixed its yellow gaze on the human outside its cage. It froze in place, its muscles tense, its jet pelt quivering. Alex took off his glasses, which he had worn since he was seven years old, and dropped them on the ground. Cat and human were so close that Alex could distinguish each golden fleck in the pupils of the beast as their eyes locked in a silent dialogue. Everything faded away. Alex was alone, facing the animal on a vast amber plane surrounded by lofty black towers, beneath a white sky in which six transparent moons were floating like the heads of medusae. He saw the cat open its jaws, he saw the gleam of its enormous pearl-white teeth, and in a human voice, but one that seemed to issue from the depths of a cavern, it spoke his name: Alexander. And he answered in his own voice, but it, too, sounded cavernous: Jaguar. The cat and its counterpart repeated those words three times: Alexander, Jaguar; Alexander, Jaguar; Alexander, Jaguar, and then the sand of the plain became phosphorescent, the sky turned black, and the six moons began to whirl in their orbits and scatter like slow-moving comets.

In the meantime, Mauro Carías had issued an order, and one of his employees came dragging in a monkey with a rope around its neck. When it saw the jaguar, it had a reaction similar to Borobá's; it began to shriek and jump up and down and wave its arms, but it could not get free. Carías took it by the collar and, before anyone could guess his intention, he had opened the cage with a single precise movement and thrown the terrorized little animal inside.

The photographers, caught by surprise, should have remembered they had cameras in their hands. Leblanc was fascinated by every movement of the unfortunate simian, which scampered up the wire looking for a way out, and of the cat, which, following the prey with its eyes, crouched and prepared to spring. Without thinking, Alex started running, stepping on his glasses, which were still on the ground, and grinding them to bits. He hurled himself at the door of the cage, intending to save both animals, the monkey from its certain death and the jaguar from its prison. When she saw her grandson opening the lock, Kate ran, too, but before she could reach him, two of Carías's employees already had him by his arms, and were struggling with him. Everything happened at once—so quickly that afterward, Alex could not remember the sequence of events. With one slash of its claws, the jaguar raked the monkey from the wire and with one snap of its terrible jaws killed it. Blood sprayed in every direction. In that same instant, César Santos pulled his pistol from his belt and fired a perfectly aimed shot to the jaguar's head. Alex felt the impact as if the bullet had struck *him* between the eyes, and he would have fallen backward if Carías's guards had not had a strong grip on him.

"What did you do, you bastard!" yelled the entrepreneur, whirling toward César Santos and pulling out his own pistol.

The guards let go of Alex, who stumbled and fell to the ground, in order to deal with the guide, but they did not dare touch him because he still had the smoking pistol in his hand.

"I set him free," César Santos replied with awesome serenity.

Mauro Carías fought to control himself. He realized he could not shoot Santos in front of the journalists and Leblanc.

"Hold it down!" Mauro Carías ordered the guards.

"He killed it! He killed it!" Leblanc babbled, red-faced with excitement. The death of the monkey, first, and then the cat, had driven him into a frenzy; he acted as if he were drunk.

"Don't concern yourself, Professor Leblanc. I can get all the animals I want. Forgive me, I fear that this was not a spectacle for soft hearts," said Carías.

Kate helped her grandson get to his feet, then took César Santos by the arm and started toward the exit before the situation could grow more violent. The guide allowed himself to be led by the writer, and they left, followed by Alex. Outside, they found Nadia with a terrified Borobá clinging to her waist.

Alex tried to explain to Nadia what had passed between the jaguar and him before Mauro Carías threw the monkey into the cage, but it was all jumbled together in his brain. The experience had been so real that he could have sworn that for a few minutes he was in a different world, a world with gleaming sand and six moons whirling through the firmament, a world where he and the jaguar blended into a single voice. Although he could not find the words to tell his friend what he had felt, she seemed to understand without the need to hear details.

"The jaguar recognized you because it is your totemic animal," she said. "We all have an animal spirit that accompanies us. It is like our soul. We don't all find our animal; usually it's only great warriors and shamans who do, but you discovered yours without looking. Your name is Jaguar," said Nadia.

"Jaguar?"

"Alexander is the name your parents gave you. Jaguar is your real name. But to use that name, you must be like a jaguar."

"And how is that? Cruel and bloody?" Alex asked, thinking of the beast's jaws as it tore the monkey apart in Carías's cage.

"Animals aren't cruel the way people are; they kill only to defend themselves, or when they are hungry."

"Do you have a totemic animal, too, Nadia?"

"Yes, but it hasn't been revealed to me yet. Finding your animal is less important for a woman, because we get our strength from the earth. We *are* nature," the girl said.

"How do you know all these things?" queried Alex, who by then was beginning to have faith in what the girl told him.

"Walimai taught me."

"The shaman is your friend?"

"Yes, Jaguar, but I haven't told anyone that I talk with Walimai, not even my papa."

"Why?"

"Because Walimai likes solitude. The only company he can bear is his wife's spirit. He shows up from time to time in a *shabono* to cure an illness or take part in a ceremony for the dead, but he never appears to the *nahab.*"

"*Nahab?*"

"Foreigners."

"You're a foreigner, Nadia."

"Walimai says that I don't belong anywhere, that I'm not an Indian and not a foreigner, not a woman and not a spirit."

"What are you then?" asked Jaguar.

"I just *am*," the girl replied.

César Santos explained to the members of the expedition that they would go upriver by motorboat, traveling through Indian territory as far as the waterfalls of the Upper Orinoco. There they would set up camp and, if possible, clear enough ground to carve out a small landing field. He would go back to Santa María de la Lluvia to pick up his plane, which they would use for speedier contact with the village. He said that by then the new engine would have arrived, and it would simply be a matter of installing it. With the plane, they would be able to go to otherwise unreachable areas of the mountains where, according to the testimony of some Indians and adventurers, the mythological Beast might have its den.

"How does a gigantic creature climb up and down terrain that supposedly we can't manage?" asked Kate.

"We are going to find out," César Santos answered.

"How do the Indians get there without a small plane?" Kate insisted.

"They know the lay of the land," the guide said. "Indians can climb those gigantic palm trees that have the trunks covered with long spines. They can also scale the rock faces of the waterfalls, which are as smooth as mirrors."

The party spent a major part of the morning loading the boats. Professor Leblanc had brought more bundles than the photographers, including a supply of bottled water to use when he shaved because he was afraid of mercury-polluted water. It was futile for César Santos to remind him that they would be camping far upstream of the gold mines. At the guide's suggestion, Leblanc had hired Karakawe, the Indian who had been fanning him the night before, as his personal assistant to look after him for the rest of the trip. Leblanc explained that he had a bad back and could not carry anything at all.

From the first day of their adventure, Alexander had been responsible for his grandmother's things. That was one aspect of his duties, for which she was paying him a minimal amount, to be collected upon their return if he did his job well. Every day, Kate jotted down the hours her grandson worked and made him sign the page; that was how they kept track of what she owed. In a moment of candor, he had told her about destroying everything in his room. She did not consider that to be terribly grave, since it was her opinion that one needs very little in this world. She offered him a salary since he planned to replace what he had demolished. His grandmother traveled with three changes of cotton clothing, vodka, tobacco, shampoo, soap, insect repellent, a mosquito net, a blanket, paper, and a box of pencils—all of it in a single canvas bag. She also had an automatic camera, so ordinary that it had provoked hoots of laughter from the professional photographers, Timothy Bruce and Joel González. Kate let them laugh. Alex had even less clothing than his grandmother, plus a map and a couple of books. He had fastened his Swiss Army knife, his flute, and a compass to his belt. When César Santos saw the compass, he commented that it would not be any help in the jungle, since it was impossible to travel in a straight line.

"Forget the compass, son. Your best bet is to not lose sight of me," he counseled.

But Alex liked the idea of being able to locate north wherever he was. His watch, on the other hand, was useless, because Amazon time was different from the rest of the planet's; it was not measured in hours, but in dawns, tides, seasons, and rains.

The five soldiers Captain Ariosto had provided, and Matuwe, the Indian guide employed by César Santos, were well armed. Matuwe and Karakawe had adopted those names in their dealings with foreigners. Only family members and close friends could call them by their true names. They both had been very young when they left their tribes to be educated in the mission schools where they were converted to Christianity, but they had maintained contact with the other Indians. No one was better in orienting himself than Matuwe, who never needed a map to know where he was. Karakawe was considered to be a "city man," because he often traveled to Manaus and Caracas, and because, like many people from the city, he was suspicious by nature.

César Santos had organized the necessities for setting up camp: tents, food, cooking utensils, a battery-operated radio and lights, tools, nets for setting traps, machetes, knives, and a few metal, glass, and plastic trinkets to exchange with the Indians. At the last moment, Santos's daughter appeared with her little black monkey on one hip, Walimai's amulet around her neck, with no luggage but a cotton cardigan tied around her shoulders, and announced that she was ready to go. She had warned her father that she did not intend to stay with the nuns at the hospital in Santa María de la Lluvia, as she had before, because Mauro Carías was hanging around and she did not like the way he looked at her and tried to touch her. She was afraid of that man who "carried his heart in a tote." Professor Leblanc threw a tantrum. He had already objected strenuously to the inclusion of Kate's grandson, but since it was impossible to send him back to the United States, he had to tolerate him. Now, however, he was not about to allow the guide's daughter to tag along, not for any reason.

"This is not a kindergarten, it is a highly dangerous scientific expedition; the eyes of the

125

world are on Ludovic Leblanc," he fumed.

When everyone ignored him, he refused to get on the boat. They could not leave without him; only the enormous prestige of his name guaranteed the backing of *International Geographic*, he reminded them. César Santos tried to convince Leblanc that his daughter went everywhere with him and that she would be no bother at all; just the opposite, she could be of great help because she spoke several Indian dialects. Leblanc was unbending. A half hour later, the temperature had climbed to one hundred degrees, moisture was dripping from every surface, and tempers were as hot as the thermometer. That was when Kate intervened.

"Like you, Professor, I have a bad back. I must have a personal assistant. I have hired Nadia Santos to carry my notebooks and fan me with a banana leaf."

Everyone burst out laughing. The girl climbed onto the boat with dignity and sat beside the writer. The monkey settled itself in her lap, and from there stuck out its tongue and made faces at Professor Leblanc, who also joined them, fiery red with indignation.

CHAPTER EIGHT

The Expedition

ONCE AGAIN THE GROUP found itself proceeding upriver. This time there were thirteen adults and two children in two motorboats, both of which belonged to Mauro Carías, who had put them at Leblanc's disposal.

Alex waited for an opportunity to talk to his grandmother in private about the strange conversation between Mauro Carías and Captain Ariosto, which Nadia had translated for him. Kate listened carefully and gave no sign that she didn't believe her grandson, as he had feared; on the contrary, she seemed very interested.

"I don't like that Carías," she said. "I wonder how he plans to exterminate the Indians."

"I don't know."

"The only thing we can do for the moment is wait and watch," the writer decided.

"Nadia said the same thing."

"That girl is smart; she should be my grand-daughter, Alexander."

The trip upriver was much like the run between Manaus and Santa María de la Lluvia, although the landscape was different. By then, Alex had decided to follow Nadia's advice and instead of battling the mosquitoes and bathing himself in insect repellent, he let them attack him, overcoming the temptation to scratch. He also took off his boots when he saw that they were always wet, and when he found out that the leeches bit him as much as if he weren't wearing them. He hadn't noticed until his grandmother pointed to his feet: his socks were bloody. He pulled them off and saw the repulsive creatures clinging to his skin, swollen with blood.

"It doesn't hurt because they inject an anesthetic before they suck your blood," César Santos explained.

Then he taught Alex how to make the leeches drop off by burning them with a cigarette; that way the heads weren't left under the skin and you avoided the risk of infection. Santos's method was somewhat complicated for Alex since he didn't smoke, but a little warm tobacco from his grandmother's pipe had the same effect. It was easier to remove the leeches than to spend all his time trying to keep them off.

From the beginning, Alex had the impression that the tension among the adults of the expedition was almost visible; no one trusted anyone. He couldn't shake the feeling that he was being spied on, as if thousands of eyes were observing every move of the motorboats. He kept looking over his shoulder, but no one was following them on the river.

The five soldiers were *caboclos,* all born in the region. The Indian guide Matuwe, hired by César Santos, served as an interpreter with the tribes. The other pure Indian was Karakawe, Leblanc's assistant. According to Dr. Omayra Torres, Karakawe did not act like other Indians, and quite possibly he would never go back to live with his tribe.

The Indians shared everything among themselves; their only possessions were the few weapons or primitive tools each carried with him. Every tribe had a *shabono,* a large, round, communal hut roofed with straw, and open to a clear space in the middle. They all lived together, sharing everything from food to the care of the children. Contact with outsiders, however, was taking its toll on the tribes. It not only poisoned their bodies with illnesses, it affected their souls. As soon as an Indian held a machete, a knife, or any other metal instrument, his life changed forever. With a single machete, they could increase productivity a thousandfold on the small plots where they cultivated cassava and maize. With a knife, any warrior felt he was a god. The Indians' obsession with steel was as powerful as the foreigners' lust for gold. Karakawe had passed the machete stage and had moved on to guns; he was never without his antiquated pistol. Someone like him, who thought more about himself than he did his community, had no place in the tribe. Individualism was thought to be a form of madness, like being possessed by a demon.

Karakawe was a gruff man who had very little to say; when someone asked a question he could not avoid, he answered in one or two words. He didn't get along well with foreigners, with the *caboclos*, or with the other Indians. He did Ludovic Leblanc's bidding reluctantly, and his eyes glittered with hatred when he had to speak to the anthropologist. He never ate with the others, he did not touch a drop of alcohol, and he went off by himself when they camped for the night. Nadia and Alex once surprised him going through Dr. Omayra Torres's baggage.

"Tarantula," he said by way of explanation.

Alex and Nadia decided to keep an eye on him.

As they continued, progress became more and more difficult because the river often narrowed and they came upon rapids that threatened to overturn the boats. In other places, the water seemed stagnant, and there they were impeded by corpses of animals and rotted tree trunks and branches. They had to kill the motors and paddle their way forward using bamboo poles to shunt aside the debris. Several times, what they poked turned out to be large caimans, which when you looked down on them resembled logs. César Santos explained that when the water was low, jaguars came to the river, and when it was high, snakes appeared. They saw a pair of gigantic turtles and a five-foot-long eel that César Santos said delivered a strong electric shock. The vegetation was very dense, and gave off the smell of decaying plant life, but sometimes at night large flowers tangled in the tree branches would open and the air would be heavy with the sweet scent of vanilla and honey. White herons watched, motionless, from the tall grass that grew by the river, and brilliantly colored butterflies were everywhere.

César Santos often slowed the boats at trees with branches stretching over the water, where all they had to do was reach out and pluck a fruit. Alex had never seen any of these strange varieties and did not want to try them, but the others ate them with pleasure. One time Santos guided the boat to the riverbank to collect a plant he said was great for healing wounds. Dr. Omayra Torres agreed, and recommended to Alex that he rub the sap over the cut on his hand, though that was not actually necessary, it had healed cleanly. All that was left was a red line, which didn't bother him at all.

Kate informed them that this was an area where many men had tried to find the mythic city of El Dorado, lured by the legend that its streets were paved with gold and children had precious stones for toys. Many adventurers had plunged into the jungle and traveled up the Amazon and the Orinoco without reaching the heart of that enchanted land where the world was as innocent as it had been at the dawn of human life on the planet. They had died or come back defeated by Indians, mosquitoes, wild animals, tropical diseases, the climate, and the difficult terrain.

The expedition members now found themselves in Venezuelan territory, but borders meant nothing there, it was all the same prehistoric paradise. Unlike the Río Negro, these waters were untraveled. They met no other boats, saw no canoes, no houses on stilts, and not a single human being. On the other hand, the flora and fauna were marvelous; the photographers were having a field day, they had never had within the focus of their cameras so many species of trees, plants, flowers, insects, birds, and animals. They saw red and green parrots, elegant flamingos, toucans with long, heavy beaks their fragile heads could scarcely support, and hundreds of canaries and cockatoos. Many of these birds were threatened with extinction because traffickers hunted them mercilessly to smuggle into other countries and sell. An assortment of monkeys, almost human in their expressions and their games, seemed to be greeting them from the trees. There were deer, bears, anteaters, and squirrels and other small mammals. Several splendid parrots—called *papagayos*—followed them for long stretches. These large multicolored birds flew with incredible grace above the boats, as if they were curious about the strange creatures traveling in them. Leblanc shot at one with his pistol, but César Santos managed to jar the professor's arm and spoil the shot. The bullet frightened the monkeys and other birds; the sky filled with wings, but soon afterward, the parrots returned, unperturbed.

"You can't eat them, Professor, the meat is bitter. There's no reason to kill them," César Santos scolded the anthropologist.

"I like the feathers," said Leblanc, annoyed by the guide's interference.

"Buy some in Manaus," César Santos said curtly.

"You can tame parrots," Dr. Omayra Torres

told them. "My mother has one at our home in Boa Vista. It goes everywhere with her, flying about six feet over her head. When my mother goes to market, the parrot follows the bus until she gets off, waits in a tree while she shops, and then comes back with her, like a lap dog."

Alex found once again that the music of his flute stirred the monkeys and birds. Borobá seemed particularly attracted. When Alex played, the little monkey sat stone still, listening with a solemn, curious expression. Sometimes he jumped up on Alex and tugged at the instrument, begging for music. Alex would oblige, delighted finally to have an interested audience after having fought for years with his sisters in order to practice in peace. The members of the expedition were comforted by the music, which accompanied them as the landscape grew more hostile and mysterious. Alex played effortlessly; the notes flowed out as if the delicate instrument had a memory and could remember the unmatched mastery of its previous owner, the celebrated Joseph Cold.

★ ★ ★

The sensation of being followed had possessed them all. Without voicing it, because what is not spoken can seem not to exist, they kept searching for signs in the jungle. Professor Leblanc, binoculars in hand, spent the day examining the passing riverbanks; tension had made him even more disagreeable. The only persons not infected by collective nerves were Kate and the Englishman, Timothy Bruce. They had worked together on many occasions; they had covered half the world for their travel articles and had experienced several wars and revolutions, and they had climbed mountains and descended to the bottoms of seas, so there was very little that robbed them of sleep. Besides, they liked to boast that they were unflappable.

"Don't you feel as if someone is watching us, Kate?" her grandson asked.

"Yes."

"Doesn't it scare you?"

"There are various ways to overcome fear, Alexander. None works," she replied.

Just as she spoke those words, one of the soldiers traveling in their boat fell at her feet without a sound. Kate bent over him, at first not comprehending what had happened until she saw a kind of long shaft buried in the man's chest. Then she knew that he had died instantly: the projectile had passed cleanly between two ribs and had pierced his heart. Alex and Kate alerted the other travelers, who were not aware of what had happened because the attack had been so silent. An instant later, half a dozen guns were fired into the thick growth along the bank. When the roar, the gunpowder, and the birds that filled the sky had settled, they could see that there was no other movement in the jungle. Whoever had shot the lethal dart was crouched down, motionless and silent. César Santos pulled the dart from the dead Indian's body; it was approximately a foot long, and as strong and flexible as steel.

The guide gave the order to continue with all speed, because this part of the river was narrow and the boats were an easy target for the attackers' arrows. They did not stop until two hours later, when they thought it safe. Only then could they examine the dart, which was painted with strange red and black designs that no one could decipher. Karakawe and

Matuwe reported that they had never seen those marks before; they were not known to their own tribes or to any others they knew, but they agreed that all the Indians of the region used blowguns. Dr. Omayra Torres explained that even if the dart had not hit the heart with such spectacular precision, the man would have died within minutes anyway—though death would have been more painful because the tip of the dart was dipped in curare, a lethal poison used by Indians for hunting and for war, and there is no known antidote.

"This is unacceptable! That arrow could have hit me!" Leblanc protested.

"That is true," César Santos admitted.

"This is your fault," the professor added.

"My fault?" César Santos repeated, confused by the unexpected turn the matter was taking.

"You're the guide! You are responsible for our safety, that is why we pay you!"

"We are not exactly on a tour, Professor," César Santos replied.

"We must turn around and return immediately. Do you realize the loss to the scientific world if anything happened to Ludovic Leblanc?" the professor exclaimed.

The other members of the expedition were too stunned to speak. No one knew what to say until Kate broke in.

"I was hired to write an article about the Beast, and I plan to do just that—with poison arrows or without them, Professor. If you want to go back, you will have to walk or swim, whichever you prefer. We will continue according to plan," she said.

"Why, you insolent old . . . How dare you . . . !" shrieked the professor.

"Remember whom you're speaking to, you little twerp," the writer calmly interrupted, seizing him firmly by the shirt and paralyzing him with the glare of her fearsome blue eyes.

Alex expected the anthropologist to take a swing at his grandmother, and he stepped forward to prevent that, but it wasn't necessary. Kate's powerful gaze had doused the rage of the irritable Leblanc as if by magic.

"What shall we do with the body of this poor fellow?" the doctor asked, pointing to the cadaver.

"We can't take it with us in this climate, Omayra; you know how quickly bodies decompose. I suppose we could throw him into the river," César Santos suggested.

"His spirit would be angry, and it would pursue us and kill us," objected Matuwe, the terrified Indian guide.

"Then we will do what Indians do when they have to postpone a cremation; we will leave it in the open for the birds and animals to pick the bones," César Santos decided.

"But there should be a ceremony," Matuwe insisted.

"We don't have time. A traditional funeral would take several days. Besides, this man was a Christian," César Santos argued.

Finally they agreed to wrap the body in a sheet of canvas and place it on a small bark platform they built in the branches of a tree. Kate, who was not a religious woman but who had a good memory and remembered her childhood prayers, improvised a brief Christian ritual. Timothy Bruce and Joel González filmed and photographed the body and the funeral, as proof of what had happened. César Santos carved crosses in the trees along the riverbank, and marked the site as well as he could on a map, in order to recognize the place when they came back later to collect the bones, which would be delivered to the family of the dead man in Santa María de la Lluvia.

From that moment, the journey went from bad to worse. The vegetation became much more dense and they saw the sun only when traveling in the middle of the river. It was so close and uncomfortable that they could not sleep on the boats and, despite the danger represented by Indians and wild animals, they had to camp onshore. César Santos distributed the food, organized the hunting and fishing parties, and assigned shifts among the men to stand guard at night. He excluded Professor Leblanc; it was obvious that the least sound set his nerves on edge. Kate and Dr. Omayra Torres demanded to take part in the guard duty; it seemed insulting to be excluded because they were females. Then the two young people insisted on being accepted, too—in part because they wanted to keep an eye on Karakawe. They had seen him put handfuls of bullets into his pockets and watched him hang around the radio equipment, which from time to time César Santos was able to use to communicate, though with great difficulty, to report their location on the map to the operator at Santa María de la Lluvia. The leafy dome of the jungle acted like an umbrella, blocking the radio frequency.

"Which is worse, the Indians or the Beast?" Alex asked Ludovic Leblanc jokingly.

"The Indians, boy. They are cannibals; they not only eat their enemies, they eat the dead of their own tribe," the professor replied emphatically.

"Oh, really? I'd never heard that," Dr. Omayra Torres said sarcastically.

"Read my book, Señorita Torres."

"Doctor," she corrected for the umpteenth time.

"These Indians kill to get women," he assured her.

"You might kill for that reason, Professor, but not the Indians," the doctor replied. "They don't need more women; the fact is, they have more than enough."

"I have seen it with my own eyes; they attack other *shabonos* and steal the women."

"As far as I am aware," César Santos interrupted, "they cannot oblige girls to stay with them against their will. If they want, they can

142

leave. When there is war between two *shabonos*, it is because one has used magic to harm the other, or out of revenge, or sometimes there are ceremonial battles in which they club each other, but not with the intention of killing anyone."

"You are mistaken, Santos. See the documentary of Ludovic Leblanc and you will understand my theory," Leblanc assured him.

"I *understand* that you handed out machetes and knives to one *shabono* and promised the Indians you would give them more gifts if they acted for the cameras according to your instructions," the guide continued.

"That is a lie! According to my theory—"

"Other anthropologists and journalists have come to the Amazon with ideas about the Indians. There was one who filmed a documentary in which the boys went around dressed like women, wore makeup, and used deodorant," César Santos added.

"Ah. That colleague was known for rather strange ideas . . . ," the professor admitted.

The guide showed Alex and Nadia how to load and fire the pistols. The girl did not show any great skill or interest; she seemed unable to hit a target three feet away. Alex, on the other hand, was fascinated. The weight of the pistol in his hand gave him a sensation of invincible power; for the first time, he understood the obsession so many people feel with firearms.

"My parents do not tolerate guns. If they saw me with this, they would faint," he commented.

"They won't see you," his grandmother assured him as she took his picture.

Alex crouched down and pretended to shoot, as he had when he had played as a little boy.

"The sure technique for missing your shot is to aim and fire in haste," said Kate. "If we are attacked, that is exactly what you will do, Alexander, but don't worry, because no one will be watching you. Most likely, by then we will all be dead."

"You don't trust me to defend you, do you?"

"No, but I would rather be murdered by Indians in the Amazon than die of old age in New York," his grandmother replied.

"You're one of a kind, Kate!" Alex said, and smiled.

"We all are, Alexander."

On the third day, they caught sight of a family

of deer in a small clearing. The animals, accustomed to the safety of the forest, did not seem disturbed by the presence of the boats. César Santos ordered a halt, and shot one deer with his rifle as the rest fled in terror. That night the party would dine very well; venison was greatly appreciated in spite of its stringy texture, and it would be a feast after so many days of the same diet of fish. Matuwe had brought a poison used by the Indians in his tribe to paralyze fish; when the poison was thrown into the river, a hunter could impale them easily with a spear or an arrow tied to a liana. The poison left no trace in the flesh of the fish or in the water, and the remaining fish recovered within minutes.

They were at a calm place where the river formed a small lake, perfect for stopping for a couple of hours to eat and regain their strength. César Santos warned them to be cautious because the water was dark and they had seen caimans several hours before, but they were all hot and thirsty. The soldiers used poles to stir the water, and since they did not see any sign of caimans, they decided to bathe—except for Professor Ludovic Leblanc, who would not get in the river for any reason. Borobá was not fond of bathing, but Nadia forced him to get wet from time to time to chase off the fleas. Perched on the top of his owner's head, the little creature squealed with pure fright every time a drop of water splashed him. The members of the expedition paddled around for a while as César Santos and two of the men dressed the deer and built a fire to roast it.

Alex watched as his grandmother took off her trousers and shirt to swim in her underwear, with absolutely no trace of embarrassment, although once she was wet she looked almost naked. He tried not to look at her, but soon he realized that there in the midst of nature, and so far from the familiar world, there was no place for shame about the body. He had grown up around his mother and his sisters, and he was used to the company of the opposite sex at school, but recently anything connected with girls or women attracted him like a remote and forbidden mystery. He knew the reason: hormones churning around, not letting him think in peace. Adolescence was the pits, the worst of the worst, he decided. They ought to invent a machine with laser beams where you could walk in for a minute, and *zap!* come out an adult. He was carrying a hurricane inside; sometimes he was euphoric, king of the world, ready to take on a lion; other times he was as wimpy as a tadpole. From the moment he had begun this journey, however, he hadn't given a thought to hormones; nor had he had time to consider whether it was worth the effort to go on living, a doubt he used to have at least once a day. Now here he was comparing his grandmother's body—wiry, knotty, leathery skin—to the smooth golden curves of Dr. Omayra Torres, who was wearing a discreet black bathing suit, and to the still childish grace of Nadia. He thought about how the body changes at different stages, and decided that the three women were equally beautiful, each in her own way. He smiled at that idea. He had never dreamed, two weeks before, that he could consider his own grandmother an attractive person. Were his hormones cooking his brain?

A bloodcurdling scream jerked Alex from these important musings. The cry had come from Joel González, one of the photographers, who was struggling desperately in the muddy water along the riverbank. At first, no one knew what was happening; all they could see were the man's arms thrashing in the air and his head disappearing and reappearing. Alex, who was a member of his school swim team, was the first to reach him with two or three strong strokes. As he came near, he saw with absolute horror that a snake as thick as a swollen fire hose was wrapped around the photographer's body. Alex seized González by one arm and tried to drag him toward land, but the weight of the man and the reptile was too much for him. With both hands, and pulling with all his strength, he tried to separate the serpent, but its coils merely tightened around its victim. He remembered the hair-raising experience with the *surucucú* that had curled around his leg a few nights before. This was a thousand times worse. The photographer was not struggling now, or screaming; he was unconscious.

"Papa! Papa! An anaconda!" Nadia yelled, adding her cries to those of Alex.

By then Kate, Timothy Bruce, and two of the soldiers had reached them, and were struggling to uncoil the powerful snake from the body of the unfortunate González. The tussle stirred up the mud from the bottom of the lake, turning the water as dark and thick as chocolate. In the confusion, they couldn't see what was happening; each was tugging and shouting instructions without result. The effort seemed futile until César Santos arrived with the knife he was using to dress the deer. He did not dare wield the knife blindly, for fear of wounding Joel González or one of the others trying to subdue the reptile. He had to wait for the precise moment the head of the anaconda thrust up from the mud to decapitate it with one well-aimed slash. Blood gushed out, turning the water the color of rust. It took five minutes more to free the photographer, because even after death the constricting coils continued to squeeze.

They dragged Joel González to the riverbank, where he lay like a dead man. Professor Leblanc was so agitated that, from a place of safety, he was firing shots into the air, contributing to the confusion and general upheaval until Kate took the pistol from him and commanded him to be still. While the others had been struggling in the water with the anaconda, Dr. Omayra Torres had gone back to the boat to look for her medical kit, and now she was kneeling beside the unconscious man with a syringe in her hand. She acted calmly, without speaking, as if the attack of an anaconda were a perfectly normal event in her life. She gave an injection of adrenaline to González, and once she was sure he was breathing, proceeded to examine him.

"He has several broken ribs, and he is in shock," she said. "We have to hope he didn't suffer a punctured lung, or a broken neck. We must immobilize him."

"How shall we do that?" asked César Santos.

"The Indians use tree bark and mud and vines," said Nadia, still trembling from what she had witnessed.

"Very good, Nadia," the doctor said approvingly.

The guide issued the necessary instructions and soon the doctor, helped by Kate and Nadia, had wrapped the injured man's torso in cloths soaked in cool mud, covered that with long strips of bark, and bound the whole with lianas. As the mud dried, that primitive cast would act like a modern orthopedic corset. Joel González, stunned and in pain, still had no idea what had happened, but he was conscious and was able to speak a few words.

"We must take Joel back to Santa María de la Lluvia. Immediately! From there, they can use Mauro Carías's plane to get him to a hospital," the doctor directed.

"This is a dreadful inconvenience," protested Professor Leblanc. "We have only two boats. We cannot send one back."

"Why not? Yesterday you wanted to use a craft to get out of here, and now you do not want to send one with my grievously injured friend?" asked Timothy Bruce, doing his best to keep calm.

"Without the proper attention, Joel can die," the doctor explained.

"Do not exaggerate, my good woman. This man is not seriously hurt, merely frightened. With a little rest, he will be himself in a day or two," said Leblanc.

"Very considerate on your part, dear Professor," muttered Bruce, closing his fists.

"Enough, señores! Tomorrow we will come to a decision. It is too late to start now; it will be dark soon. We must camp here," was César

Santos's conclusion.

Dr. Omayra Torres ordered a fire to be built near the injured man, to keep him dry and warm during the night, for nights were always cool. For his pain, she gave him morphine, and to prevent infection, she began a course of antibiotics. She mixed a few teaspoons of sugar and a little salt in a bottle of water and instructed Timothy Bruce to give the liquid by spoonfuls to his friend, to help keep him from getting dehydrated, since it was clear that he would not be able to swallow solid food for the next few days. The English photographer, whose face usually suggested a placid draft horse, was openly worried, and he obeyed the orders with the solicitude of a mother. Even the bad-tempered Professor Leblanc had to admit to himself that the presence of the doctor was indispensable on an adventure like this.

In the meantime, three of the soldiers and Karakawe had dragged the body of the anaconda up on the bank. When they measured it, they found that it was nearly eighteen feet long. Professor Leblanc insisted on being photographed with the anaconda coiled around his body in such a way that it was not apparent the head had been cut off. Afterward, the soldiers skinned the reptile and nailed the skin on a trunk to dry; that technique increased the length by twenty percent, and there were tourists who would pay a good price for it. They did not have to take it back to town, however, because Professor Leblanç offered to buy it on the spot, once he was certain he could not acquire it gratis. Kate whispered nastily into her grandson's ear that she bet that within a few weeks the anthropologist would be exhibiting the anaconda as a trophy in his lectures, telling how he had killed it with his own hands. That was how he had won a hero's reputation among anthropology students, who were fascinated with the theory that killers had twice as many women and three times as many sons as peaceful men. Leblanc's theory on the advantages of the dominant male, able to commit any act of brutality in order to transmit his genes, was like a stimulant to bored students condemned to living tame lives in the lap of civilization.

The soldiers looked in the lake for the head of the anaconda but couldn't find it; it had either sunk into the mud on the bottom or the current had carried it off. They didn't dare probe around too much, because those reptiles were known to travel in pairs, and no one was inclined to chance another confrontation. Dr. Omayra Torres explained that Indians and *caboclos* both attributed curative and prophetic powers to serpents. They dried the head, ground it up, and used the powder to treat tuberculosis, baldness, and bone disease, as well as using it as an aid for interpreting dreams. A head that size would be greatly prized, she assured them, it was a shame it had been lost.

The men cut up the flesh of the anaconda, salted it, and then roasted it on sticks. Alex, who up till then had refused to taste *pirarucú*, anteater, toucan, monkey, or tapir, was struck with a sudden curiosity to know how that enormous water snake would taste. He was particularly aware of how his prestige with Cecilia Burns and his friends in California would balloon when they learned he had eaten anaconda in the middle of an Amazon jungle. He posed in front of the serpent's skin, with a piece of its flesh in his hand, and asked his grandmother to provide photographic evidence. The serpent, roasted to a cinder, since none of the crew was a good cook, turned out to have the texture of chicken and a slight taste of tuna fish. Compared to venison, it was rather bland, but Alex decided that in any case it was better than the rubbery pancakes his father prepared. A sudden recollection of his family hit him like a fist. He stood holding the chunk of burned anaconda on a stick, gazing into the night, thoughtful.

"What do you see?" Nadia asked in a whisper.

"I see my mother," Alex replied, and could not hold back a sob.

"How is she?"

"Ill, very ill," he replied.

"Your mother is ill in her body, mine is ill in her soul."

"Can you see her?" Alex asked.

"Sometimes," she answered.

"This is the first time I've ever seen someone this way," Alex explained. "I had a strange sensation: I was seeing my mother as clear as day, but I wasn't able to touch her or speak to her."

"It's just a matter of practice, Jaguar. You can learn to see with your heart. Shamans like Walimai can touch and speak, too. From afar, with the heart."

CHAPTER NINE

People of the Mist

THAT NIGHT THEY hung their hammocks between trees and César Santos assigned turns of two-hour shifts to stand guard and keep the fire going. Following the death of the man struck by the arrow, and Joel González's accident, there were now ten adults and the two younger members of the party—Leblanc didn't count for anything—to cover the eight hours of darkness. Ludovic Leblanc thought of himself as the leader of the expedition, and as such had to "stay fresh." Without a good night's sleep, he argued, he would not be clear-headed enough to make decisions. The others were relieved, because, in truth, none of them wanted to stand guard with a man who panicked at the sight of a squirrel. The first shift, which normally was the easiest, because people were still alert and it wasn't as yet cold, was assigned to Dr. Omayra Torres, a *coboclo*, and Timothy Bruce, who was inconsolable about what had happened to his colleague. Bruce and González had worked together over the years and felt like brothers. The second shift went to Alex, Kate, and another soldier, the third to Matuwe, César Santos, and his daughter, Nadia. The dawn shift was assigned to two soldiers and Karakawe.

It was difficult for everyone to fall asleep because of the moans of the unfortunate Joel González and, additionally, a strange and persistent odor that seemed to saturate the forest. They had heard about the stench that all sources said was characteristic of the Beast. César Santos explained that they had probably set up camp near a family of *iraras*, a kind of weasel with a very sweet face but a smell similar to that of a skunk. That interpretation did not make anyone feel easier.

"It makes me dizzy, and nauseated," Alex said. He looked pale.

"If the smell doesn't kill you, it will make you strong," said Kate, who was the only one unaffected by the stink.

"It's awful!"

157

"Let's say that it's different. Senses are sub-jective, Alexander. Something that you find revolting may be attractive to someone else. Maybe the Beast emits that smell as his love song to call to his mate." Kate smiled.

"Phew! It smells like a dead rat mixed with elephant urine, rotten food, and—"

"Oh, you mean like your socks," his grand-mother interrupted.

The party still had the feeling that they were being observed by hundreds of eyes from the thicket. They felt exposed, lighted as they were by the flickering flames of the bonfire as well as a pair of kerosene lanterns. The first part of the night went by without any major alarms, until Kate, Alexander, and the soldier were on duty. Alex had been sitting for more than an hour, bored, gazing at the night and the reflec-tions on the water, watching over the sleep of his companions, thinking about how much he had changed in a few days. Now he could sit quietly for a long time, in silence, concentrat-ing on his thoughts, forgetting his video games, his bicycle, and television. He discov-ered he could transport himself to that private place of stillness and silence that he had to reach when he climbed mountains. His father's first lesson in climbing had been that when you are tense or anxious or hurrying, you lose half your strength. It takes calm to conquer a mountain. Alex had learned to apply that lesson when he climbed, but until now it hadn't been of much help in other areas of his life. He realized that he had many things to think about, but his most recurrent image was of his mother. If she died . . . He always stopped himself there. He had decided not to allow that thought, because it was like tempting disaster. He concentrated, instead, on sending her positive energy; it was his way of helping her.

Suddenly, a loud noise interrupted his thoughts. As clear as a bell, he heard giant steps crashing through the nearby undergrowth. His chest contracted as if he were suffocating. For the first time since he had lost his glasses at Mauro Carías's headquarters, he missed them, because his vision was much worse at night. Holding the pistol in both hands to steady the trembling, as he had seen in movies, he waited, not knowing what to do. When he saw leaves moving, as if a band of enemies were stalking through them, he let out an earsplitting yell that sounded like the siren of a sinking ship and woke up everybody in camp. In one instant, his grandmother was by his side, rifle at the ready. The two of them found themselves facing the huge head of an animal that it took a few instants to identify. It was a wild pig, a humongous boar. No one moved, paralyzed with surprise, and that saved them because the animal, like Alex, did not see well in the dark. By luck, the breeze was blowing in the opposite direction, so it didn't smell them. César Santos was the first to slip cautiously from his hammock and evaluate the situation, despite the poor visibility.

"Don't anyone move," he ordered, almost in a whisper so as not to attract the boar.

The meat of the wild boar is very tasty, and there would have been enough to feast on for several days, but it was still too dark to get off a good shot, and no one cared to take up a machete and tangle with such a dangerous animal. The pig strolled calmly among the hammocks, sniffed the provisions suspended by ropes to keep them out of the reach of mice and ants, and finally poked its nose into the tent of Professor Ludovic Leblanc, who came within an inch of cardiac arrest. There was nothing they could do but wait until the hefty visitor got bored with checking out their camp and left, in the process passing so close to Alex that he could have reached out and touched its bristly coat.

After the tension was broken, and everyone could laugh and joke, the young American felt like a chicken-heart for having shouted as he had, but César Santos assured him that he had done the right thing. The guide repeated the instructions for an alarm: crouch down and yell first; shoot later. He had just got the words out when they did hear a shot; it was Ludovic Leblanc firing into the air a good ten minutes after all danger had passed. The professor definitely had an itchy trigger finger, as Kate described it.

César Santos, Nadia, and one of the soldiers had responsibility for the third shift, when it was even colder and darker. The guide hesitated to wake his daughter, who was sleeping soundly, hugging Borobá, but he knew that she would not forgive him if he didn't. The girl shook off sleep with two swallows of heavily sugared black coffee, and bundled up the best she could in a couple of T-shirts, her light cardigan, and her father's jacket. Alex had slept only two hours and was very weary, but when he saw that Nadia was getting ready to stand her shift, he got up, too, prepared to keep her company.

"I'm fine, you don't have to worry. I have the talisman to protect me," she whispered, to ease his concern.

"Go back to your hammock," César Santos ordered. "We all need sleep, that's why we set up turns."

Grudgingly, Alex obeyed. He vowed to stay awake, but within a few minutes, sleep overcame him. He could not calculate how long he had slept, but it must have been more than two hours because when he awakened, startled by the uproar around him, Nadia's stint had been over for some time. It was just beginning to get light; the mist was milky and the cold intense, but everyone was up. There was an odor in the air so thick it could be cut with a knife.

"What happened?" he asked, rolling out of his hammock, still groggy with sleep.

"Don't anyone leave camp for any reason!

Throw more wood on the fire!" ordered César Santos, who had tied a kerchief around his face and was standing with a rifle in one hand and a lantern in the other, staring into the swirling gray mist that rose from the jungle at dawn.

Kate, Nadia, and Alex hurried to feed more wood to the fire, adding a little more light. Karakawe had raised the alarm: somehow one of the *caboclos* on his shift had disappeared. César Santos shot twice into the air, to call him in, but as there was no answer, he decided to go with Timothy Bruce and two soldiers to search the surrounding area, leaving the others around the fire, armed with pistols. Everyone followed their guide's example and tied a handkerchief over their noses in order to breathe.

Minutes dragged by that seemed eternal, without a sound from anyone. At that hour, the monkeys normally would be waking up in the treetops, their cries, which sounded like dogs barking, announcing the coming of day. That early morning, however, a spinechilling silence reigned. The animals, even the birds, had all fled. Suddenly they heard a shot, followed by the voice of César Santos, and then shouts from the other men. A minute later Timothy Bruce ran into camp, out of breath; they had found the *caboclo*.

The man was lying facedown among some ferns. His head, however, was facing upward, as if a powerful hand had twisted it ninety degrees, breaking the bones in his neck. His eyes were wide open, and an expression of absolute terror deformed his face. When they rolled him over, they saw that his chest and abdomen were striped with deep gashes. There were hundreds of strange insects, ticks, and small beetles swarming over the body. Dr. Omayra Torres confirmed what was obvious: the man was dead. Timothy Bruce ran to get his camera, to record evidence of what had happened, while César Santos picked off some of the insects and put them in a little plastic bag to take to Padre Valdomero in Santa María de la Lluvia, who knew a lot about entomology and collected species from the region. The stench near the body was much worse, and it took a great effort of will not to run away.

César Santos gave instructions to one of the soldiers to go back and keep an eye on Joel González, whom they had left alone at the camp, and to Karakawe and another soldier to sweep the area. Matuwe, the other Indian guide, was profoundly affected by the corpse. He had turned gray, as if he were seeing a ghost. Nadia hugged her father and hid her face in his chest so she wouldn't have to look at the dreadful spectacle.

"The Beast!" Matuwe exclaimed.

"Beast, nothing. The Indians did this," Professor Leblanc differed, pale from shock and holding a cologne-soaked handkerchief in one trembling hand and a pistol in the other.

At that instant, Leblanc stepped back, stumbled, and plopped down in the mud. He yelled a curse, and tried to get up, but with every movement slipped and flailed, struggling to get out of the dark, soft, lumpy goo. From the horrendous odor, those watching knew it wasn't mud but a monumental bed of excrement; from head to foot, the famous anthropologist was literally covered in manure. César Santos and Timothy Bruce held out a tree branch for him to grab on to. They helped him up, then—at a prudent distance, trying not to come in contact—went with him to the river. Leblanc had no choice but to get thoroughly

165

wet, shivering from humiliation, cold, fear, and rage. Karakawe, his personal assistant, flatly refused to soap him or to wash his clothing and, despite the tragic circumstances, all the others had to contain themselves to keep from exploding with nervous laughter. The same thought was on everyone's mind: the being that produced that deposit must be as big as an elephant.

"I am almost sure that the creature that passed this eats a varied diet: plants and fruit, along with some raw meat," said the doctor, who had tied a handkerchief around her nose and mouth as she examined the sample under her magnifying glass.

Kate was on all fours, exploring the ground and vegetation; her grandson imitated her.

"Look, Kate, here are broken branches, and in places it looks like the bushes were crushed by enormous feet. And I found some wiry black hairs," Alex said, pointing to them.

"It could have been the boar," said Kate.

"But there are a lot of insects, too, the same ones we saw on the body. I've not seen them before."

★ ★ ★

As soon as it was daylight, César Santos and Karakawe strung the body of the unfortunate soldier, netted in a hammock, high in a tree, as high as they were able. The professor, who had developed a tic in his right eye, and was so nervous that his knees were knocking, prepared to issue a decision. He said that all of them were running a serious risk of being killed, and that he, Ludovic Leblanc, as the person responsible for the group, should be the one to give the orders. The murder of the first soldier confirmed his theory that the Indians were natural killers, sly and treacherous. The death of the second, in such rare circumstances, could also be attributed to the Indians —though he admitted that the Beast could not be ruled out. The best thing to do would be to set traps and see whether with a little luck the creature they sought might fall in before it came back to kill someone else, then return to Santa María de la Lluvia where they would call for helicopters. His companions concluded that this strange little man had learned something from his wallow in the puddle of excrement.

"Captain Ariosto would never dare to refuse

aid to Ludovic Leblanc," said the professor. The farther they traveled into unknown territory, and the more the Beast gave signs of life, the greater the tendency of the anthropologist to refer to himself in the third person.

Several members of the group agreed with him. Kate, however, declared that she was determined to continue, and she urged Timothy Bruce to stay with her, since it would be pointless to find the creature if they did not have photographs to prove it. The professor suggested that the group break up, and that those who wanted to leave take one of the boats back to the village with him. The soldiers, and Matuwe, wanted to go as soon as possible; they were terrorized. Dr. Omayra Torres, on the other hand, said that she had come with the intention of vaccinating Indians, that she might not have another opportunity to do so in the near future, and that she was not going to turn back at the first obstacle.

"You are a very brave woman, Omayra," commented César Santos with admiration. "I'm staying. I am the guide, I can't leave you here," he added.

Alex and Nadia exchanged knowing glances;

they had noticed how César Santos followed the doctor with his eyes and never lost an opportunity to be near her. They both knew, before he spoke, that if she stayed, he would do the same.

"And how do we get back without you?" Leblanc asked uneasily.

"Karakawe can lead you," said César Santos.

"I stay," the Indian stated, as always, stingy with words.

"Me, too, I'm not leaving my grandmother here alone," said Alex.

"I don't need you, and I don't need kids tagging along, Alexander," Kate grumbled, but in those eagle-sharp eyes everyone could see the glint of pride at her grandson's decision.

"I am going back for reinforcements," said Leblanc.

"Are you not in charge of this expedition, Professor?" Kate asked icily.

"I am more useful there than here . . . ," he gabbled.

"Do whatever you wish, but if you leave, I personally will publish that information in *International Geographic* so all the world will know just how courageous Professor Leblanc really is," she threatened.

Finally they agreed that Matuwe and one of the soldiers would take Joel González back to Santa María de la Lluvia. The trip would be faster than it had been coming, since they would be traveling with the current. The other members of the party, including Ludovic Leblanc, who did not have the nerve to defy Kate, would stay where they were until reinforcements arrived. By midmorning everything was ready; those staying told the others good-bye, and the boat with the injured man started down the river.

The remainder of that day and a good part of the next were spent in setting a trap for the Beast, following Professor Leblanc's instructions. It was of childlike simplicity: a huge hole in the ground covered with a net camouflaged with leaves and branches. The thought was that when the creature stepped onto the snare, it would fall in, dragging the net with it. At the bottom of the pit was a battery-powered alarm, which would sound and immediately alert the expedition. The plan was to get to the trap before the Beast could disentangle itself and get free, and to shoot several darts with an anesthesia powerful enough to down a rhinoceros.

The most difficult part was digging a pit deep enough to hold a creature as tall as the Beast. Everyone took turns with the shovel except Nadia and Leblanc, the former because she was opposed to the idea of hurting an animal, and the latter because his back was hurting again. The ground was very different from what the professor, comfortably installed at a desk in his home thousands of miles away, had expected when he designed his trap. There was a thin layer of humus, and beneath that a thick tangle of roots, then clay as slippery as soap, and as they dug deeper, the hole filled with reddish water in which all sorts of tiny things were swimming. Finally they quit, overcome by obstacles. Alex suggested using a system of ropes to hang nets from the trees, with a lure below. When their prey moved in to take the bait, the alarm would go off and the net would drop over the Beast. Everyone, except Leblanc, thought that that plan might work in theory, but they were too exhausted to test it and decided to postpone the project until the following morning.

"I hope your idea doesn't work, Jaguar," said Nadia.

"The Beast is dangerous," Alex replied.

"What will they do with it if they catch it? Kill it? Cut it up in little pieces to study? Put it in a cage for the rest of its life?"

"What's your solution, Nadia?"

"Talk with it and ask what it wants."

"Now there's a brilliant idea! We could invite it for tea," he jeered.

"All animals can communicate," she insisted.

"That's what my sister Nicole says, but she's only nine."

"I see that she knows more at nine than you do at fifteen," Nadia replied.

They had camped in a very beautiful spot. The dense tangle of growth along the river-bank opened up farther inland into a majestic forest, the straight, soaring tree trunks forming the pillars of a magnificent green cathedral. Orchids and other flowers hung from the branches and glittering ferns covered the ground. Animal life was so varied that there was never a moment of silence; from dawn to late day, the songs of toucans and parrots filled the air, replaced at night by the clamor of tree frogs and howler monkeys. This Garden of Eden hid many dangers, however: distances were enormous, the solitude absolute, and without long experience it was impossible to get your bearings. According to Leblanc—and in this César Santos was in agreement—the only way to get around in this region was with the help of Indians. Contact with them was essential. Dr. Omayra Torres was the one most eager to find them because, as she explained, she first had to fulfill her mission—the vaccinations—and then establish a basic health care system.

"I don't think the Indians will voluntarily offer their arms for you to stick, Omayra. They have never seen a needle in their lives." César Santos smiled. There was a strong current of sympathy between them, and by then they were acting like old friends.

"We will tell them that it is powerful magic sent by the white man," she said, and winked.

"Which is absolutely true," approved César Santos.

According to the guide, there were several tribes in the vicinity that had almost surely had contact, if brief, with the outside world. From his airplane, he had sighted *shabonos*, but since there was nowhere to land, all he could do was mark them on his map. The communal huts he had seen were rather small, which meant that each tribe was composed of only a few families. Professor Leblanc, who declared himself an expert on the matter, assured them that the minimal number of inhabitants per shabono was around fifty—otherwise they would not be able to defend themselves against enemy attack—and, very rarely, more than two hundred and fifty. César Santos also suspected that there were isolated tribes that had never been seen, which was what Dr. Torres expected; the only way these groups could be reached was by air. They would have to fly to the rain forests on the high plain, the enchanted region of the waterfalls, where outsiders had never traveled before the invention of airplanes and helicopters.

With the hope of attracting the Indians, the guide tied a cord between two trees and hung a number of gifts from it: bead necklaces, bright scarves, mirrors, and plastic trinkets. He held the machetes, knives, and steel tools for later, when the real negotiations and exchange of gifts would begin.

That afternoon, César Santos tried to reach Captain Ariosto and Mauro Carías in Santa María de la Lluvia, but the radio was out of order. Professor Leblanc strode around the camp, furious at this new difficulty, while the others took turns in vain to try to send or receive a message. Nadia took Alex aside to tell him that last night, before the soldier had been murdered during Karakawe's shift, she had seen the Indian fooling with the set. She said she had gone to bed when her turn was over, but hadn't fallen asleep immediately, and from her hammock had seen Karakawe near the apparatus.

"Did you see him clearly, Nadia?"

"No, because it was dark, but the only ones up during that shift were the two soldiers and him. I'm almost sure it wasn't either of the soldiers," she replied. "I think Karakawe is the person Mauro Carías mentioned. Maybe it's part of the plan for us not to be able to call for help in case of an emergency."

"We should warn your father," Alex determined.

César Santos was not interested in their

report; he merely warned them that before they accused anyone, they should be very sure. There were many reasons why such antiquated radio equipment might fail. Besides, why would Karakawe put it out of commission? There was no reason he would want to be without communication. He calmed Alex and Nadia, saying that reinforcements would be there in only three or four days.

"We aren't lost, just isolated," he concluded.

"And the Beast, Papa?" Nadia asked, troubled.

"We don't know if it even exists, child. On the other hand, we can be sure about the Indians. Sooner or later they will appear, and we hope they will come in peace. In any case, we're well armed."

"The soldier who died had a rifle, but it didn't help him," Alex rebutted.

"He was distracted. From now on we have to be much more cautious. Unfortunately, there are only seven adults to stand guard."

"I count as an adult," Alex assured him.

"That's fine, but not Nadia. The only time she can help is during my shift," César Santos decided.

★ ★ ★

That day, Nadia discovered an *urucu* pod tree near the camp. She picked some of its fruit, which looked like shelled almonds, opened them, and took out the red seeds. When she squeezed them and mixed them with a little saliva, she formed a red paste that had the consistency of soap. This, along with other vegetable dyes, was what the Indians used to decorate their bodies. Nadia and Alex painted lines, circles, and dots on their faces, then tied feathers and seeds onto their arms. When Timothy Bruce and Kate saw them, they insisted on taking photographs, and Omayra combed the girl's curly hair and adorned it with tiny orchids. César Santos, in contrast, did not approve; the vision of his daughter painted like an Indian girl seemed to fill him with sadness.

As the light began to fade, they knew that somewhere the sun was preparing to disappear below the horizon, yielding to night. Beneath the treetops the sun was rarely seen; its brilliance was hazy when filtered through the green lace of vegetation. Only occasionally, where a tree had fallen, could the blue eye of the sky be seen. At that hour, the shadows of the trees began to close around them like a fence. In less than an hour, the jungle would be black. Nadia asked Alex to play the flute to entertain them, and for a while the music, delicate and crystalline, filled the jungle. Borobá, the little monkey, followed the melody, moving its head in time to the notes. César Santos and Dr. Omayra Torres, kneeling at the bonfire, were roasting fish for dinner. Kate, Timothy Bruce, and one of the soldiers were securing the tents to protect their provisions from monkeys and ants. Karakawe and the other soldier, armed and alert, were standing watch. Professor Leblanc was dictating ideas that flashed through his mind into a pocket recorder he always carried for the times he was gifted with a transcendent thought that must be preserved for humanity. This happened so frequently that Alex and Nadia, bored, were just awaiting their chance to steal the batteries. About fifteen minutes into the flute concert, Borobá's attention suddenly shifted: he began to jump up and down, fidgeting and tugging at Nadia's clothing. At first Nadia tried to ignore her pet, but the animal kept bothering her until she got up. After she peered into the thick growth, she signaled Alex, who had just come to the end of a song, and led him outside the circle of firelight without attracting the others' attention.

"Shhhh," she whispered, putting a finger to her lips.

There was still a trace of twilight but the colors had faded; the world lay in tones of gray and black. Alex had felt he was being observed ever since he left Santa María de la Lluvia, but just that evening the impression of being spied upon had disappeared. He had been filled with a sensation of calm and safety he hadn't felt for many days. Also, the penetrating odor at the place where the soldier had been killed the previous night had dispersed. Alex, Nadia, and Borobá walked a few yards into the thicket and waited there, more curious than uneasy. Without having stated it, they supposed that if there were Indians about, and if they had any intention of harming them, they would already have done so, because the members of the expedition, lighted by the campfire, were exposed to the aim of arrows and poisoned darts of the dwellers of the jungle.

They stood very quietly, feeling they were sinking into a cottony mist, as if when night fell the normal dimensions of reality were lost to them. Then gradually Alex began to see, one by one, the beings that surrounded them. They were naked, painted with stripes and spots, with feathers and leather thongs tied around their arms—silent, airy, motionless. Even though they were right beside him, they were difficult to see; they blended perfectly into nature, which made them invisible, like stealthy ghosts. Once he could see them, Alex figured that there had to be at least twenty, all men, all with their primitive weapons in their hands.

"Ah-ee-ah," whispered Nadia.

No one answered, but a barely perceptible movement of the leaves indicated that the Indians were moving closer. In the darkness, and without his eyeglasses, Alex wasn't sure what he was seeing, but his heart was pounding wildly and he could feel the blood throbbing at his temples. He had the same hallucinatory sensation of being in a dream that he had felt in the presence of the black jaguar in Mauro Carías's patio. There was a similar tension, as if things were happening in a glass bubble that might shatter at any instant. Danger was in the air, just as it had been with the jaguar, but he was not afraid. He did not feel threatened by those transparent beings floating among the trees. The idea of pulling out his knife or calling for help never occurred to him. Like lightning, a scene flashed through his mind that he had seen years before at the movies: a young boy's encounter with an alien. He was living in a similar moment. Through his amazement, he realized that he would not trade this experience for anything in the world.

"Ah-ee-ah," Nadia repeated.

"Ah-ee-ah," Alex murmured, too.

No response.

They waited, hand in hand, still as statues. Even Borobá was quiet, expectant, as if he knew he was participating in a precious instant. Endless minutes passed and night fell rapidly, completely cloaking them in black. At some point, they realized they were alone; the Indians had evaporated with the same airiness with which they had emerged from nothing.

"Who are they?" Alex asked as they

returned to camp.

"They must be the People of the Mist, the invisible ones, the most remote and mysterious Indians of the Amazon. It's been known they exist, but no one has ever spoken with them."

"What do they want of us?" Alex asked.

"To see what we're like, maybe," she suggested.

"That's what I want, too," he said.

"We mustn't tell anyone what we've seen, Jaguar."

"It's strange they didn't attack us, and that they don't seem to be interested in the gifts your father put out," Alex commented.

"Do you think they're the ones who killed the soldier on the boat?" Nadia asked.

"I don't know, but if they are, why didn't they attack us today?"

That night Alex stood guard with his grandmother, totally unafraid, because he didn't perceive any scent of the Beast, and he wasn't worried about the Indians. After their strange encounter, he was convinced that pistols would be of little use in case the natives wanted to attack. How would you aim at nearly invisible beings? The Indians dissolved like shadows in the night; they were mute ghosts that could be on top of them and murder them in an instant, before their victims realized they were even there. Deep down, however, he was sure that killing them was not what the People of the Mist intended to do.

CHAPTER TEN

Kidnapped

THE FOLLOWING DAY was slow and boring. It rained so much that they could not dry their clothes before the next cloudburst came along. That same night, the two soldiers disappeared during their watch, and it didn't take long to discover that the boat was gone, too. The two men, who had been terrified since the death of their companions, had fled downriver. They had been near mutiny when they'd not been allowed to go back to Santa María de la Lluvia with the first boat; no one was paying them to risk their lives, they said. César Santos had replied that it was precisely what they were being paid for, they were soldiers, weren't they? The decision to desert could cost them dearly, but they preferred to face a court-martial rather than die at the hands of the Indians or the Beast. For the rest of the expedition group, that boat represented the only possibility of returning to civilization; without it or the radio, they were completely isolated.

"The Indians know where we are. We can't stay here!" exclaimed Professor Leblanc.

"Where do you plan to go, Professor? If we leave this place, the helicopters won't be able to find us when they come. From the air, all you can see is a mass of green; they'll never find us," César Santos explained.

"Can't we follow the river and try to get back to Santa María de la Lluvia on our own?" asked Kate.

"Impossible on foot. There are too many obstacles and detours," the guide replied.

"This is your fault, Cold! We should all have gone back to Santa María de la Lluvia as I proposed," accused the professor.

"All right, it's my fault. What are you going to do about it?" the writer asked.

"I'm going to denounce you! I'm going to ruin your career!"

"Maybe I'm going to ruin *yours*, Professor," she replied, not giving an inch.

César Santos interrupted, saying that instead of arguing they should join forces and analyze the situation: the Indians were distrustful and had not shown any interest in the gifts; they were simply watching them—but at least they hadn't attacked.

"You don't call what they did to that poor soldier an attack?" Leblanc asked sarcastically.

"I don't believe it was the Indians, that isn't their way of fighting. If we're lucky, this may be a peaceful tribe," the guide replied.

"But if we're not lucky, they will eat us," grumbled the anthropologist.

"That would be perfect, Professor. That would prove your theory about how ferocious they are," said Kate.

"All right, enough foolishness," cut in the photographer, Timothy Bruce. "We have to make a decision. Do we stay or do we go?"

César Santos took control. "It's been nearly three days since the first boat left. Since they were traveling with the current and Matuwe knows the way, they must be in Santa María de la Lluvia by now. Tomorrow, or two days more at the most, Captain Ariosto's helicopters will be here. They fly by day, and we will have to keep a bonfire going all the time so they can sight the smoke. The situation is difficult, as I said, but it isn't desperate. Lots of people know where we are; they will come look for us."

Nadia was calm, hugging her little monkey as if she didn't understand the magnitude of what was happening. Alex, on the other hand, concluded that he had never been in such danger, not even when he was hanging off the face of El Capitán, a sheer cliff that only the most expert dare to climb. If he hadn't been roped to his father's waist, he could have died.

César Santos had warned all of them about various insects and animals in the jungle, from tarantulas to serpents, but he had forgotten to mention ants. Alex had stopped wearing his boots; not only were they always damp and foul smelling, they were also too tight; he supposed they'd shrunk from being wet. Even though he rarely took off the sandals César Santos had given him, his feet were covered with scabs and abrasions.

"This is no place for delicate feet," was his grandmother's only comment when he showed her the bleeding cuts.

Her indifference turned to concern when Alex was bitten by a fire ant. He hadn't been able to choke back a yell; he felt as if someone had burned his ankle with a cigarette. The ant had left a small white mark that within a few minutes had turned as hard and round as a cherry. Pain rose up his leg like flames, and he couldn't take another step. Dr. Omayra Torres warned him that the poison would last for several hours and he would have to bear it with no relief but warm-water compresses.

"I hope you're not allergic, because if you are, the consequences will be more serious," the doctor observed.

He wasn't, but the bite ruined a good part of the day nevertheless. By evening, as soon as he could put weight on his foot and take a few steps, Nadia told him that while the others had been doing their chores, she had seen Karakawe hanging around the boxes of vaccines. When the Indian realized that she had spied him, he took her by the arms so brutally that he left his finger marks on her skin, and he warned her that if she said one word about what she'd seen, she would pay for it. Nadia was sure that the man would do what he threatened, but Alex thought they couldn't *not* tell, they needed to warn the doctor. The girl, who admired the doctor as much as she did her father and was beginning to cherish the fantasy of seeing her become her stepmother, also wanted to tell her about the conversation they'd heard in Santa María de la Lluvia between Mauro Carías and Captain Ariosto. She was still convinced that Karakawe was the person sent to carry out Carías's sinister plans.

"Let's not say anything just yet," Alex urged.

They waited for the right moment, when Karakawe had gone off to fish at the river, and presented the situation to Dr. Omayra Torres. She listened very closely, showing signs of uneasiness for the first time since they had met her. Even at the most dramatic moments of their adventure, this delightful woman had not lost her calm; she had the steely nerves of a samurai. She was not shaken this time, either, but she did want to know every detail. When she found that Karakawe had opened the cases but not broken the seals on the vials, she sighed with relief.

"These vaccines are the only hope for the Indians. We must guard them like a treasure," she said.

"Alex and I have been watching Karakawe;

we think he's the one who tampered with the radio, but my father says that we can't accuse him without proof," said Nadia.

"Let's not worry your father with these suspicions, Nadia, he already has enough problems. Among the three of us, we can neutralize Karakawe. I want you two to keep an eye on him every minute," Dr. Torres said, and they promised that they would.

That day went by without incident. César Santos continued his attempts to repair the radio transmitter, without results. Timothy Bruce had brought a radio they had used to listen to news from Manaus during the early part of the trip, but the signal was too weak to pick up now. They were bored, because once they had caught some birds and a couple of fish for the day's meals, there was nothing more to do; it was pointless to hunt or fish anymore because the catch would be covered with ants or rotted in a matter of hours. Finally Alex could understand the mentality of the Indians, and why they never accumulated anything. The members of the expedition took turns keeping the campfire smoking as a signal in case their rescuers were looking for them, although according to César Santos, it was still too early for that. Timothy Bruce produced a worn pack of cards and they played poker, blackjack, and gin rummy until the light began to fade. There was no hint of the penetrating odor of the Beast.

Nadia, Kate, and the doctor went to the river to relieve themselves and bathe; it had been agreed that no one would venture alone outside the camp. For their most private needs, the three women went together; for everything else they all took turns in pairs. César Santos arranged things so that he was always with Omayra Torres, which annoyed Timothy Bruce considerably since he, too, was captivated by the doctor. Even though Kate had warned the Englishman to save the film for the Beast and the Indians, he had taken so many photographs of Dr. Torres that she refused to pose any more. The writer and Karakawe were the only ones who did not seem to be impressed by the young woman. Kate muttered that she was too old to notice a pretty face, a comment that to Alex sounded like a hint of jealousy unworthy of someone as cool as his grandmother. Professor Leblanc, who could not compete in looks with César Santos, or youth with Timothy Bruce, tried to impress the young beauty with the weight of his celebrity, and never lost an opportunity to read aloud paragraphs from his book, in which he outlined in detail the hair-raising dangers he had faced among the Indians. It was difficult for her to imagine the cowardly Leblanc dressed only in a loincloth, fighting hand to hand with Indians and wild beasts, hunting with arrows and surviving unaided in the midst of all kinds of natural catastrophes, as he described. In any case, the rivalry over Dr. Omayra Torres's attention had created a certain tension among the men in the group, which increased as the hours went by anxiously waiting for the helicopter.

Alex checked his ankle; it still hurt and was a little swollen, but the hard red cherry where the ant had bitten him was smaller. The compresses of warm water had helped a lot. To entertain himself, he took up his flute and began to play his mother's favorite concerto, the sweet and romantic music of a European composer dead for more than a century but a melody that seemed suited to the jungle around them. His grandfather Joseph was right; music is a universal language. At the first notes, Borobá came bounding up and sat at Alex's feet, as absorbed as a music critic, and after only a few minutes, Nadia returned with the doctor and Kate. The girl waited until the others were busy preparing the camp for the night, then signaled to Alex, who casually followed her.

"They're here again, Jaguar," she whispered into his ear.

"The Indians?"

"Yes, the People of the Mist. I think they came to hear the music. Be still, and follow me."

They walked about twenty yards into the thicket, then stopped, just as they had before. As hard as Alex tried to see, he could not make out anyone among the trees; the Indians blended into the background. Suddenly he felt firm hands on his arms, and when he looked around, he saw that Nadia and he were surrounded. This time the Indians were not staying at a distance, as they had before; now Alex could smell the sweetish scent of their bodies.

Again he noticed how short and slim they were, but this time he could also see that they were very strong, and that there was something fierce in their attitude. Could Leblanc be right when he claimed they were violent and cruel?

"Ah-ee-ah," he said tentatively in greeting.

A hand clamped over his mouth, and before he could realize what was happening, he felt himself lifted off the ground by his ankles and upper arms. He started to twist and kick, but the hands did not let go. He felt a sharp blow to his head, whether a fist or a rock he couldn't tell, but he realized that if he was smart, he would let himself be carried or they would knock him senseless or kill him. He thought about Nadia and wondered if she, too, had been taken by force. He seemed to hear his grandmother's voice in the distance, calling him, as the Indians—and he—vanished into the darkness like spirits of the night.

Alexander felt sharp stabs in the ankle where the fire ant had bitten him. He was now in the strong grasp of one of the four Indians carrying him. His captors were trotting, and with each step his body jounced brutally; the pain in his shoulders felt as if he were being torn limb from limb. The Indians had pulled off his T-shirt and wrapped it around his head, blinding and silencing him. He could barely breathe and his head hurt, but he was relieved that he hadn't lost consciousness; that meant that the warriors had not hit him very hard, and did not intend to kill him. At least, not for the moment. . . . It seemed to him that they traveled a long way before finally they stopped and dropped him to the ground like a sack of potatoes. The relief to his muscles and bones was almost immediate, although his ankle was burning terribly. He was afraid that if he pulled off the T-shirt, it would provoke his attackers, but he waited awhile and when nothing happened he went ahead and removed it. No one stopped him. When his eyes got used to the pale light of the moon, he saw that he was in the middle of the forest, lying on a cushion of humus. All around him, in a tight circle, he sensed the presence of the Indians, although he couldn't actually see them in the faint light and without his eyeglasses. He remembered his Swiss Army knife and casually put his hand to his belt, but he was checked by a firm hand on his wrist. Then he heard Nadia's voice and felt the tiny hands of Borobá on his neck. Alex yipped as the monkey put his fingers on the bump where he had been hit.

"Be quiet, Jaguar, or they may hurt us," said the girl.

"What happened?"

"They were frightened; they thought you were going to yell, that's why they had to carry you by force. All they want is for us to come with them."

"Where? Why?" Alex mumbled, trying to sit up. His head was pounding like a drum.

Nadia helped him up, and gave him water from a gourd. By now, Alex's eyes had adjusted, and he saw that the Indians were very near, watching him and talking loudly, with no fear of being heard or overtaken. Alex was sure the other members of the group would be looking for them, although no one would dare venture too far at night. For once, he thought, his grandmother would be worried. How would she explain to her son John that she had lost her grandson in the jungle? Apparently the Indians had treated Nadia more gently, because she was moving among them freely. As he sat up he felt something warm running down his right temple and dripping onto his shoulder. He put a finger to his forehead and then to his lips: blood.

"They split my head open," he murmured, frightened.

"Pretend it doesn't hurt, Jaguar, like a true warrior," Nadia advised him.

Alex decided that he must make a show of courage. He staggered to his feet, trying to ignore the trembling in his knees, stood as straight as he could, and beat his chest the way he had seen Tarzan do in the movies, at the same time bellowing like King Kong. The Indians stepped back and clutched their weapons more tightly, astonished. Alex repeated the chest thumping and bellowing, confident that he had caused panic in the enemy ranks, but instead of running off in fear, the warriors burst out laughing. Nadia smiled, and Borobá jumped and bared his teeth, chattering hysterically. The laughter rose in volume; some warriors plopped down, too weak to stand, others rolled on their backs and kicked their feet with pure delight, and others imitated Alex's Tarzan yell. The merriment lasted a long time, until Alex, feeling absolutely ridiculous, was himself caught up in it. Finally everyone calmed down, wiped the tears from their eyes, and slapped each other's backs like old friends.

One of the Indians, who in the shadows appeared to be the smallest and oldest and was distinguished by a feather crown, the only adornment of an otherwise naked body, began a long diatribe. Nadia caught the sense of it, because she knew several Indian tongues, and although the People of the Mist had their own language, many words were similar. She felt sure she could communicate with them. From the oration of the feather-crowned chief she picked up references to Rahakanariwa, the spirit of the cannibal-bird Walimai had mentioned, the *nahab*, the Indians' word for non-Indians, and a powerful shaman. Although he wasn't named, since it would have been discourteous to do that, she deduced that they were talking about Walimai. Calling on the vocabulary she knew, and on gestures and mimicry, Nadia communicated that the carved bone she wore around her neck was a gift from the witch man. The Indian chief examined the talisman for a long while, showing signs of admiration and respect, then started speaking again, but this time directing it to the warriors, who came up one by one to touch the amulet.

Afterward, the Indians sat down in a circle and continued to talk as they handed around pieces of something like unleavened bread. Alex realized that he hadn't eaten for many hours and was extremely hungry; he took his portion without noticing the dirt and without asking how it was made; his fussiness with regard to food was now history. Following the bread, the warriors circulated an animal bladder containing a thick, sharp-smelling liquid that tasted like vinegar, as they sang a chant to defy the ghosts that bring nightmares in the night. They did not offer the brew to Nadia, but they were sociable enough to share it with Alex, who was not particularly tempted by the smell and even less by the idea of sharing the bladder with the others. He recalled the story César Santos had told of an entire tribe infected by one puff from a journalist's cigarette. The last thing he wanted was to pass his germs to these Indians, whose immune systems might not withstand them, but Nadia warned him that not accepting would be an insult. She explained that *masato* was a fermented drink made of chewed cassava root and saliva, something only the men drank. When Alex heard the description, he was afraid he would vomit, but he didn't dare refuse.

Between the blow to his head and the *masato,* Alex was speedily borne off to the planet of the golden sands and the phosphorescent sky with six moons that he had seen in Mauro Carías's patio. He was so blurry and intoxicated that he could not have walked a single step, but fortunately he didn't have to because the warriors were also feeling the influence of the liquor and soon were stretched out on the ground, snoring. Alex concluded that they would not be going anywhere before first light, and consoled himself with the vague hope that his grandmother would catch up with him by dawn. Curled up on the ground, the ghosts of nightmares, the fire ants, the tarantulas, and the snakes all forgotten, he abandoned himself to sleep. Not even the dreadful odor of the Beast alerted him when it began to spread through the air.

The only ones who were sober and awake when the Beast appeared were Nadia and Borobá. The monkey was petrified, as if turned to stone, and the girl managed to glimpse a gigantic figure in the moonlight before the odor made her lose consciousness. Later she would tell her friend exactly what Padre Valdomero had said: she had seen a creature with human form, erect, about nine feet tall, with a small head out of proportion to the size of its body and powerful arms that ended in claws curved like scimitars. To Nadia, it seemed that it moved very, very slowly, but if it had chosen, the Beast could have gutted them all. The stench it emitted—or maybe the absolute terror it inspired in its victims—paralyzed like a drug. Before fainting, she had wanted to scream or run away, but she couldn't move a muscle; in a flash of consciousness she saw the body of the soldier cut open like a slaughtered steer and could image the man's horror, his helplessness and his terrifying death.

Alex awakened in confusion, trying to remember what had happened; his body was trembling from the strange liquor he'd drunk the night before and the stench, which was still floating on the air. He saw Nadia with Borobá in her lap, sitting cross-legged and staring into space. He crawled to her, barely controlling his lurching innards.

"I saw it, Jaguar," the girl said in a remote voice, as if she were in a trance.

"What did you see?"

"The Beast. It was here. It's enormous, a giant. . . ."

Alex went behind a fern to throw up, after which he felt greatly improved even though the Beast's stench made him nauseated all over again. When he returned, the warriors were ready to get started. In the dawn light, he saw them clearly for the first time. Their fearsome appearance corresponded exactly to Leblanc's descriptions: their naked bodies were painted red, black, and green; they wore feather bracelets and had bowl haircuts, with the crown of the skull shaved like a priest's tonsure. Their bows and arrows were strapped to their backs, along with small, hide-covered gourds that Nadia said contained the lethal curare for their arrows and darts. Several of them were carrying thick clubs, and all of them had scars on their heads, proud badges of war, since courage and strength were measured by the marks of blows survived.

Alex had to shake Nadia out of her trance because her fright at having seen the Beast the night before had left her dazed. She managed to explain what she'd seen, and the warriors listened attentively but gave no sign of surprise, just as they had made no comment about the odor.

Immediately thereafter, the Indians set off, trotting single file behind their chief, whom Nadia had decided to call Mokarita since she couldn't ask his real name. To judge by the condition of his skin, his teeth, and his misshapen feet, Mokarita was much older than Alex had thought when he had seen him in the dark, but he had the agility and endurance of the other warriors. One of the young men stood out from the rest; he was taller and huskier and unlike the others was painted all over with black except for a kind of red mask across his eyes and forehead. He always walked beside the chief, as if he were his lieutenant, and he referred to himself as Tahama; Nadia and Alex learned later that that was his honorary title, earned by being the best hunter in the tribe.

Although the landscape seemed never to change, and there were no landmarks, the Indians knew exactly where they were going. Not once did they turn around to see whether the alien boy and girl were following, because they knew they had no other choice; it was follow or be lost. At times it seemed to Alex and Nadia that they were alone, because the People of the Mist simply faded into the vegetation, but that impression wouldn't last long; just the way they had vanished, the Indians would reappear at any moment, as if they were practicing the art of becoming invisible. Alex concluded that their talent for disappearing could not be attributed solely to the paint that camouflaged them; more than anything, it was a mental attitude. How did they do it? He thought how useful the trick of invisibility could be in his life, and determined to learn it. During the next few days he would realize that it was not a question of magic but a talent achieved with great practice and concentration, like playing the flute.

They kept up the rapid pace for several hours, stopping only occasionally to drink at a stream. Alex was hungry, but he was grateful that at least the bite on his ankle wasn't hurting anymore. César Santos had told him that the Indians eat when they can—not necessarily every day—and that their bodies are used to storing energy. He, on the other hand, had always had a refrigerator stuffed with food, at least when his mother was well, and if he had to skip a meal, it made him uneasy. He could only smile when he thought of the complete upheaval in his habits. Among other things, he hadn't brushed his teeth or changed his clothes for days. He decided to ignore the gnawing in his stomach and kill hunger with indifference. Once or twice he looked at his compass and noted that they were heading northeast. Would anyone come to their rescue? How could he leave signs along the way? Would they be seen from a helicopter? He did not feel optimistic; in fact, their situation was desperate. He was surprised that Nadia wasn't showing signs of fatigue; his friend seemed completely wrapped up in the journey.

Four or five hours later—it was impossible to measure time in that place—they came to a deep, clear river. They followed it for a couple of miles, and, suddenly, before Alex's astounded eyes appeared a towering mountain and a magnificent waterfall that fell with the roar of a battle, forming at its base an enormous cloud of foam and spray.

"This is the river that falls from the sky," said Tahama.

CHAPTER ELEVEN

The Invisible Village

MOKARITA, THE CHIEF with the yellow feathers, gave permission for the group to rest a while before beginning the climb up the mountain. He had a face like wood, the skin scored like tree bark, but the effect was serene and kindly.

"I can't climb," Nadia said when she saw the smooth, wet, black rock.

It was the first time Alex had seen her defeated by an obstacle, and he sympathized with her because he was afraid, too, even though he had climbed mountains and rocks for years with his father. John Cold was one of the most experienced and daring climbers in the United States; he had taken part in famous expeditions to almost inaccessible sites, and had even been called on a couple of times to rescue people stranded on the highest peaks of Austria and Chile. Alex knew he did not have his father's ability or courage, much less his experience, and he had never seen a rock as sheer as what stood before him now. To climb up the sides of that waterfall, without ropes and without help, was practically impossible.

Nadia went over to Mokarita and with signs and the words they had in common tried to explain that she was not capable of making that climb. The chief seemed very angry; he shouted, and shook his weapons and waved his arms. The other Indians joined in, surrounding Nadia threateningly. Alex went to stand beside his friend and try to calm the warriors with gestures, but the only thing he accomplished was to see Tahama grab Nadia by the hair and drag her toward the falls, while Borobá shrieked and slapped at him. With a flash of inspiration—or desperation—Alex unfastened his flute from his belt and began to play. The Indians stopped instantly, as if they were hyp-notized; Tahama released Nadia and they gath-ered in a circle around Alex.

Once the men were calm, Alex convinced Nadia that with a rope, he could help her make the climb. He repeated what he had heard his father say so many times: Before you conquer the mountain, you must learn to overcome your fear.

"I'm afraid of heights, Jaguar, I get dizzy. Every time I get into my father's airplane, I'm so scared that I get sick," Nadia moaned.

"My father says that fear is good; it's the body's alarm system, it warns us of danger. But sometimes danger can't be avoided, and then you have to forget about being afraid."

"I can't!"

"Nadia, listen to me," Alex said, taking her shoulders and forcing her to look into his eyes. "Take a deep breath. I will teach you to use your fear. I trust you and I trust myself. I will help you climb; we will do it together, I promise," Alex assured her.

Nadia's response was to burst into tears and rest her head on Alex's shoulder. He didn't know what to do, he had never been that close to a girl. In his fantasies, he had put his arms around Cecilia Burns a thousand times; she was his dream love, but in reality, he would have run for his life if she had touched him. Cecilia Burns was so far away that it was as if she didn't exist; he couldn't remember her face. Almost as a reflex, Alex's arms closed around

Nadia. He felt his heart pounding in his chest like a stampede of buffalo, but he had enough sense to realize how absurd the situation was. Here he was in the middle of the jungle, surrounded by strange, gaudily painted warriors, with a terrified girl in his arms, and what was he thinking about? Love! He pulled himself together, pushed Nadia away, and faced her with determination.

"Stop crying, and tell these guys that we need rope," he ordered, pointing to the Indians. "And remember that the talisman will protect you."

"Walimai said it would protect me from people, animals, and ghosts, but he didn't mention the danger of falling and breaking my neck," Nadia protested.

"Well, my grandmother always says that you have to die of something," he consoled his friend, trying to smile. And he added, "Didn't you tell me that I should learn to see with my heart? This is a good opportunity."

Nadia found a way to communicate Alex's request to the Indians. When finally they understood, several of them sprang into action and soon produced a rope made of braided lianas.

When they saw that Alex was tying one end of the rope to the girl's waist and rolling the rest around his chest, they showed signs of great curiosity. They could not imagine why these foreigners would do anything that crazy: if one slipped, the other would be dragged down, too.

Now they were right by the waterfall, which tumbled freely from a height of more than a hundred and sixty feet to explode at its base in an impressive cloud of water crowned by a magnificent rainbow. Hundreds of black birds swept through the waterfall in every direction. The Indians greeted the river that falls from the sky by waving their weapons and yelling; they were very close to their homeland. Once they climbed to the high country, they felt safe from any danger. Three of them went briefly into the rain forest and returned with balls of a substance that when inspected turned out to be a white, thick, and very sticky resin. Imitating the Indians, Alex and Nadia rubbed the palms of their hands and soles of their feet with the paste. When their feet touched the ground, the humus stuck to the resin, creating a rough surface. Their first steps were difficult,

211

but as soon as they were beneath the mist from the fall, they recognized its usefulness: it was like wearing rubber boots and gloves.

Following the edge of the water that formed into a lake, they quickly came to the fall itself, a solid curtain of water that arched several yards away from the cliff. They were soaking wet, and the roar of the water was so loud that it was impossible to communicate. They could not sign to one another since visibility was almost zero; the water vapor turned the air to white foam. They felt as if they were feeling their way through a cloud. Following Nadia's command, Borobá was clinging to Alex like a large, warm, hairy Band-Aid, while she followed behind—only because she was tied to Alex, otherwise she would have turned back. The warriors knew the terrain and moved forward slowly but without hesitation, knowing where to set each foot. The two friends followed as closely as they could, because falling only a couple of steps behind would mean losing sight of their guides altogether. Alex saw why they were named the People of the Mist, for the heavy spray formed from the impact of the water.

This and other waterfalls of the Upper Orinoco had always defeated outsiders, but the Indians had turned obstacles into allies. They knew exactly where to step; they used natural toeholds, or notches they had hollowed out and used for hundreds of years. Those grooves in the cliff formed a stairway behind the cascade that led to the very top. Unless you knew of its existence, and the exact location, there was no way you could climb those smooth, wet, slippery walls with the thundering noise of the falls at your back. One slip and the fall ended in sure death, surrounded by roaring foam.

Before they were isolated by the noise, Alex had instructed Nadia not to look down; she was to concentrate on imitating his every movement, holding where he took hold, just as he imitated Tahama, who was in front of him. He also had explained that the first part would be the most difficult because of the mist rising from the foaming water, and that as they climbed farther, it would not be as slick and they would be able to see better. That did nothing to encourage Nadia; her worst problem wasn't seeing, it was dizziness. She tried not to think of the height and the deafening rumble of the falls, but to convince herself that the resin on her hands and feet would help her cling to the wet rock. The rope that joined her to Alex gave her a faint sense of security, although it was all too easy to imagine how one false step by either of them would pitch them both into empty space. She tried to follow Alex's instructions: concentrate on the next move, on the precise place where she was to put her foot or hand, one at a time, without hurrying and without losing the rhythm.

As soon as she was certain of her balance, she made a cautious move toward a higher crack or protruding stone, then felt with a foot to find another and inch her body upward. The fissures in the cliff were deep enough to get a good hold, the greatest danger was pushing away from the rock; you had to keep pressed against it. Borobá passed through her mind in a flash: if she was that frightened, imagine what the poor monkey clamped on Alex's back was feeling.

As Alex and Nadia moved upward, the visibility improved but the distance between the waterfall and the cliff decreased. The water fell

214

closer and closer to their backs. Just when they were wondering how they could finish the last part of the climb, the notches in the rock curved off to the right. Alex could feel nothing but smooth surface, then he felt someone take his wrist and pull upward. He gathered his strength and landed in a cave in the side of the mountain; the warriors were all waiting there. Pulling on the rope, Alex brought up Nadia, who landed on top of him, stupefied by strain and fear. Poor Borobá didn't even move; he was stuck to Alex's back like a barnacle, frozen with terror. The black birds swooped through the solid curtain of water before the mouth of the cave, ready to defend their nests from invaders. Alex could only admire the incredible courage of the first Indians who had ventured behind the fall, maybe in prehistoric times, and had discovered some toeholds and chipped out others, found the cave, and opened the route for their descendants.

The long, narrow grotto was not high enough for them to stand; they had to crawl or pull themselves forward with their elbows. A milky-white sun filtered through the waterfall; it barely lighted the entrance, and farther on it was dark. Alex, holding Nadia and Borobá tight, watched Tahama come over to him, waving his arms and pointing to the falling water. He couldn't hear, but realized that someone had fallen or stayed behind. Tahama showed him the rope, and finally he understood that the Indian wanted to use it to go down to look for the missing person. He was heavier than Alex and, regardless of his athleticism, he had no experience in mountain rescue. Alex was no expert himself, but at least he had accompanied his father on a couple of risky missions; he knew how to use a rope and had read a lot on the subject. Climbing was, after all, his passion, comparable only to his love for the flute. With sign language, he indicated that he would go down as far as the rope would reach. He untied Nadia and signed to Tahama and the others to lower him over the precipice.

The descent, hanging by a fragile rope above the sheer drop, with a sea of water roaring around him, seemed worse to Alex than the climb. He could scarcely see and had no idea who had fallen or where to look for him. The operation was one of a practically pointless daring since anyone who had taken a false step during the ascent would by now be a bloody pulp at the bottom. What would his father do in such a circumstance? John would think first of all of the victim, then himself. John would not be defeated without trying everything possible. As Alex was being lowered, he struggled to see farther than his nose and to breathe, but it was all he could do to open his eyes and he inhaled more water than air. He was swinging in empty space, praying that the liana rope would hold together.

Suddenly one of his feet touched something soft, and an instant later his fingertips were following the shape of a man apparently hanging from nothing. With a shock he realized it was the chief, Mokarita. He recognized him by the crown of yellow feathers that was still planted firmly on his head, even though the unfortunate old man was hung up like a steer on a thick root growing out of the cliff that had miraculously stopped his fall. Alex could not find a purchase for his feet and he was afraid that if he added his weight to the root, it would break and Mokarita would plummet to the rock below. He calculated that the only possible salvation was for him to grab the chief, and he knew he would have to do it with precision, for as wet as he was, the Indian could slip through his hands like a fish.

Alex pumped hard, swinging almost blindly, and wrapped his arms and legs about the limp figure. Up in the cave, the warriors felt the tug, and the added weight on the rope, and began to haul it in, carefully, very slowly, to keep from fraying the rope or swinging Alex and Mokarita against the cliff. The young rescuer had no idea how long the operation lasted, perhaps only a few minutes, but it seemed hours to him. Finally he felt himself seized by several hands and lifted into the cave. The Indians had to pry him away from Mokarita: he had locked onto him with the doggedness of a piranha.

The chief adjusted his feathers and smiled weakly. Threads of blood trickled from his nose and mouth, but he seemed otherwise intact. It was clear that the Indians were greatly impressed by the rescue, and they passed the rope from hand to hand with admiration, but it did not occur to any of them to attribute their chief's rescue to the young stranger. Instead they congratulated Tahama for having had the idea. Exhausted and aching all over, Alex wished that someone would thank him, but even Nadia ignored him. Curled up with Borobá in a corner, she was not even aware of her friend's heroism because she was still recovering from the ascent.

The rest of their journey was easier. At a certain distance from the falls, the tunnel opened onto a place where it was possible to climb with less risk. The Indians used the rope to pull Mokarita up, because his legs were weak, and Nadia, because her spirit was shaken. Finally all of them reached the top safely.

"Didn't I tell you that the talisman would save you from dangerous heights?" Alex joked.

"You did!" Nadia admitted, convinced.

Before them lay the Eye of the World, which was what the People of the Mist called their land. It was a paradise of magnificent waterfalls, a vast rain forest filled with animals, birds, and butterflies, with a benign climate free of the clouds of mosquitoes that tormented them in the lowlands. In the distance strange formations rose like very tall drums of black granite

219

and red earth. Lying on the ground, unable to move, Mokarita pointed to them with reverence: "*Tepuis,*" he said in a thread of a voice as Nadia translated, the homes of the gods. Alex recognized them immediately: those impressive mesas were identical to the majestic towers he had seen when he'd faced the black jaguar in Mauro Carías's courtyard.

"They are the oldest and most mysterious mountains on earth," he said.

"How do you know that? Have you seen them before?" Nadia asked.

"I saw them in a dream," Alex answered.

The chief did not exhibit any pain, as befitting a warrior of his stature, but he had little strength left; at times he closed his eyes and seemed to have fainted. Alex couldn't know whether he had broken bones or unidentifiable internal injuries, but it was clear he couldn't stand. Using Nadia as an interpreter, he was able to get the Indians to improvise a litter from two long poles with some lianas woven between them and covered by a large strip of tree bark. The warriors, troubled by the weakness of the ancient who had guided the tribe for several decades, accepted Alex's guidance without arguing. Two of them picked up the stretcher and they continued along the riverbank for half an hour, led by Tahama, until Mokarita indicated they should stop to rest.

Their ascent up the side of the waterfall had taken several hours, and by now everyone was exhausted and hungry. Tahama and two other men went into the forest with their bows and arrows and returned shortly afterward with a few birds, an armadillo, and a monkey. The monkey, still alive, but paralyzed by the curare, was finished off with a rock, to the horror of Borobá, who ran over to Nadia and crawled beneath her T-shirt. The Indians started a fire by striking two rocks together—something Alex had vainly attempted when he was a Boy Scout—and roasted their prey on sticks over the fire. The hunter never tasted the flesh of his victim, because it was bad manners and bad luck; he had to wait until another hunter offered his. Tahama had caught everything but the armadillo, so the meal was delayed while the strict formalities of the exchange of food was carried out. When Alex finally had his portion in his hand, he devoured it without a thought for the feathers and hair that remained, and it tasted delicious.

It was still an hour or two until sunset, and on the altiplano, where the vegetation was less dense, the light lasted longer than in the valley. After long consultation with Tahama and Mokarita, the group again started walking.

Without warning, Tapirawa-teri, the village of the People of the Mist, appeared right in the middle of the forest, as if it had the same ability as its dwellers: to make itself visible or invisible at will. It was protected by a clump of gigantic chestnut trees—the tallest in the jungle—some of whose trunks measured more than thirty feet around. Their domed tops covered the village like enormous umbrellas. Tapirawa-teri was not like the typical *shabono,* which confirmed Alex's suspicion that the People of the Mist were different from other Indians and had had very little contact with other Amazon tribes. The village did not have the usual circular hut with an open space in the center, the place the entire tribe lived, but was composed of small mud, stone, stick, and straw constructions roofed with branches and shrubs that blended perfectly with nature. You could be ten feet away without having any idea that a human habitation stood there. Alex realized that if it was this difficult to see their small settlement when you were standing right in the middle of it, it would be impossible to sight from the air in the way that the large round roof and cleared central space of a *shabono* could be seen. That might be the reason the People of the Mist had been able to remain absolutely isolated. His hope of being rescued by army helicopters or César Santos's little plane went up in smoke.

The village was as unreal as the Indians. Just as the huts were invisible, everything around them also seemed hazy or transparent. Objects, like persons, lost their precise contours, fading to the plane of illusion. Out of thin air, like ghosts, came women and children to welcome the warriors. They were very short, with amber eyes and skin paler than that of the Indians of the valley. They moved with extraordinary lightness, floating, almost as if they were not flesh and bone. Instead of clothing, they wore designs painted on their bodies and sometimes feathers or flowers tied to their arms or threaded through an ear. Frightened by the two strangers, the smallest children began to cry and the women stayed back, afraid, even though their men were there, and armed.

"Take off your clothes, Jaguar," Nadia ordered as she stripped off her shorts, her T-shirt, and even her underwear.

Alex imitated her without thinking about what he was doing. The idea of being naked in public would have horrified him a couple of weeks before, but in this place it was natural. Wearing clothes was indecent when everyone else was naked. He did not feel strange about seeing his friend's body, although he would have blushed at seeing either of his sisters without clothes. The women and children immediately shed their fear and slowly came closer. They had never seen such strange-looking people, especially the young American male, who was so white in places. Alex could tell they were particularly curious about the difference in color between the skin usually covered by his swimsuit and the rest of his suntanned body. They rubbed him with their fingers to see if it was paint, and then laughed real belly laughs.

The warriors set Mokarita's litter on the ground, where it was quickly surrounded by all the people of the village. They were talking in whispers, in melodious tones that imitated the sounds of the forest, the rain, the water running over river rocks . . . the way Walimai spoke. To his amazement, Alex realized that he could pretty much understand as long as he didn't try, but "listened with his heart." According to Nadia, who had an astounding gift for languages, words are not that important when you recognize intentions.

Iyomi, Mokarita's wife, even more ancient than he, came forward. Everyone stepped aside with respect, and she knelt beside her husband without a tear, murmuring comforting words in his ear as the other women, serious and silent, gathered around them, supporting them with their closeness but not interfering.

Very soon it was night, and the air turned cold. Normally in a *shabono* there was always a ring of bonfires beneath the common roof for cooking and providing heat, but in Tapirawa-teri, fire, like everything else, was not obvious. Small fires were lighted only at night, always inside the huts on stone altars, in order not to attract the attention of possible enemies or bad spirits. Smoke escaped through holes in the roof, dissipating in the air. At first Alex had the impression that the huts were scattered among the trees haphazardly, but soon he realized that they were distributed more or less in a circle, as in a *shabono*, and were connected by tunnels or roofs made of branches, giving unity to the village. The Indians could move about using that network of hidden paths, protected in case of attack and sheltered from the sun and the rain.

The Indians were grouped in families, but the adolescent boys and unwed men lived apart from the others in a common hut provided with mats on the ground and hammocks strung between poles. That was where they put Alex, while Nadia was taken to Mokarita's dwelling. The chief had been wed in his puberty to Iyomi, his life companion, but he also had two young wives and a large number of children and grandchildren. He did not keep track of his offspring; because who the parents were didn't actually matter, the children were all raised together, protected and looked after by the members of the tribe.

Nadia found out that among the People of the Mist it was normal to have several wives or several husbands; no one had to be alone. If a man died, his children and wives were immediately adopted by another man who could protect them and provide for them. That was the case with Tahama, who must have been a good hunter, because he was responsible for several women and a dozen young. A mother whose husband was a bad hunter could choose other spouses to help feed her children. Parents usually promised their girls in marriage at birth, but none was forced to marry or stay with a man against her will. Abuse of women and children was taboo, and anyone who violated that rule lost his family and was condemned to sleep alone; he was also excluded from the hut of the bachelors. The one punishment among the People of the Mist was isolation; nothing was so greatly feared as being ostracized from the community. The concept of reward and punishment did not exist; children learned by imitating the adults, and if they didn't, they were destined to perish. They had to learn to hunt, fish, plant, and harvest, to respect nature and their fellows, to be helpful, and to maintain their position in the village. They learned at their own rhythm and in accordance with their ability.

There were times that not enough girls were born in a generation, so the men would go out on long forays looking for wives. The girls of the village, in turn, were allowed to find a husband on the rare times they visited other areas. The Indians also adopted families abandoned following a battle with another tribe, because if a community was too small, it could not survive in the jungle. From time to time, it was necessary to declare war on another *shabono*; that guaranteed strong warriors and new pairings. It was very sad when the young said good-bye to go off and live in another tribe; only rarely would they would see their families again. The People of the Mist jealously guarded the secret of their village, a defense against being attacked or acquiring new customs. They had lived the same way for thousands of years and did not want to change.

The huts were very bare inside: hammocks, gourds, stone axes, and knives fashioned from teeth or claws. Assorted domesticated animals that belonged to the community wandered in and out at will. Bows, arrows, blowguns, and darts were kept in the hut shared by the bachelors. Everything had a purpose. There was no art, only what was essential for strict survival; nature provided the rest. Alex did not see a single metal object that indicated contact with the outside world, and he remembered that the People of the Mist had not touched the gifts César Santos had strung up to attract them. In that, too, they differed from the other tribes of the region, which succumbed one by one to a greed for steel and other goods brought by the foreigners.

When the temperature went down that night, Alex put his clothes back on, but he shivered all the same. He observed that his roommates slept two to a hammock or huddled together on the ground to keep warm, but he came from a culture in which physical contact among men was not tolerated, where most men touched only in fits of violence or in the roughest sports. He lay alone in a corner feeling insignificant, less than a flea. That small group of humans in a tiny village in the jungle was invisible in the immensity of astral space.

His lifetime was less than a fraction of a second in infinity. Or maybe he did not even exist; maybe human beings, the planets, everything in Creation were a dream . . . an illusion. He smiled with humility when he remembered that a few days before he had thought he was the center of the universe. He was cold and hungry; he had the feeling it was going to be a very long night, but in less than five minutes he was sleeping as if he had been anesthetized.

When he woke, he was curled up on a straw mat between two husky warriors who were snoring and snorting in his ear the way his dog, Poncho, always did. He untangled himself, with difficulty, from the arms of the Indians and quietly got up, but he didn't go very far because a thick snake more than six feet long was stretched across the doorway. He stood there rooted like stone, not daring to take a step even though the serpent gave no sign of life; it was either dead or sleeping. Almost immediately, the Indians began to stir and go about their activities with absolute calm, stepping over the snake as if it weren't there. It was a domesticated boa constrictor whose mission was to rid the place of mice,

bats, and scorpions, and to frighten away poisonous snakes. The People of the Mist had
many pets: monkeys that were raised with the
children, little dogs the women nursed along
with their own offspring, toucans, parrots,
iguanas, and even a decrepit old yellow jaguar,
meek and lame in one foot. The boas, well fed
and generally lethargic, allowed the children to
play with them. Alex thought how happy his
sister Nicole would be in the midst of that
exotic domestic zoo.

A good part of the day was spent preparing the
celebration for the return of the warriors and
the visit of the two "white souls," as they called
Nadia and Alex. Everyone participated, with
the exception of one man who sat at the far
edge of the village, apart from the others. That
Indian was performing the *unokaimú*—rite of
purification—required after killing another
human. Alex learned that *unokaimú* consisted
of a total fasting, silence, and immobility that
lasted for several days; if that was done, the
spirit of the dead person, which escaped
through the nostrils of the corpse and attached
itself to the breastbone of the killer, would

gradually let go. If the person who had killed ate anything, the ghost of his victim grew fat and its weight would eventually crush him. In front of the motionless warrior fulfilling *unokaimú* was a large bamboo blowgun decorated with strange symbols identical to those on the poison dart that had pierced the heart of the soldier as the expedition had traveled upriver.

Some of the men left to hunt and fish, led by Tahama; several women went to bring maize and plantains from the small gardens hidden in the forest and others were responsible for grinding cassava. The smallest children hunted for ants and other insects to roast; teenagers collected nuts and fruits and some, with amazing agility, swarmed up trees to take honey from a honeycomb, the jungle's only source of sugar. As soon as a boy child could stand alone, he learned to climb. These people were capable of running across the highest tree branches without losing their balance. Just seeing them up so high, like monkeys, made Nadia feel dizzy.

Alex was handed a basket, taught how to bear its weight by placing its long strap across his forehead, then with signs directed to follow the other young males his age. They walked some distance into the rain forest, crossed the river by holding on to branches and lianas, and finally came to a group of slender palm trees whose trunks were covered with long, sharp spines. Beneath the leaves, more than forty feet overhead, shone clusters of a yellow fruit that looked a little like peaches. The Indians bound poles together to make two strong crosses, then pushed the fork of one cross tight against the tree trunk and did the same with the other, but higher up the trunk. One of the boys stepped onto the first cross, climbed from it to the second, reached down and pulled the lower cross out and placed it farther up, and, using this technique, and with the agility of an acrobat, quickly climbed to the top. Alex had heard about the feat, but until he saw it done had not understood how anyone could climb without wounding himself on the thorns. The climber tossed down fruit that the others caught in baskets. Later the women of the village ground them and mixed them with plantains to make a soup that was highly treasured among the People of the Mist.

Even though everyone was busy with preparations, the atmosphere was relaxed and festive. No one hurried, and there was more than enough time to play for a couple of pleasant hours in the river. As he was paddling with the other young people, Alex thought the world had never seemed so beautiful, and felt he would never again be so free. After the long bath, the girls of Tapirawa-teri mixed vegetal paints of various colors and decorated all the members of the tribe, including babies, with intricate designs. In the meantime, the older males ground and mixed leaves and bark from different trees to obtain *yopo*, the magic powder used in their ceremonies.

CHAPTER TWELVE

Rites of Passage

THE CELEBRATION STARTED in the afternoon and lasted through the night. The Indians, painted from head to foot, sang, danced, and stuffed themselves with food. It was considered discourteous for a guest to refuse an offering of food or drink, so Alex and Nadia, imitating the others, filled their bellies until they had to throw up, which was thought to be evidence of very good manners. The village children ran around with large butterflies and phosphorescent beetles tied to their fingers with long hairs. The women, adorned with fireflies and orchids, and with feathers in their ears and long picks through their lips, began the festivities by dividing into two facing groups to engage in a friendly singing competition. Then they invited the men to join in a dance inspired by the displays animals made at mating time, during the rainy season. Finally the men took the forefront, first dancing in a circle, imitating monkeys, jaguars, and caimans, then offering a demonstration of strength and skill, shaking their weapons and making flamboyant leaps. Nadia's and Alex's heads were whirling; they were dizzied by the spectacle—the *tam-tam* of the drums, the songs, the cries, and the noises of the jungle around them.

Mokarita lay in the center of the village, where he received the ceremonial greetings of everyone present. Although he took small sips of *masato*, he could not swallow food. Another ancient, famed as a *curandero*, or healer, came to treat Mokarita. He was coated with dried mud and resin, to which he had stuck small white feathers, giving him the look of a strange bird just out of its egg. For a long time, the *curandero* leaped and shouted to drive away the demons in the body of his chief. He sucked several places on his belly and chest, making motions of drawing out the bad humors and spitting them away. Then he rubbed the dying man with a paste of *paranary*, a plant used in the Amazon to heal wounds. Mokarita's injuries were not external, however, and the remedy had no effect whatsoever. Alex suspected that the fall had burst some internal organ, maybe the liver, for as the hours went by, the aged chief was growing weaker and weaker as a thread of blood trickled from the corner of his mouth.

At dawn, Mokarita called Nadia and Alex to his side, and with his remaining strength explained to them that they were the only foreigners to enter Tapirawa-teri since the village had been founded.

"The souls of the People of the Mist and of our ancestors dwell here. The *nahab* speak lies and do not know justice; they have the power to stain our souls," he said.

They had been invited there, he added, by the instruction of the great shaman, who had told them that Nadia was destined to aid them. He did not know what role Alex played in events yet to come, but as companion to the girl, he, too, was welcome in Tapirawa-teri. Alex and Nadia knew that when Mokarita said "shaman" he was referring to Walimai, and to his prophecy about the Rahakanariwa.

"What form does the Rahakanariwa take?" Alex asked.

"Many forms. It is a blood-sucking bird. It is not human; it acts crazed; you cannot know what it will do. It is always thirsty for blood; it is quick to anger and to punishment," Mokarita explained.

"Have you seen the birds?" Alex asked.

"We have seen the birds that make noise and wind, but they have not seen us," Mokarita replied. "We know that they are not the Rahakanariwa, although they are much like it; those are the birds of the *nahab*. They fly only by day, never at night. That is why we are careful when we make fire, so that the bird will not see the smoke. That is why we live hidden. That is why we are the invisible people."

"The *nahab* will come sooner or later, it is inevitable. What will the People of the Mist do then?"

"My time in the Eye of the World is ended. The chief who comes after me must decide," Mokarita replied weakly.

Mokarita died at dawn. Waves of laments swept through Tapirawa-teri for hours; no one could remember a time before this chief who had guided the tribe for many decades. His yellow-feather crown, the symbol of his authority, was placed on a post until a successor could be chosen. In the meantime, the People of the Mist removed their adornments and painted their bodies with mud, charcoal, and ash as a sign of mourning. There was a great uneasiness, because they believed that death seldom occurred for natural reasons; usually the cause was an enemy that had used bad magic to inflict harm. The way to satisfy the spirit of the dead person was to find the enemy and eliminate him; otherwise the victim's ghost would remain in the world to bedevil the living. If the enemy was from another tribe, that could lead to a battle, but if he was from their own village, he could be "killed" symbolically through an appropriate ceremony. The warriors, who had spent the night drinking masato, were fired up, eager to settle the score with the one who had caused Mokarita's death. Finding him and destroying him was a matter of honor. No one was eager to replace the chief since there was no caste system among them; no one was more important than anyone else, the chief merely had more responsibilities. Mokarita was not respected for his position of command but for being very, very old; that signified experience and knowledge. But now the men, drunken and inflamed, could become violent at any moment.

"I believe this is the time to call on Walimai," Nadia whispered to Alex.

She went off to the edge of the village, took the amulet from her neck, and began to blow. The high-pitched owl's screech that came from the carved bone sounded strange in that place. Nadia had thought that all she had to do was use the talisman and Walimai would appear by magic, but now no matter how hard she blew, the shaman did not come.

The tension in the village was mounting by the hour. One of the warriors attacked Tahama, and he struck back, drawing blood. Several men had to step in to separate and calm the two hotheads. They decided to resolve the conflict with *yopo*, the green powder that, like *masato*, was used only by the men. They lined up two by two in pairs, facing one another; each was furnished with a long hollow reed, pointed at the tip, and used to blow the powder directly into the opposite person's nose.

The *yopo* slammed into the brain like an ax. The affected person fell backward, screaming with pain, and then began to vomit, hop around, grunt, and see visions as green mucus drained from his nostrils and mouth. It was not a pleasant spectacle, but the powder transported the user to the world of the spirits. Some men became demons, some absorbed the soul of an animal, others looked into the future; but the ghost of Mokarita did not appear to any of them to designate his successor.

Alex and Nadia feared that this pandemonium would end in violence, and they tried to keep themselves in the background, hoping that if they didn't make any noise, no one would remember they were there. They were out of luck, though, because suddenly one of the warriors had a vision that the enemy of Mokarita—the cause for his death—was the young foreigner. In one instant, all the men, as one, joined to punish the supposed murderer of their chief, raising their clubs and giving chase. That was not the moment for Alex to think of the flute as a way of soothing spirits; instead, he started sprinting like a gazelle. His one advantage was desperation, which gave him wings—that, and the fact that his pursuers were not in the best condition. In the confusion, the intoxicated Indians tripped, and ran into, and clubbed each other as the women and children urged them on. Alex thought that his hour had come, and the image of his mother flashed through his mind as he ran blindly through the forest.

The young American was no competition for these Indian warriors in speed or skill, but they were drugged and one by one they dropped out of the chase. Finally Alex was able to take refuge beneath a tree, gasping and drained. But just when he thought he was safe, he realized he was surrounded, and before he could start running again the women of the tribe were upon him. They were laughing, as if having caught him was just a joke, but they tied him up firmly and in spite of his swinging his fists and kicking, they dragged him back to Tapirawa-teri and tied him to a tree. More than one girl tickled him, and several put bits of fruit in his mouth, but despite these attentions, they left the rope tightly knotted. By then, the effect of the *yopo* was beginning to wear off, and the exhausted men were slowly leaving their visions behind to return to reality. It would be several hours before they completely recovered their senses and their strength.

Alex, sore from having been dragged over the ground and humiliated by the teasing of the women, remembered Professor Ludovic Leblanc's hair-raising tales. If his theory was correct, he would wind up as a meal. And what would happen to Nadia? He felt responsible for her. In a movie or a novel, this would be the moment that the helicopters arrived to rescue him and he looked toward the sky, but without hope; in real life, helicopters never come in time. In the meantime, Nadia had come over to his tree; no one stopped her because none of the warriors could imagine that a girl would dare to defy them. Alex and Nadia had put their clothes on when the evening first turned cold, and since by now the People of the Mist were used to seeing them dressed, they felt no reason to take them off. So Alex was wearing the belt to which his flute, his compass, and the knife Nadia used to cut him free were attached. In the movies, it takes only one slash to cut a rope, but Alex sweated with impatience as Nadia sawed away for a long time at the leather thongs that bound Alex to the tree. Children, and some of the women of the tribe, came to see what they were doing, astonished at their daring, but Nadia acted with such confidence, waving the knife before the noses of the curious, that no one intervened, and after ten minutes, Alex was free. The two friends began quietly to walk away, not daring to run for fear of attracting the warriors' attention. That was a time when the art of invisibility would have been very useful.

The young foreigners did not get very far because at just that moment, Walimai made his entrance into the village. The aged witch man appeared with his staff and collection of little bags, his short spear, and the quartz cylinder that sounded like a rattle. It contained small stones taken from a place where lightning had struck; it was the symbol of curanderos and shamans, and represented the power of Sun Father. The shaman was accompanied by a young girl with hair to her waist, like a black shawl; her eyebrows were shaved and she was wearing necklaces of beads and polished picks that pierced her cheeks and nose. She was very beautiful and seemed happy, and, though she never said a word, she was always smiling. Alex realized that this was the shaman's angel-wife and was thrilled that he could see her; that meant that something had opened in his mind or his intuition. As Nadia had taught him, he had to see with his heart. She had told him that many years before, when Walimai was still young, he had used a poison knife to kill this girl, as it was the only way to free her from slavery. Though it was a favor, not a crime, when her soul escaped it had clung to his breastbone. Walimai had fled into the deepest part of the jungle, carrying the soul of the girl to a place where no one could ever find her. There he had fulfilled the required rites of purification: fasting and immobility. However, during the journey, he and the woman had fallen in love, and once the rite of unokaimú had been performed, her spirit had not wanted to leave him but had chosen to stay in this world beside the man she loved. That had happened nearly half a century ago, and, ever since, she had accompanied Walimai, waiting for the moment that he could fly away with her, he, too, a spirit.

Walimai's presence dissolved the tension in Tapirawa-teri, and the same warriors who only shortly before had been ready to massacre Alex now were relaxed and friendly. The tribe respected and feared the great shaman because he had the supernatural ability to interpret signs. Everyone dreamed and had visions, but only the chosen like Walimai traveled to the world of the great spirits, where they learned the meaning of visions and could guide others and change the course of natural disasters.

The ancient told the tribe that Alex had the soul of a black jaguar, a sacred animal, and that he had come from far away to help the People of the Mist. He explained that these were very strange times, times in which the boundary between this world and the world of the beyond was unclear, times when the Rahakanariwa could devour them all. He reminded them of the existence of the *nahab*, which most of them knew only through stories told them by brothers from tribes in the lowlands. The warriors of Tapirawa-teri had spied on the expedition of the *International*

Geographic for days, but they had not understood the activities or customs of those strange foreigners. Walimai, who in the century of his lifetime had seen many things, told them what he knew.

"The *nahab* are like the dead; their souls have escaped their breasts," he said. "The *nahab* have no knowledge, they know nothing; they cannot spear a fish with a lance or fell a monkey with a dart, or climb a tree. They do not go dressed in air and light, as we do, but wear stinking cloth. They do not bathe in the river, they do not know the rules of decency or courtesy, they do not share their house, their food, their children, or their women. They have soft bones and their skulls split at the least blow. They kill animals and do not eat them, leaving them on the ground to rot. Wherever they pass they leave a trail of filth and poison, even in water. The *nahab* are so crazed that they try to take with them the stones of the earth, the sand of the rivers, and the trees of the forest. Some want the earth itself. We tell them that the jungle cannot be carried away on their backs like a dead tapir, but they do not listen. They speak to us of their gods but they do not want to hear of ours. Their appetites are unbounded, like the caimans's. These terrible things I have seen with my own eyes, and I have heard with my own ears, and touched with my own hands."

"We will never allow these demons to come to the Eye of the World; we will kill them with our darts and arrows as they climb the waterfall, as we have done to all foreigners who have tried since the times of the grandfathers of our grandfathers," Tahama proclaimed.

"But they will come no matter," Alex said. "The *nahab* have birds of noise and wind; they can fly above the mountains. They will come because they want the stones and the trees and the earth."

"True," Walimai admitted.

"The *nahab* can also kill with sickness," said Nadia. "Many tribes have died in this way, but the People of the Mist can be saved."

"This honey-colored girl knows what she is saying; we must listen to her. The Rahaka-nariwa can adopt the form of deadly sickness," Walimai assured them.

"She is more powerful than the Rahakana-riwa?" asked Tahama, dumbfounded.

"I am not, but there is another woman who is very powerful. She has serums that can prevent epidemics," said Nadia.

Nadia and Alex spent an hour trying to convince the Indians that not all *nahab* were evil demons, that some were friends, like Dr. Omayra Torres. The limitations of language were difficult enough, but added to that were cultural differences. How could they explain to these Indians what a serum was? They themselves did not completely understand, which is why they chose to say that it was very strong magic.

"The only way to save the tribe is for this woman to come and use her needle on the People of the Mist," Nadia argued. "That way, even if the *nahab* or the Rahakanariwa should come, thirsty for blood, they cannot do harm with sickness."

"They can threaten us in other ways. Then we will go to war," Tahama swore.

"War against the *nahab* is not a good idea . . . ," Nadia tried to say.

"The new chief must decide," Tahama concluded.

★ ★ ★

Walimai took charge of conducting Mokarita's funeral rites in accordance with the ancient traditions. Despite the danger of being seen from the air, the Indians built a huge bonfire to cremate the body, and for hours the chief's remains were consumed by fire as the inhabitants of the village mourned his parting. Walimai prepared a magic potion, the powerful *ayahuasca,* to help the men of the tribe see deep into their hearts. The young foreigners were invited as well because they had a heroic mission to fulfill, the most important of their lives, and for that they would not only need the help of the gods, they would need to know their own strength. They did not dare refuse, although the taste of the potion was nauseating and they had to make a great effort to swallow it and keep it down. They did not feel its effects until sometime later, when suddenly the ground gave way beneath their feet and the sky filled with geometric figures and brilliant colors and their bodies began to whirl and dissolve, and panic invaded their every cell. Just when they believed they were dead, they felt themselves propelled at dizzying speed through countless chambers of light, and soon the doors of the kingdom of the totemic gods opened, and they were bidden to enter.

Alex felt his limbs grow longer, and burning heat spread inside him. He looked at his hands and saw two paws ending with sharp claws. He opened his mouth to call out and a terrible roar rumbled from his belly. He was transformed into a large, black, sleek cat, the magnificent male jaguar he had seen in the courtyard of Mauro Carías. The animal was not in him, or he in it; the two of them had blended into a single being, simultaneously animal and youth. Alex took a few steps, stretching, and testing his muscles, and realized that he was endowed with the lightness, the speed, and the strength of the jaguar. He made a few great leaps through the forest, possessed with supernatural energy. With a bound, he sprang up to the limb of a tree and from there observed the jungle around him through golden eyes, slowly switching his coal-black tail. He knew he was powerful, feared, solitary, invincible; the king of the South American jungle. No other animal was as fierce as he was.

Nadia soared upward and in a few instants' time lost the fear of heights that had always plagued her. Her powerful eagle wings barely stroked; the cold air held her and the slightest movement was enough to change the direction or speed of her course. She was flying at a great height, calm, unworried, detached, observing the earth beneath her without curiosity. From above, she saw the jungle and the flat peaks of the *tepuis*, many covered with clouds like crowns of foam; she also saw the faint column of smoke from the bonfire where the remains of chief Mokarita were burning. Borne by the wind, the eagle was as invincible as the jaguar was on land: nothing could reach her. The girl-bird swooped in Olympian fashion above the Eye of the World, observing from on high the lives of the Indians. Her head feathers stood up like hundreds of antennae, capturing the warmth of the sun, the vastness of the wind, the dramatic emotion of height. She knew that she was the protector of these Indians, the mother-eagle of the People of the Mist. She flew over the village of Tapirawa-teri and the shadow of her magnificent wings, like a mantle, covered the nearly invisible roofs of the small dwellings hidden in the forest. Finally the great bird flew to the summit of the highest *tepui*, where in her nest, exposed to the winds, shone three crystal eggs.

The next morning, when the two foreigners had returned from the world of totemic animals, they told each other their experiences.

"What is the meaning of those three eggs?" Alex asked.

"I don't know, but they are very important. Those eggs are not mine, Jaguar, but I must find them in order to save the People of the Mist."

"I don't understand. What do eggs have to do with Indians?"

"I don't really know, but I think they have everything to do with them," Nadia replied.

When the coals of the funeral pyre cooled, Iyomi, Mokarita's wife, pulled out the residue from his bones, ground it until it was a fine powder, and mixed that with water and plantains to make a soup. The gourd with this gray liquid passed from hand to hand, and everyone, even Alex and Nadia, drank a sip. Then they buried the gourd and the name of the chief was to be forgotten, so that no one would ever speak it again. The memory of the man, like the particles of courage and wisdom left in his ashes, passed on to his descendants and friends. A part of him would always remain among the living. Nadia and Alex had been asked to drink the soup of his bones as a form of baptism: now they belonged to the tribe. When Alex held the gourd to his lips, he remembered that he had read about an illness caused by "eating the brain of one's ancestors." He closed his eyes and drank with respect.

Once the funeral ceremony was concluded, Walimai directed the tribe to elect its new chief. According to tradition, only men could aspire to that position, but Walimai explained that this time they must choose with extreme care because they were living in very strange times and they would need a chief capable of understanding the mysteries of other worlds, of communicating with the gods, and of holding the Rahakanariwa at bay. He said that these were the times of a sky with six moons, times when the gods had seen it necessary to abandon their dwelling. At the mention of the gods, the Indians put their hands to their heads and began to rock back and forth, chanting something that to Nadia and Alex sounded like a prayer.

"Everyone in Tapirawa-teri, including children, must participate in the election of a new chief," Walimai instructed.

The tribe spent one whole day in proposing candidates and negotiating. By dusk, Nadia and Alex fell asleep, tired, hungry, and bored. The American had tried in vain to explain the method of choosing by vote, as in a democracy, but the Indians did not know how to count, and the idea of voting seemed as incomprehensible as the function of the serum. They elected through "visions."

Late that night, the young people were wakened by Walimai with the news that the strongest vision had been of Iyomi, which meant that Mokarita's widow was now chief in Tapirawa-teri. It was the first time in memory that a woman had acted in that position.

The first order the ancient Iyomi gave when she put on the crown of yellow feathers her husband had worn for so many years was for food to be prepared. That was acted upon immediately because the People of the Mist had gone two days with nothing more to eat than a sip of the soup made from the bones.

Tahama and the other hunters went off into the jungle with their weapons and a few hours later returned with a giant anteater and a deer, which they cut up and roasted over coals. In the meantime, the women had made cassava bread and cooked plantains. When her people's stomachs were full, Iyomi invited them to sit in a circle; she then issued her second edict.

"I am going to name other chiefs. A chief for war and hunting: Tahama. A chief for soothing the Rahakanariwa: the honey-colored girl called Eagle. A chief for negotiating with the *nahab* and their birds of noise and wind: the foreigner named Jaguar. A chief for visiting the gods: Walimai. A chief for the chiefs: Iyomi."

This was how the wise woman distributed power and organized the People of the Mist for confronting the terrible times drawing near. And that was how Nadia and Alex found themselves saddled with a responsibility that neither felt capable of fulfilling.

And then came Iyomi's third order. She said that the girl Eagle must conserve her "pure soul" to face the Rahakanariwa, the only way to keep from being devoured by the cannibal-bird, but that the young foreigner Jaguar must become a man and receive his warrior's weapons. Every young male, before taking up weapons or considering marriage, had to die as a boy and be born as a man. There was not enough time for the traditional ceremony, which lasted three days and normally included all the males of the tribe who had reached puberty. In Jaguar's case, they would have to improvise something much briefer, Iyomi explained, because he was to accompany Eagle on her journey to the mountain of the gods. The People of the Mist were in danger; only these two outsiders could save them, and it was their duty to leave quickly.

Walimai and Tahama were chosen to organize Alex's rite of initiation, in which only adult males participated. Afterward, Alex told Nadia that if he had known what the ceremony held in store, the experience might have been less terrifying. Under Iyomi's direction, the women shaved the crown of Alex's head with a sharpened stone, a rather painful process since he still had the unhealed cut from being clubbed when he and Nadia had been kidnapped. As they shaved that place, the stone reopened the wound, but the women dabbed on a little clay and soon the bleeding stopped. Then they painted him from head to toe with a paste of wax and charcoal. At that point, Alex had to tell his friend and Iyomi good-bye because the women could not be present during the ceremony and went off to spend the day in the forest with the children. They would not return to the village until night, when the warriors had taken him to undergo the trials of initiation.

Tahama and his men went to the river and from the mud unearthed the sacred musical instruments used only in ceremonies of virility. These were large hollow tubes about five feet long that produced a low, hoarse sound when blown, like the bellowing of a bull. The women, and the boys as yet to be initiated, were not allowed to see them, lest through magic they would fall ill and die. The instruments represented male power in the tribe, the bond between fathers and sons. Without those horns, all the power would be vested in the women, who already possessed the divine ability to have children, or "make people," as they called it.

The rite began in the morning and would

last all that day and that night. Alex was given some bitter berries to eat, and was left curled up on the ground in the fetal position. The warriors, directed by Walimai and decorated with the symbols of demons, formed a tight circle around him and beat the ground with their feet and smoked cigars made of leaves. Among the bitter berries, his fear, and the smoke, Alex soon began to feel rather ill.

For a long time, the warriors danced and chanted around him, blowing the large sacred horns, which were so long they dragged on the ground. The sound echoed through Alex's confused brain. For hours he heard the chants repeating the story of the Sun Father, who dwelled beyond the everyday sun that lighted the sky; he was invisible fire, the origin of Creation; he listened about the drop of blood that had dripped from the moon to give life to the first man. They sang about the River of Milk, which contained all the seeds of life— but also of decay and death; they told of how this river led to the kingdom where shamans like Walimai met with the spirits and other supernatural beings to receive wisdom and the power of healing. They told of how everything that exists is dreamed by Mother Earth, how each star dreams its inhabitants, and how all that happens in the universe is an illusion, dreams within dreams. Even in his confusion, Alexander felt that those words described concepts that he himself had sensed, then he ceased to reason and gave himself to the strange experience of thinking with his heart.

As the hours went by, Alex was losing his sense of time, space, and his own reality, and sinking into a state of terror and profound fatigue. At some point, he felt himself being lifted to his feet and forced to walk; that was when he realized that night had fallen. They walked in a long line toward the river, playing their instruments and brandishing their weapons; there he was submerged several times, until he thought he was drowning. They rubbed him with rough leaves to remove the black paint and then dusted pepper on his burning skin. With earsplitting yells, they beat his legs, arms, chest, and stomach with twigs, but not to inflict injury; they threatened him with their spears, sometimes touching him with the tips but not wounding him. They tried in every possible way to frighten him, and they succeeded, because the American did not understand what was happening and was afraid that at any moment his attackers would go too far and actually kill him. He tried to defend himself from the pounding and pushing of the warriors of Tapirawa-teri, but instinct told him not to try to escape; it would be futile, there was nowhere to go in that unfamiliar and hostile terrain. That was a wise decision; had he tried, he would have looked like a coward, the unpardonable flaw for a warrior.

When he was close to losing control and yelling hysterically, Alex suddenly remembered his totemic animal. He did not have to do anything extraordinary to enter the body of the black jaguar, the transformation happened quickly and easily; the sound that burst from his throat was the same he had roared before, the slash of his claws he already knew, the leap over the heads of his enemies was a natural act. The Indians celebrated the arrival of the jaguar with a deafening clamor, and soon they led him in a solemn procession to the sacred tree, where Tahama was waiting with the final test.

It was nearly dawn. Fire ants were trapped in a kind of tube or sieve of woven straw, like those used to press the prussic acid from cassava. Tahama was holding the tube with two sticks to avoid contact with the insects. It took Alex, exhausted after that long and frightening night, a moment to understand what was expected of him. He took a deep, deep breath, filling his lungs with the cold air, called on the courage of his father, the mountain climber, the endurance of his mother, who never gave up, and the strength of his totemic animal, and plunged his left arm, to the elbow, into the tube.

The fire ants crawled over his skin for a few seconds before biting him. When they did, he felt as if acid had eaten his flesh to the bone. Horrific pain stunned him for several instants, but through a brutal effort of will, he kept from pulling his arm from the sieve. He remembered Nadia's words when she was trying to teach him to live with mosquitoes: Don't try to defend yourself; ignore them. It was impossible to ignore fire ants, but after a few moments of absolute desperation, in which it was all he could do not to run and jump in the river, he realized it was possible to control the impulse to flee, to choke back his howls, to open himself to suffering without resisting, to allow the pain to penetrate his body and his consciousness. And then the searing pain went through him like a sword, emerged from his back, and, miraculously, he was able to bear it. Alex would never be able to explain the sense of power he felt during that torture. He felt as strong and invincible as he had in the form of the black jaguar, after drinking Walimai's magic potion. That was his reward for having survived the test. He knew that, in truth, he had left his childhood behind and that from that night on he would be able to look after himself.

"Welcome among men," said Tahama, removing the sieve from Alex's arm.

The warriors led the semiconscious young man back to the village.

CHAPTER THIRTEEN

The Sacred Mountain

BATHED IN SWEAT, battered, and burning with fever, Alexander—Jaguar—walked down a long green corridor, stepped across an aluminum threshold, and saw his mother. Lisa was lying back among pillows in a large chair with a sheet pulled across her body, in a room where the light was as clear as moonlight. She was wearing a blue wool cap over her bald head and headphones on her ears. She was very pale and thin, with dark shadows around her eyes. Yellow liquid dripped from a plastic bag into the IV inserted into a vein beneath her collarbone. Each drop penetrated, like the fire of the ants, directly into the bloodstream to his mother's heart.

Thousands of miles away in a hospital in Texas, Lisa was receiving her chemotherapy. She tried not to think about the drug that, like a poison, flowed through her veins to fight the worse poison of her illness. To distract herself, she was concentrating on each note of the flute concerto she was listening to, the one she had heard her son rehearsing so many times. At the same moment that Alex, in his delirium, was dreaming about her deep in the jungle, Lisa saw her son with absolute clarity. She saw him in the doorway of her room, taller and stronger, more mature and more handsome than she remembered. Lisa had called him so often in her thoughts that she was not surprised to see him. She didn't ask how or why he had come, she simply gave herself to the pleasure of having him at her side. "Alexander . . . Alexander . . . ," she murmured. She held out her hands and he moved forward to touch her; he knelt beside the chair and put his head on her knees. As Lisa repeated her son's name and stroked the back of his neck, from the earphones, through the diaphanous notes of the flute, she heard his voice asking her to fight, not to give in to death, telling her over and over, *I love you, Momma.*

Alexander's meeting with his mother might have lasted an instant or several hours, neither of the two knew for sure. When finally they said good-bye and returned to the material world, they were strengthened. Shortly afterward, John entered his wife's room and was surprised to find her smiling, and with color in her cheeks.

"How do you feel, Lisa?" he asked with concern.

"Happy, John, because Alex was here," she replied.

"Lisa, what are you saying . . . ? Alexander is in the Amazon with my mother, don't you remember?" her husband murmured, frightened about the effect the medication might be having on his wife.

"Yes, I remember, but that doesn't change the fact that he was here a moment ago."

"That isn't possible," her husband rebutted.

"He's grown, he looks much taller and stronger, but his left arm is very swollen . . . ," she told John, and closed her eyes to rest.

In the middle of the South American continent, in the Eye of the World, Alexander awoke. It was several minutes before he recognized the golden girl bending over him to give him water.

"You are a man now, Jaguar," said Nadia, smiling to see him back among the living.

Walimai prepared a paste of medicinal plants and applied it to Alex's arm, and within a matter of hours, the fever and swelling had subsided. The shaman explained that just as there are poisons in the jungle that kill without leaving a trace, there are thousands and thousands of natural remedies. Alex described his mother's illness and asked Walimai if he knew of any plant that could help her.

"There is a sacred plant, but it must be mixed with the water of health," the shaman replied.

"Can I find the water and that plant?"

"Maybe yes and maybe no. You must perform many labors."

"I will do anything I have to!" Alex exclaimed.

The next day Alex was bruised, and a red pimple marked each ant bite, but he was on his feet and hungry. When he recounted his experience to Nadia, she told him that the girls of the tribe did not go through an initiation ceremony because they didn't need it; women know when they have left their childhood behind because their body bleeds and tells them.

This was one of those days when Tahama and his companions had not had good luck with the hunt, and the tribe had only maize and a few fish. Alex decided that if he had eaten anaconda on a spit, he should be able to eat the fish, even though it was covered with scales and spines. Surprised, he discovered that he liked it. "And to think that I have deprived myself of this delicious treat for more than fifteen years!" he exclaimed at the second mouthful. Nadia told him to eat well; they would be leaving the following day with Walimai on a journey to the world of the spirits, where there might not be food for the body.

"Walimai says we're going to the sacred mountain where the gods live," she said.

"What will we do there?"

"We're going to look for the three crystal eggs I saw in my vision. Walimai believes that the eggs will save the People of the Mist."

Their journey began at dawn, as soon as the first light appeared in the sky. Walimai went first, accompanied by his beautiful angel-wife, who sometimes walked hand in hand with the shaman and other times fluttered like a butterfly over his head, always silent and smiling. Alexander was proudly armed with a bow and some arrows, new weapons given to him by Tahama at the end of the rite of initiation. Nadia carried a gourd with plantain soup and some cassava flatbread Iyomi had given them for the trek. The witch man did not need provisions, everyone said that in old age he ate very little. He did not seem human: He nourished himself with sips of water and a few nuts that he sucked for long periods between his toothless gums, and he scarcely slept, yet he had strength enough to keep going when the young people were dropping with fatigue.

They started off through the tree-covered plains of the altiplano in the direction of the highest of the *tepuis*, a black, shining tower like an obsidian sculpture. Alex consulted his compass and learned that they were heading due east. There was no visible path, but Walimai plunged through the undergrowth with awesome certainty, orienting himself among trees, valleys, hills, rivers, and waterfalls as if he were carrying a map in his hand.

As they advanced, the landscape changed. Walimai told them that this was the kingdom of the Mother of Waters, and in truth there was an incredible wealth of cascades and waterfalls. As yet, the *garimpeiros* had not arrived here in search of gold and precious stones, but it was only a question of time. The miners worked in groups of four or five and were too poor to pay for transport by air; they explored the obstacle-filled terrain on foot or paddled the rivers in canoes. There were, however, men like Mauro Carías who had modern resources and who knew about the enormous riches in this part of the country. The only thing that stopped them from exploiting the land, mining with giant pressure hoses that destroyed the forests and transformed the countryside into a mud pit, were new laws that protected the environment and the indigenous peoples. The former were violated constantly, but it was not as easy any longer to do that with the latter; the eyes of the world were on these Indians of the Amazon, the last survivors of the Stone Age. They could not be gunned down—as they had been until only recently—

without causing an international reaction.

Alex thought once again how important Dr. Omayra Torres's vaccines were, and about his grandmother's reporting for *International Geographic*, which would alert other countries to the situation of the Indians.

What did those three crystal eggs mean that Nadia had seen in her dream? Why did they have to make this journey with the shaman? It seemed to Alex that it would be more useful to try to rejoin the expedition, recover the vaccines, and have his grandmother publish her article. Iyomi had appointed him "chief for negotiating with the *nahab* and their birds of noise and wind," but instead of fulfilling that purpose, he was getting farther and farther away from civilization. There was no logic at all in what they were doing, he thought with a sigh. Before him rose the mysterious and solitary *tepuis*, like constructs from another planet.

The three travelers walked from sunup to sunset, maintaining a fast pace, stopping only to rest their feet or drink from the rivers. Alex tried to shoot a toucan perched a few feet away on a branch, but missed. Then he aimed at a monkey that was so close he could see its yellow teeth, but again missed the mark. The monkey made openly sarcastic faces in response. He considered what little good his brand-new warrior's weapons were; if his companions had to depend on him for food, they would die of starvation. Walimai pointed to some nuts, which were very tasty, and fruit on a tree that they were unable to reach.

The toes on the Indians' feet were widely separated, strong, and flexible; they could climb smooth trunks with incredible agility. Those same feet, with skin as tough as crocodile hide, were also very sensitive; they used their toes even in weaving baskets or rope. In the village, children began to climb as soon as they could stand; Alex, in contrast, with all his experience in climbing mountains, could not get up a tree to pick fruit. Walimai, Nadia, and Borobá were weeping with laughter at his failed attempts, and not one of them showed a drop of sympathy when he took a fall, bruising his bottom and his pride. He felt as heavy and clumsy as an elephant.

At dusk, after many hours of walking, Walimai indicated they could rest. He walked into the river up to his knees and stood motionless and silent until the fish forgot his presence and began to dart around him. When he had the prey within reach, he speared it with his short lance and handed Nadia a beautiful silvery fish, its tail still flicking.

"How did he do that so easily?" Alex wanted to know, humiliated by his earlier failures.

"He asks the fish's permission and explains that he has to kill it out of necessity. Afterward he thanks it for offering its life so that we can live," she clarified.

Before this journey, Alex would have jeered at such thoughts. Now he was absorbing what Nadia was saying.

"It understands because that fish has eaten other fish; now it is its turn to be eaten. That's how it goes," she added.

The shaman built a small fire for them to cook their meal, which revived them, but he took nothing but water. Nadia and Alex slept curled together among the strong roots of a tree. There was no time to set up the hammocks made with strips of bark, as they had in the village; they were tired and they had to start early the next day. Every time one of them moved, the other wiggled around to get as close as possible and share their warmth during the night. In the meantime, the aged Walimai, squatting motionless on his haunches, spent those hours observing the heavens; his wife stayed by his side like a transparent fairy, clothed in nothing but her dark hair.

When the young people awakened, the Indian was in exactly the same position he had been the night before; invulnerable to cold or exhaustion. Through Nadia, Alex asked him how long he had lived, and where he got his energy and amazing health. The ancient explained that he had seen many children born who became grandfathers, and had seen those grandfathers die and their grandchildren born. How many years? He shrugged his shoulders; it didn't matter and he didn't know. He said that he was the messenger of the gods; he was used to going to the world of the immortals where the illnesses that kill men do not exist. Alex remembered the legend of El Dorado, where there was not only fabulous wealth but also the fountain of eternal youth.

"My mother is very sick . . . ," Alex murmured, moved by the memory. The experience of having been mentally transported to the hospital in Texas to be with her had been so real that he recalled every detail, from the medicinal smell of the room to Lisa's thin legs beneath the sheet, where he had laid his head.

"We all die," said the shaman.

"Yes, but she is young."

"Some go young, others when they are ancient. I have lived too long, I would like for my bones to rest in the memory of others," said Walimai.

At noon on the following day, they reached the base of the highest *tepui* in the Eye of the World, a giant whose peak was lost in a thick crown of white clouds. Walimai explained that the peak was never cloudless and that no one, not even the powerful Rahakanariwa, had visited that place without being invited by the gods. He added that for thousands of years, from the beginning of life, when human beings were formed from the heat of the Sun Father, the blood of the Moon, and the clay of Mother Earth, the People of the Mist had known of the existence of the dwelling of the gods on that mountain. In every generation, there was one person, always a shaman who had performed many acts of penance, who was chosen to visit the *tepui* and serve as messenger. That role had fallen to him. He had been there many times, he had lived with the gods, and he knew their customs. He was worried, he told them, because he had not as yet trained his successor. If he should die, who would that messenger be? On each of his spiritual voyages, he had looked for him, but no vision had come to his aid. Not just anyone could be trained, it had to be someone born with the soul of a shaman, someone who had the power to heal, to give counsel, and to interpret dreams. That person demonstrated his talent from an early age; he had to be very disciplined to resist temptations and govern his body: a good shaman was free of desires and needs. This, in brief, is what the young people understood of the witch man's long oration; he spoke in circles, repeating himself, as if he were reciting an endless poem. It was clear to them, however, that only he was authorized to cross the threshold of the world of the gods, although on one or two extraordinary occasions, other Indians had entered with him. This would be the first time foreign visitors had been admitted since the beginning of time.

"What is it like, the land of the gods?" Alex asked.

"Larger than the largest of the *shabonos*, gleaming and yellow like the sun."

"El Dorado! Could it be the legendary city of gold the conquistadors were looking for?" Alex asked eagerly.

"Maybe yes and maybe no," answered Walimai. He had no point of reference with which to compare a city, to recognize gold, or to imagine the conquistadors.

"And what are the gods like? Are they like the creature we call the Beast?"

"Maybe yes and maybe no."

"Why have you brought us here?"

"Because of the visions. The People of the Mist can be saved by an eagle and a jaguar; that is why you have been invited to the secret dwelling of the gods."

"We will be worthy of that confidence. We will never reveal the entrance," Alex promised.

"You will not be able to. If you come out alive, you will forget it," the Indian replied simply.

If I come out alive . . . Alex hadn't ever considered dying young. Deep down, he thought of death as something disagreeable that happened to other people. Despite the dangers he had confronted during the last weeks, he had never doubted he would be reunited with his family. He had, in fact, been shaping the stories of his adventures to tell, although he did not have much hope of being believed when he told them. Who among his friends would be able to imagine that he had been among Indians of the Stone Age and that he might even have found El Dorado?

There at the base of the *tepui*, Alex realized that life is filled with surprises. He had never believed in destiny, it seemed a fatalistic concept; instead he had believed that each of us is free to make of his life what he will, and he was determined to do something very good with his; to triumph and to be happy. Now all of that seemed absurd. He couldn't put his trust in reason after having experienced the hazy territory of dreams, intuition, and magic. Destiny was a fact, and there were times you had to jump into an adventure and get out whatever way you could, the way he had when he was four and his grandmother had pushed him into the pool and he had had to swim or else. There was no other way but to dive into the mysteries that lay ahead. Once again, he was aware of the risks. He was alone in the middle of the most remote region of the planet, where the rules he was used to didn't count. He had to admit it: His grandmother had done him a huge favor when she dragged him from the security of California and threw him out into this strange world. It wasn't only Tahama and his fire ants that had initiated him into adulthood, the ineffable Kate had done her part, too.

Walimai left his two companions on this journey resting beside a stream with instructions to wait for him. In this area of the altiplano, the trees were less dense, and the midday sun fell on their heads like lead. Nadia and Alex jumped into the water, frightening the electric eels and turtles resting on the bottom, while Borobá hunted flies and scratched his fleas on the bank. Alex felt absolutely comfortable with this girl; he enjoyed being with her and trusted her, and in this setting she knew much more than he did. It seemed strange to feel so much admiration for someone his sister's age. At times he was tempted to compare her with Cecilia Burns, but he didn't know how to begin; they were totally different. Cecilia Burns would be as lost in the jungle as Nadia Santos would be in a city.

Cecilia had developed early, and at fifteen she already looked like a young woman. He was not the only one in love with her, all the guys in their school had the same fantasies. Nadia, in contrast, was still as tall and slim as a reed, without any feminine curves, nothing but bone and tanned skin, an androgynous being who carried the scent of the jungle. Despite her childish looks, she inspired respect: She had poise and dignity. Maybe because she didn't have any sisters or friends her own age, she acted like an adult. She was serious, silent, focused, and did not have the annoying ways that bothered Alex so much in other girls. He hated it when the girls whispered and giggled among themselves; it made him feel insecure, sure that they were making fun of him. "We're not always talking about you, Alexander. We have more interesting things to think of," Cecilia Burns had said once in front of the whole class. He knew Nadia would never embarrass him that way.

The aged shaman returned a few hours later, as fresh and serene as always, with two thick sticks dipped in a resin similar to the one the Indians had used when climbing the sides of the waterfall. He announced that he had found the entrance to the mountain of the gods, and then after hiding the bow and arrows, which could not be carried there, he bid them follow him.

At the base of the *tepui*, the primary growth was enormous ferns, which grew as tangled as burlap. They moved forward cautiously and slowly, parting the leaves and opening a path with difficulty. Once beneath those gigantic plants, the sky disappeared and they sank into a universe of green; time stopped and reality lost its familiar forms. They were in a labyrinth of palpitating leaves, of sweet-scented dew, of phosphorescent insects and succulent flowers that dripped a thick blue honey. The air was as heavy as the breath of a beast. There was a constant humming, stones burned like coals, and the earth was the color of blood. Alexander held on to Walimai's shoulder with one hand and grasped Nadia with the other, aware that if they got separated by a few inches, the ferns would swallow them up and they would never find each other again. Borobá was clinging to his mistress, silent and alert. They had to brush away from their eyes the delicate spiderwebs embroidered with mosquitoes and dewdrops suspended like lace among the leaves. They could barely see their own feet, so they stopped wondering about the sticky, warm substance that they were sinking into up to their ankles.

Alex could not imagine how the shaman knew where they were going; perhaps his wife-spirit was guiding him; sometimes he was sure that they were traveling in circles, not moving forward at all. There were no points of reference, only the endless vegetation enfolding them in its glossy embrace. He tried to read his compass but the needle was quivering madly, reinforcing the impression that they were going in circles. Suddenly Walimai stopped, moved a fern leaf that seemed no different from the others, and they were standing before an opening in the side of the mountain, something resembling a fox's den.

The witch man dropped down and crawled, and they followed him. The passage was a narrow ten or twelve feet in length, then opened into a spacious cave dimly lighted by some ray from outside; here they were able to stand up. Walimai began patiently to strike his stones to make fire, as Alex promised himself never to leave home again without matches. Finally the stones sparked, some straw blazed, and Walimai used that to light the resin on one of his torches.

They watched as a compact, dark cloud of thousands and thousands of bats lifted up in the flickering light. They were in a rock cavern with water streaming down the walls on all sides and spreading across the floor like a black lake. Several natural tunnels, some wider than others, branched off in different directions, creating an intricate subterranean labyrinth. With no hesitation, the Indian started down one of the passages, Alex and Nadia right on his heels.

Alex remembered the story of Ariadne's thread that, according to Greek mythology, allowed Theseus to find his way back from the depths of the labyrinth after slaying the fierce Minotaur. He did not have a spool of thread to mark the way, and he asked himself how they would get out should something happen to Walimai. Since the needle of his compass was whirling aimlessly, he deduced they were in a magnetic field. He tried to use his knife to blaze a trail on the walls, but the rock was as hard as granite and it would have taken hours to chip out markers. They moved from tunnel to tunnel, always climbing upward inside the *tepui*, with the improvised torch as their only defense against the total blackness surrounding them. There in the bowels of the Earth it was not silent as a tomb, as he had imagined; they heard the fluttering of bats, the squeaking of mice, the racing footsteps of small animals, the dripping of water, and a muted, rhythmic thumping like a heartbeat, as if they were inside a living organism, an enormous animal in repose. No one said a word, but from time to time Borobá shrieked with fright and then the echo of the labyrinth returned the sound multiplied over and over. Alex asked himself what nature of creatures such depths might harbor, maybe snakes or poisonous scorpions, then determined he would not think about such things but keep a cool head, taking his cue from Nadia, who was marching along behind Walimai, silent and confident.

Gradually they could make out the end of the long passageway. They saw a faint green glow and, when they emerged, found themselves in a large cavern whose beauty was impossible to describe. Enough light filtered in from somewhere to illuminate a space as large as a vast church, with marvelous sculptural rock and mineral formations. The labyrinth they had left behind was dark stone, but now they were in a round, lighted hall beneath a cathedral-like dome, surrounded by crystal and precious stones. Alex knew very little about minerals, but he recognized opals, topazes, agates, formations of quartz and alabaster, jade and tourmaline. He saw crystals like diamonds, others that were milky, some that seemed to shine from within, and still others veined with green, purple, and red, as if they were encrusted with emeralds, amethysts, and rubies. Transparent stalactites hung from the ceiling like daggers of ice, dripping lime-rich water. The smell was of dampness and, surprisingly, flowers. The mixture was rancid, intense, and penetrating . . . slightly nauseating; a blend of perfume and tomb. The air was cold and crisp, as in winter after a snow.

At the far end of the grotto, something moved, and an instant later broke away from a rock of blue crystal, something that resembled a strange bird, or a winged reptile. The creature stretched its wings, preparing to fly, and Alex could see it clearly. It was very like the drawings he had seen of legendary dragons, only about the size of a large pelican and very beautiful. The terrible dragons of European legends, which always guarded a treasure or an imprisoned damsel, were definitely repulsive. The one before his eyes, however, was like the dragons he had seen at festivals in San Francisco's Chinatown, pure joy and vitality. Even so, he whipped out his Swiss Army knife and prepared to defend himself, but Walimai calmed him with a gesture.

The shaman's wife-spirit, as delicate as a dragonfly, flew across the grotto and descended between the animal's wings, riding it like a horse. Borobá screeched with terror and bared his teeth, but Nadia, enchanted by the dragon, made him stop. She began to call in the language of birds and reptiles, hoping to summon it to her, but the fabulous creature examined the visitors from a distance with its ruby-red eyes and ignored Nadia's enticement. Then it rose up in flight, elegant and airy, and flew in a majestic circle around the dome of the grotto, with Walimai's wife on its back, as if it merely wanted to show off the beauty of its lines and its phosphorescent scales. Finally it again settled on the rock of blue crystal, folded its wings, and waited with the impassive attitude of a cat.

The spirit of the woman flew back to her husband and hovered there, suspended in air. Alex wondered how he could describe what his eyes had seen. If only he had his grandmother's camera to prove that this place and these creatures really did exist, and that he had not drowned in the storm of his own hallucinations.

They left the enchanted cave and the winged dragon with a certain reluctance, not knowing whether they would see them again. Alex was still trying to find rational explanations for what he had witnessed. In contrast, Nadia accepted all of its wonder without question. Alex reasoned that those *tepuis*, so isolated from the rest of the planet, were the last enclaves of the Paleolithic era, where the flora and fauna of thousands and thousands of years ago had been preserved. They must have been led to a kind of Galápagos Island, where the most ancient of species had escaped genetic mutation or extinction. That "dragon" was probably some kind of unknown bird. Such creatures appeared in the folklore and mythology of many different regions. In China, where they were the symbol of good luck, and in England, they had served to prove the courage of knights like St. George. Possibly, Alex concluded, they were animals that had coexisted with the first human beings on the planet, and popular superstition had remembered them as gigantic reptiles spewing fire from their nostrils. The dragon of the grotto did not emit flames, but the penetrating perfume of a courtesan. However, Alex could not come up with an explanation for Walimai's wife, that human-looking fairy creature accompanying them on their strange journey. Perhaps he would find an explanation later, somewhere.

They followed Walimai through new tunnels, the light of his torch growing weaker and weaker. They passed through other grottos, but none as spectacular as the first, and they saw other strange creatures: birds, with red plumage and four wings, that growled like dogs; and white cats, with blind eyes, which were on the verge of attacking but backed off when Nadia soothed them in the language of felines. They passed through a flooded cave where they had to walk through water up to their necks with Borobá perched on Nadia's head. They saw golden winged fish that swam between their legs and suddenly took flight, disappearing into the darkness of the tunnels.

In another cave, which emitted a thick purple fog the color of certain twilights, indescribable flowers were growing out of living rock. Walimai brushed one of them with his spear and fleshy tentacles flashed from among its petals, reaching out for its prey. At a bend in one of the passages, in the orange, wavering light of the torch, they saw a niche in the wall that contained something that seemed to be a small child encased in resin, like an insect trapped in a piece of amber. Alex imagined that the infant had been in his sealed tomb since the dawn of humankind, and that he would lie intact in that place for thousands of years. How had he got there? How had he died?

Finally the group reached the last passage of that enormous labyrinth. They peered into open space, blinded for a few instants by a blast of white light. Then they saw that they were on a kind of balcony, a rock projecting over the hollow interior of the mountain, like the crater of a volcano. The labyrinth they had followed through the depths of the *tepui* joined the outside world with the fabulous universe inside. They realized they had climbed a long way through the tunnels. Overhead rose the vertical faces of the mountain, covered with vegetation and disappearing among the clouds. They could not see the sky, only a ceiling as thick and white as cotton, where the sunlight filtering through created a strange optical phenomenon: six transparent moons floating in a milky sky. They were the moons

Alex had seen in his vision. Wheeling in the air were birds he had never seen before, some as translucid and filmy as jellyfish, others as solid as black condors, some like the dragon they had seen in the grotto.

Far below was a large circular valley, which from where they stood looked like a blue-green garden blanketed in haze. Waterfalls, trickles of water, and small streams slipped down the sides of the verdant walls to feed the lakes of the valley, so symmetrical and perfect that they did not seem natural. And in the center, gleaming like a crown, rose the proud city of El Dorado. Nadia and Alex choked back cries of amazement as they were blinded by the unbelievable splendor of the city of gold, the dwelling of the gods.

Walimai gave them time to recover from their surprise and then pointed to the steps carved into the mountainside, curving down from the overhang where they stood to the valley floor. As they descended, they realized that the flora was as extraordinary as the fauna they had seen; the plants, flowers, and shrubs were unique. The lower they went, the hotter and more humid it became; the vegetation was thicker and more exuberant, the trees taller and leafier, the flowers more perfumed, the fruit more succulent. Although it was very beautiful, the overall impression was not peaceful, but was, in fact, vaguely threatening, like a mysterious landscape on Venus. Nature throbbed, panted, grew before their eyes, as if waiting to ambush them. They saw yellow flies as transparent as topaz, blue beetles sporting horns, large snails so colorful that from a distance they looked like flowers, exotic striped lizards, rodents with sharp, curved fangs, and hairless squirrels leaping among the branches like naked gnomes.

As they neared the valley, closer and closer to El Dorado, it became obvious that this was not a city, nor was it gold. It was a group of natural geometric formations, like the crystals they had seen in the grottos. The golden color came from mica, a mineral with little value, and pyrite, called—with good reason—"fool's gold." Alex smiled quietly, thinking that if the conquistadors and countless other adventurers had succeeded in conquering the incredible obstacles on the road to El Dorado, they would have gone home poorer than they'd come.

CHAPTER FOURTEEN

The Beasts

MINUTES LATER, Alex and Nadia saw the Beast. It was about thirty yards away, heading in the direction of the city. It looked like a gigantic man-ape, more than ten feet tall, upright, with powerful arms that dragged on the ground and a melancholy face on a head too small for its body. It was covered with thick, wiry hair and had three long, curved, knife-sharp claws on each hand. It moved with incredible slowness, almost as if it were not moving at all. Nadia recognized it immediately as the Beast, since she had seen it before. Paralyzed with terror and surprise, they froze in place, studying the creature. It reminded them of some familiar animal, but they couldn't think what.

"I know, it looks like a sloth," Nadia whispered finally.

And then Alex remembered that in the San

Francisco zoo he had seen an animal something like an ape or a bear that lived in trees and moved at the same sluggish pace as the Beast—which is how it got a name that means laziness, "sloth." It had no defenses. It lacked the speed to attack, escape, or protect itself, but it had very few predators; its hairy hide and bitter flesh were not appetizing to even the hungriest carnivore.

"And the smell? The Beast I saw had a terrible stink," said Nadia, still speaking in a whisper.

"Well, this one doesn't. At least we're not smelling it from here," Alex commented. "Maybe it has a scent gland, like a skunk, and it sprays the smell when it wants to defend itself or stop prey in its tracks."

Their whispering reached the ears of the Beast, which turned very slowly to see where the sound was coming from. Alex and Nadia stepped back, but Walimai, with his wife-spirit just behind him, moved forward slowly, as if imitating the astonishing lethargy of the creature. The shaman was a small man; he came no higher than the hipbone of the Beast, which loomed like a tower over the ancient. He and his wife fell to their knees before this extraordinary being, and then, as clear as a bell, the youngsters heard a deep and cavernous voice speaking in the language of the People of the Mist.

"It talks like a human!" Alex muttered, convinced he was dreaming.

"Padre Valdomero was right, Jaguar."

"That means it has human intelligence. Do you think you can communicate with it?"

"If Walimai can, I probably can, too, but I'm too afraid to go closer," Nadia whispered.

They stood quietly a long while, because words issued from the creature's mouth one at a time, in the same deliberate way it moved.

"It's asking who we are," Nadia translated.

"I got that. I understand almost everything," Alex murmured, stepping a little closer. Walimai gestured him to stop.

The dialogue between the shaman and the Beast advanced at the same imperceptible pace; no one moved as the light in the white sky began to change to an orange glow. That, Alex and Nadia assumed, meant that outside the crater the sun was descending toward the horizon. Finally Walimai got to his feet and came back to where they were standing.

"There will be a council of the gods," he announced.

"Council? Are there more of these creatures? How many are there?" Alex asked, but Walimai could not clarify this because he did not know how to count.

The witch man led them around the edge of the valley lying in the heart of the *tepui* to a small natural cavern in the rock, where they made themselves as comfortable as possible, then he went to look for food. He returned with some very aromatic fruit that neither of them had ever seen before, but they were so hungry that they devoured it without a question. Suddenly it was night and they were sunk in fathomless darkness. The city of fool's gold, which during the day had been blindingly brilliant, had disappeared into the shadows. Walimai made no effort to light his second torch; he was undoubtedly keeping that for their return through the labyrinth, and there was no other source of light. Alex concluded that though human in their language, and maybe in some other habits, the creatures were more primitive than cavemen, for they hadn't as yet discovered fire. Compared to the Beasts, the Indians were quite sophisticated. Why did the People of the Mist think of the creatures as gods, if they themselves had evolved further?

There was no relief from the heat and humidity; it came from the mountain itself, reminding them that they might be in the crater of a dormant volcano. The idea of being on a thin layer of dirt and rock formed over molten flames of lava was not very reassuring, but Alex reasoned that if the volcano had been inactive for thousands of years, as proved by the luxuriant growth inside it, it would indeed be unusually bad luck if it erupted the one night he was there. The next hours dragged painfully by. The two young people found it difficult to sleep in that unfamiliar place. They remembered the murdered soldier's horrible wounds all too well. The Beast must have used those enormous claws to gut him. Why hadn't the man run away, or fired his weapon? The creature was so unbelievably slow that his victim should have had more than enough time. The explanation could only be the paralyzing stench it sprayed. There was no way to protect yourself if the creatures decided to use their scent glands. It didn't help to hold your nose, the odor penetrated every pore of the body, overpowering brain and will; it was a poison as deadly as curare.

"Are they human or animal?" Alex asked, but again Walimai couldn't answer; to him there was no difference.

"Where do they come from?"

"They have been here always, they are gods."

Alex imagined the interior of the *tepui* as an ecological archive where species that had vanished from the rest of the earth still survived. He told Nadia that these must be the ancestors of the sloths they knew.

"They don't seem like humans, Eagle. We haven't seen any sign of dwellings, or tools, or weapons; nothing that suggests an organized society," he added.

"But they speak like people, Jaguar," the girl said.

"They must have an unbelievably slow metabolism, and live hundreds of years. If they have memory, then in such a long life they would be able to learn many things, even to speak, right?" Alex ventured.

"They speak the language of the People of the Mist. Who invented it? Did the Indians teach the Beasts? Or did the Beasts teach the Indians?"

"Whichever it was, I am guessing that the Indians and these *sloths* have had a symbiotic relationship for centuries," Alex replied.

"What?" she asked, for she had never heard that word.

"That means they need each other to survive."

"Why?"

"I don't know, but I'm going to find out. I read once that the gods need humans as much as humans need their gods," said Alex.

"I know that the Beasts' council will be very long and very boring. We'd better try to get a little rest now, that way we'll be fresh in the morning," Nadia suggested, settling down to go to sleep. She had to make Borobá move away a little because it was too hot to have him right next to her. The monkey was like an extension of her being: they were both so accustomed to the contact between their bodies that a separation, however brief, felt like a premonition of death.

With the dawn, life stirred in the city of gold and the valley of the gods was illuminated with every tone of red and orange and pink. The Beasts, nevertheless, lingered many hours before they brushed the sleep from their eyes and one by one emerged from their dens among the rock and crystal formations. Alex and Nadia counted eleven creatures, three males and eight females, some taller than others, but all adults. They did not see any examples of the young of that unique species, and wondered how often they reproduced. Walimai said it was very rare for one to be born; it had never happened in his lifetime. He added that he had never seen one die, either, although he knew a grotto in the labyrinth that held their skeletons. Alex concluded that this information fit with his theory about their living for centuries, and he imagined that these prehistoric mammals had only one or two offspring in their lifetimes, so that witnessing a birth would be a rare event indeed.

When he observed the creatures at closer range, he realized that given their limitations in mobility, they would not be good hunters, and so must be vegetarians. Their tremendous claws were not for killing but for climbing. That explained how they were able to go up and down the vertical trail the three of them had climbed at the waterfall. The sloths used the same niches, bumps, and cracks in the rock the Indians did. How many of them were there outside the *tepui*? Only one, or several? He wished he could bring back proof of what he was seeing.

Many hours later, the council began. The Beasts gathered in a semicircle in the center of the city of gold, and Walimai, Alex, and Nadia stood opposite them. They looked tiny among these giants. They had the strange impression that the bodies of the creatures were vibrating, and that their outlines were fuzzy; later they realized that in those centuries-old hides nested entire colonies of insects of various sorts, some flitting around them like fruit flies. In the steamy air, that motion gave the illusion that the Beasts were enveloped in individual clouds. The young visitors were not far from the creatures, close enough to see them in detail, but also far enough to escape should they have to—although they both knew that if any of those eleven giants decided to spray their scent, there was no power in the world that could save them. Walimai's attitude was solemn and reverent, but he did not appear to be frightened.

"This is Eagle, and this is Jaguar," said the ancient. "They are friends of the People of the Mist, and they are here to receive instructions."

An eternal silence greeted this introduction, as if the words took forever to make an impact in the brains of these creatures. Then Walimai recited a long poem that contained news of the tribe, from recent births to the death of their chief, Mokarita, and included the visions in which the Rahakanariwa had appeared, the Indians' visit to the lowlands, the arrival of the foreigners, and the election of Iyomi as chief of chiefs.

A painfully slow dialogue began between the witch man and the creatures, which Nadia and Alex had no difficulty understanding because there was time to think and consult after every word. That was how they learned that for centuries and centuries the People of the Mist had known the location of the city of

302

gold and had zealously guarded the secret, protecting the gods from the outside world, while in turn those extraordinary beings had served as the storehouse of every word of the tribe's history. There had been times of great catastrophes in which the ecological bubble of the *tepui* had suffered serious imbalances and there hadn't been enough food to satisfy the needs of the species that lived in its interior. During those periods, the Indians had brought "sacrifices": maize, potatoes, cassava, fruit, nuts. They left their offerings near the *tepui*, not entering the secret labyrinth but sending a messenger to inform the gods. The offerings included eggs, fish, and animals killed by the Indians; over the course of time, the vegetarian diet of the Beasts had changed.

Alexander reasoned that had these ancient creatures with their slowed-down intelligence needed a sense of the divine, their gods would have been the invisible Indians of Tapirawateri, the only human beings they knew of. For them, the Indians were magical: they moved quickly, they could reproduce with ease, they had weapons and tools, they were masters of fire and of the vast universe outside the *tepui*;

they were all-powerful. But the giant sloths had not as yet reached the stage of evolution in which they contemplated death, and so had no need of gods. Their infinitely long lives were lived on a purely material plane.

The memory of the Beasts contained all the information the messengers of man had given them; they were living archives. The Indians did not know writing, but their history was never lost because the Beasts forgot nothing. By questioning them, patiently and over long periods, they could retrieve the tribe's past from its beginnings twenty thousand years before. Shamans like Walimai visited to keep them up to date by reciting the epic poems recounting the past and recent history of the tribe. Messengers died and were replaced by others, but every word of those poems was stored in the brains of the Beasts.

Only twice since the beginning of history had the tribe come inside the *tepui*, and on both occasions they had been fleeing from a powerful enemy. The first time had been four hundred years before, when the People of the Mist had had to hide for several weeks from a party of Spanish soldiers that had succeeded in reaching the Eye of the World. When the warriors saw that the strangers could kill from afar, with no effort beyond pointing sticks of smoke and noise, they realized that their weapons were useless against the invaders. They dismantled their huts, buried their few belongings, covered the rubble of the village with dirt and branches, erased their tracks, and with their women and children retreated to the sacred *tepui*. There they were sheltered by the gods until, one by one, the foreigners were all dead. The soldiers were searching for El Dorado, so blind with greed that they ended up murdering each other. Those few who were left were exterminated by the Beasts and the Indian warriors. Only one lived to get away, and somehow managed to find his compatriots. He spent the rest of his life insane, tied to a post in a madhouse in Navarre, ranting about mythological giants and a city of pure gold. The legend survived in the pages of the chroniclers of the Spanish empire, feeding the fantasy of adventurers to the present day.

The second time had been three years before, when the *nahab*'s great birds of noise and wind had landed in the Eye of the World.

Once again, the People of the Mist had hidden until the foreigners left, disillusioned at not finding the mines they were searching for. The Indians, however, warned by Walimai's visions, were preparing for their return. This time it would not be four hundred years before the *nahab* came to the altiplano, because now they could fly. That was when the Beasts had decided to come out from the *tepui* and kill them, never suspecting that they numbered in the hundreds of millions. Accustomed to the reduced number of their own species, they believed they could eliminate their enemies one by one.

Alex and Nadia listened to the Beasts recount their history, drawing many conclusions along the way.

"And that's why there haven't been any dead Indians, only outsiders," Alex marveled.

"What about Padre Valdomero?" Nadia reminded him.

"Padre Valdomero lived with the Indians. The Beasts must have identified the scent and so didn't attack him."

"And me? He didn't attack me that night . . . ," she added.

"We were with Indians. If the Beast had seen us when we were with the expedition, we would have died like the soldier."

"So if I understand it right, the Beasts have come out in order to punish the foreigners," the girl concluded.

"Exactly, but the result has been just the opposite. You see what's happened? They have focused attention on the Indians and on the Eye of the World. I wouldn't be here if my grandmother hadn't been hired by a magazine to look for the Beast," Alex said.

The afternoon went by, and then it was night, and still the participants in the council had not come to an agreement. Alex asked how many gods had gone out from the mountain, and Walimai said two, which was not information that could be trusted, it could just as easily be a dozen. With the help of Nadia, who translated for him, the American explained to the Beasts that their one hope of salvation was to stay inside the *tepui*, and, for the Indians, to establish some controlled form of contact with civilization. Contact was inevitable, he said. Sooner or later the helicopters would land again in the Eye of the World, and this time the *nahab* would come to stay. There were some *nahab* who wanted to destroy the People of the Mist and claim the Eye of the World for themselves. It was very difficult to make this point, because neither the Beasts nor Walimai could comprehend how anyone could *own* land. Alex said that there were still other *nahab* who wanted to save the Indians, and that because the gods were the last of their species on the planet, they would do everything they could to save them, too. He reminded the shaman that Iyomi had named him, Alexander, chief of negotiating with the *nahab,* and that he was here to ask permission and seek help in carrying out his mission.

"We do not believe that the *nahab* can be more powerful than the gods," said Walimai.

"Sometimes they are. The gods will not be able to defend themselves against the *nahab*, nor will the People of the Mist. But the good *nahab* can stop other *nahab,*" Alexander replied.

"In my visions the Rahakanariwa is always thirsty for blood," said Walimai.

"I have been named chief to pacify the

Rahakanariwa," said Nadia.

"There must be no more war. The gods must go back to the mountain. Nadia and I will see that the People of the Mist and the dwelling of the gods are respected by the *nahab*," Alex promised, trying to sound convincing.

In truth, he had no idea how he could restrain Mauro Carías, Captain Ariosto, and all the other adventurers who coveted the wealth of the region. He didn't even know Mauro Carías's plan, or the part the members of the *International Geographic* expedition were to play in exterminating the Indians. The entrepreneur had said very clearly that they were to be witnesses, but Alex could not imagine to what.

In his heart of hearts, Alex believed there would be worldwide excitement when his grandmother published information about the existence of the Beasts, and about the ecological paradise inside the *tepui*. With luck, and skillful management of the press, Kate could have the Eye of the World declared a nature preserve protected by world governments. That solution, however, might come too late. If Mauro Carías got his way, "before three months have gone by," as he had said in his conversation with Captain Ariosto, "there won't be a living soul left in that area." The one hope was that international protection would get there first. Even though it would not be possible to prevent the curiosity of scientists or television reporters, at least they could stop the invasion of adventurers and settlers planning to tame the jungle and wipe out its inhabitants. He also had a terrible premonition of some Hollywood impresario trying to turn the *tepui* into a kind of theme park. He hoped that the pressure created by his grandmother's reporting could delay or totally prevent that sort of nightmare.

The Beasts lived in separate chambers in their fabulous city. They were solitary creatures that did not share space. Despite their enormous size, they ate very little, chewing for hours: vegetables, fruit, roots, and occasionally a small animal they found dead or wounded. Nadia could communicate with them better than Walimai. A couple of the females showed interest in her and allowed her to come close to them—she wanted more than anything to touch them. But when she put her hand on the wiry pelt, a hundred assorted insects swarmed up her arm and covered her entire body. Horrified, she tried to shake them off; many clung to her clothing and her skin and she couldn't get rid of them. Walimai pointed to one of the many lakes in the city and she jumped in. The water was warm and bubbly, and as she sank down she felt the tickle of the carbonation on her skin. She invited Alex in, and they soaked for a long time, clean, finally, after so many days of crawling through tunnels and sweating.

In the meantime, in a large gourd Walimai had crushed the pulp of a fruit with big black seeds and mixed that with the juice of shiny blue grapes. The result was a purple brew about the consistency of the soup from Mokarita's bones they had drunk during the funeral, but this had a delicious flavor and a lingering aroma of honey and nectar. The shaman offered it to the Beasts, then he drank and gave some to Alexander, Nadia, and Borobá. That porridgelike beverage satisfied their hunger immediately, though they felt slightly dizzy, as if they had drunk alcohol.

That night they were given one of the chambers in the city of gold where the heat was less oppressive than it had been in the cave the first night. Strange orchids grew among the mineral formations, some so fragrant that it was difficult to breathe near them. For a long time a warm, dense rain fell, soaking everything and pouring like a river through channels in the crystal with a persistent thrumming, like drums. When finally it stopped, the air was cooler and the exhausted pair finally fell asleep on the hard ground of El Dorado with the sensation that their stomachs were filled with perfumed flowers.

The brew Walimai had prepared had the magical power to carry them to the kingdom of myths and collective dream, where everyone—gods and humans—could share the same visions. In that way, many words and many explanations were spared. They all dreamed that the Rahakanariwa was a prisoner in a locked wooden cage, desperately trying to free itself with its formidable beak and terrible talons, as gods and humans tied to trees awaited their fate. They dreamed that the *nahab,* all of them wearing masks, were killing

312

each other. They watched as the cannibal-bird destroyed the cage and was free to devour everything in its path, but a white eagle and a black jaguar stood in its way, challenging it to a fight to the death. There was no resolution in that contest, as there rarely is in dreams. Alexander recognized the Rahakanariwa because he had seen it before in a nightmare in which it appeared as a vulture; it had broken a window in his house and carried off his mother in its monstrous talons.

When they awakened in the morning, they did not have to tell each other what they had seen since they had all been together in the same dream, even Borobá. When the council of the gods reconvened to continue its deliberations, it wasn't necessary to spend hours repeating the same ideas, as they had the day before. They knew what they had to do; each knew his role in the events to come.

"Jaguar and Eagle . . . will do battle . . . with the Rahakanariwa. . . . If they win . . . what will be . . . their reward?" one of the sloths asked, after intermittent silences.

"The three eggs in the nest," Nadia said without hesitation.

"And the water of health," Alex added, thinking of his mother.

Frightened, Walimai told the visitors that they had violated the basic law of exchange: you do not take without giving. It was the law of nature. They had dared ask the gods for something without offering anything in exchange. The Beasts' question had been only a formality and the correct response was that no reward was expected, that they were doing it out of reverence for the gods and compassion for humans. It was obvious that the Beasts were bothered by the foreigners' requests. Some laboriously rose to their feet, threatening, grunting, raising arms as thick as oak branches. Walimai fell to the ground on his face before the council, mumbling explanations and apologies, but he could not calm them. Fearing that one of the Beasts might decide to douse them with its scent, Alex held out the only possible peace offering he could think of: his grandfather's flute.

"I bring something for the gods," he said, trembling.

The sweet notes of the instrument floated tentatively on the warm air of the *tepui*. The

Beasts, caught by surprise, took several moments to react, and by the time they did, Alex was into it, abandoned to the pleasure of making music. His flute seemed to have acquired Walimai's supernatural powers. The notes multiplied over and over in the strange theater of the city of gold, ricocheted, transformed into endless arpeggios that set the orchids among the tall crystal formations vibrating. Alex had never played like this before, had never felt so much in control; he could tame creatures with the magic of his flute. He felt as if he were connected to an enormous synthesizer, that his melody was accompanied by a whole orchestra of strings, woodwinds, and percussion. The Beasts, at first motionless, began to move like large trees blown by the wind; their ancient feet thumped the ground and the fertile valley of the *tepui* resonated like a great bell. Then Nadia, on an impulse, leaped into the center of the council semicircle, leaving Borobá sitting quietly at Alex's feet, as if he understood that this was a crucial moment.

Nadia began to dance with the energy of the earth, an energy that shone through her fine bones like a light. She had never seen a ballet, but she had stored all the rhythms she had so often heard: the samba of Brazil, the salsa and *joropo* of Venezuela, the American music that came to them on the radio. She had seen Blacks, mulattoes, *caboclos*, and Whites dance till they dropped during Carnival in Manaus, watched solemn Indians dance during their ceremonies. With no conscious knowledge, she improvised her gift to the gods out of pure instinct. She soared. Her body moved on its own, in a trance, with no awareness or premeditation on her part. She swayed like the slimmest palm tree, she effervesced like the foam of the waterfall, she whirled like the wind. She imitated the flight of the parrot, the fleet course of the jaguar, the leaping of the dolphin, the buzzing of the insect, the undulation of the serpent.

For thousands and thousands of years, there had been life in the hollow cylinder of the *tepui*, but until that moment, music had never been heard, not even the *tam-tam* of a drum. The two times the People of the Mist had taken shelter in the legendary city, they had done so in a way not to irritate the Beasts; in silence, and making use of their talent to become invisible. The Beasts had no sense of a human's ability to create music; they had never seen a body move with the airiness, the passion, the speed, and grace of Nadia's dance. In truth, these heavy creatures had never received such a grand offering. Their sluggish brains absorbed each note and each movement and stored them for future centuries. The gift of these two young people would stay with them as part of their legend.

CHAPTER FIFTEEN

The Crystal Eggs

IN EXCHANGE FOR THE gifts of music and dance they had received, the Beasts granted Alex and Nadia what they had asked for. They told them that Nadia must climb to the highest part of the *tepui*, to the very top, where she would find the nest of the three magnificent eggs of her vision. As for Alex, he was to descend into the depths of the earth, where he would find the water of health.

"Can we go together, first to the top of the *tepui* and then to the depths of the crater?" Alex asked, thinking that their tasks would be easier if they shared them.

Lethargically, the sloths shook their heads no, and Walimai explained that every journey to the realm of the spirits is made alone. He added that they had only the next day to complete their missions, because by nightfall—

without fail—they must return to the outside world; that was their agreement with the gods. If they were not back, they would be trapped in the sacred *tepui*; they would never find the way out of the labyrinth by themselves.

The pair spent the rest of the day wandering around El Dorado and telling each other about their brief lives; each wanted to know as much as possible about the other before they went their separate ways. It was difficult for Nadia to imagine her friend's life in California with his family. She had never seen a computer or gone to school or known what winter was. For his part, the American envied the girl's free and quiet life in such close contact with nature. Nadia possessed a common sense and a wisdom that to him seemed beyond reach.

Both were enchanted by the city's magnificent formations of mica and other minerals, and with the unreal flowers blooming everywhere and the unique animals and insects. They found out that the dragons they saw swooping through the air, the creatures like the one in the cavern, were as tame as pet parrots. They called to one and it landed gracefully at their feet; they could touch it. Its skin was smooth and cold, like that of a fish; it had the gaze of a falcon and the perfumed breath of flowers. The friends swam in the warm lake waters and stuffed themselves with fruit—but only what Walimai approved. Certain fruits and mushrooms were deadly, the shaman explained. Others induced nightmarish visions or sapped the will, and some erased memory forever.

From time to time during their wanderings, they came across the Beasts, which spent the greatest part of their lives in a stupor. Once they had eaten enough leaves and fruit to be nourished, they spent the rest of the day sitting and gazing at the lush landscape around them and the cover of clouds that closed the mouth of the *tepui*. "They believe that sky is white and the size of that circle," Nadia commented, and Alex replied that they themselves had only a partial vision of the sky, which astronauts knew was not blue, but black, and infinite. They were weary that night when they went to bed. They slept side by side, not touching since it was so hot, but sharing the same dream, as they had learned to do with Walimai's magical fruit.

★ ★ ★

At dawn the next day, the ancient shaman handed Alexander a hollow gourd and gave Nadia a gourd filled with water and a basket that she strapped to her back. He warned them that once the journey was begun, either toward the heights or toward the depths, there was no turning back. They must conquer every obstacle or perish in the undertaking, because it was not possible to return with empty hands.

"Are you sure this is what you want to do?" asked the shaman.

"I am," Nadia declared.

She had no idea what she would do with the eggs or why she was the one to look for them, but she did not doubt her vision. They had to be very valuable, or very magical. To get them, she was ready to conquer her most deeply rooted fear: heights.

"I am sure, too," Alex added, thinking that he would go to hell itself if it would save his mother.

"You may return and you may not," said the witch man as he bid them good-bye; he was unmoved, because to him the boundary between life and death was no more than a film of smoke that the slightest breeze could disperse.

Nadia unclasped Borobá from her waist and explained to him that she could not take him where she was going. The monkey clung to Walimai's leg, moaning and pounding his little fists, but he did not try to disobey. Alex and Nadia gave each other a strong hug, frightened and excited. Then each set off in the direction Walimai indicated.

Nadia climbed up the same stairway carved from rock that she had come down with Walimai and Alex when they had emerged from the labyrinth and descended to the valley of the *tepui*. Getting up to that balcony was not difficult, even though the way was very steep, there was no handrail to hold on to, and the steps themselves were irregular, worn, and not very deep. Fighting against dizziness, she took one quick glance down and saw the extraordinary blue-green valley floor wreathed in a light mist, with the magnificent city of gold in the center. Then she looked up and her gaze was lost in the clouds. The mouth of the *tepui* seemed narrower than the base. How would she climb those inward-tilting walls? She would have to have little feet, like a beetle. How high was the *tepui*, really, and how much was covered in clouds? Where exactly was the nest? She decided to think about solutions, not problems. She would confront the obstacles one by one, as she came to them. If she had managed to climb the waterfall, she could do this, she thought—even if she wasn't tied to Jaguar by a rope, and even if she was all by herself.

When she reached the balcony, she realized that the stairs ended there; from then on she would have to climb by holding on to anything she could find. She settled the basket on her back, closed her eyes, and searched for internal calm. Jaguar had explained that vital energy and courage were concentrated in the center of her being. She breathed in with all her strength so clean air would fill her lungs and travel through her body to the tips of her fingers and toes. She repeated that breath three times without opening her eyes, visualizing the eagle, her totemic animal. She imagined her arms stretching out, growing longer, turning into feathered wings; she pictured her legs, and her feet ending in talons like grappling hooks; her nose hardening into a ferocious beak; and her eyes growing wider apart until they were at the sides of her head. She felt her soft and curly hair changing into strong feathers that lay flat against her skull but that bristled when she willed, feathers that contained everything eagles know, antennae that perceived anything in the air, even the invisible. Her body lost its muscled flexibility and in exchange acquired an airiness so absolute that she could lift up from the earth and float with the stars. She experienced a tremendous sense of power, with all the eagle's strength flowing in her blood. She felt that strength penetrating her cells, her whole awareness. "I am Eagle!" she cried aloud, and opened her eyes.

Nadia placed her fingers in a small crack in the rock above her head and her foot in another at the level of her waist. She pulled her body up and paused until she was sure of her balance. She felt with the other hand until she found a root, and with the opposite foot, until she could ease her toes into a crack. She followed with the other hand, looking for something she could grasp, and when she found it, she raised her body a little farther. The vegetation growing on the sides of the *tepui* helped: roots, shrubs, lianas. She saw deep scratches on the rocks and on some trunks; they looked like the marks of claws. The Beasts must have climbed this way searching for food, or maybe they didn't know the route through the labyrinth and every time they went in or out they climbed up one side of the *tepui* and down the other. She calculated that would take days, maybe weeks, considering the ponderous progress of those gigantic sloths.

Some conscious part of her mind registered that the hollow of the *tepui* was not cone-shaped, as the optical illusion of looking at it from below had made her believe, but, in fact, opened slightly outward. The mouth of the crater was actually wider than the base. She would not need beetle claws, after all, just concentration and courage. So, foot by foot, she made her way upward, for hours, with admirable determination and newly acquired skill. That ability came from a hidden and mysterious place, a place of calm inside her heart, where she found the noble qualities of her totemic animal. She was an eagle, the highest-flying bird, the queen of the sky, the bird that builds a nest only angels can reach.

The eagle-girl continued upward, little by little. The warm, humid air of the lower valley turned into a cool breeze, which pushed her higher. She paused often, exhausted, fighting the temptation to look down or calculate the distance to the top, concentrating only on the next move. She was burning with thirst; her mouth felt as if it were coated with sand and had a bitter taste, but she could not let go to drink from the water gourd Walimai had given her. "I'll drink when I get to the top," she muttered, thinking about cool, clean water bathing the lining of her parched throat. If only it would rain, she thought, but not a drop fell from the clouds. When she thought she could not climb a step farther, she felt Walimai's magic talisman around her neck and that gave her courage. It was her protection. It had helped her climb the smooth black rocks of the waterfall, it had made her a friend to the Indians, it had saved her from the Beasts; as long as she had that, she was safe.

Much later, the first clouds, as thick as meringue, brushed her head, and then she was enveloped in milky white. She climbed by feeling her way, clinging to rock and to the vegetation that was growing sparser the farther she climbed. She was not aware that her hands and knees and feet were bleeding; she was focused on the magic power sustaining her ... and then one hand was exploring a very wide opening. She was able to pull her whole body into it; though the *tepui* was still hidden in the piled-up clouds, she was at the top! A loud cry of triumph, a savage, ancestral screech like a hundred eagles in unison, burst from the breast of Nadia and crashed against the rocks of other peaks, echoing and spreading until it passed over the horizon.

The girl waited, motionless, on that summit until her cry was lost in the farthest chasms of the large mesa. Then her heart stopped its drumming and she could breathe deeply. As soon as she felt solid rock beneath her feet, she took the water gourd and drank all it held. She had never wanted anything so much. The cool liquid ran down her throat, cleaning away the sand and bitter taste in her mouth, moistening her tongue and cracked lips, spreading through her body like a miraculous balm capable of curing anxiety and erasing pain. She understood that happiness consists of achieving something we have wanted for a long time.

The height, and the brutal effort of getting there and of conquering her fears, acted like a drug more powerful than any given to her by the Indians in Tapirawa-teri or Walimai's potion for collective dreams. Again she felt she was flying, but now she was not even an eagle, she was detached from everything physical, she had become pure spirit. She was suspended in glorious space. The world was far away, below her on the plane of illusions. She floated there for a time that could not be measured, until she noticed an opening in the radiant sky. Without hesitation, she sped like an arrow through that hole into dark, empty space that reminded her of the infinite firmament of a moonless night. This was the absolute space of the divine and of death, the space where even spirit is dissolved. She was the void, empty of desire, of memory. There was nothing to fear. She was outside time.

But on the heights of the *tepui*, the body of

Nadia began to call her back, reclaiming her. Oxygen flowing to her brain carried with it a sensation of physical reality. The water she'd drunk furnished the energy she needed to move. So finally Nadia's spirit made the reverse journey: again it flew like an arrow through the opening in the void back into the glorious dome where it floated a few instants in limitless white, then passed into the form of the eagle. It fought to resist the temptation to glide forever on the wind and with a last effort returned to the body of the girl. Once again, Nadia was sitting on top of the world, looking all around.

Nadia was at the highest point on a large mesa, encircled by the silence of the clouds. Although she could not see the true height or expanse of where she was, it was her impression that the hollow center of the *tepui* was small in comparison with the size of the mountain that contained it. The terrain she could see, partly smooth rock and in other places covered with thick growth, was rough, with deep crevices. She felt sure that it would be a long time before the steel birds of the *nahab* explored this place, because landing here would be unthinkable even for a helicopter, as was the near impossibility of walking across that irregular surface. She felt her confidence weaken. She could look for the nest the rest of her days without finding it among all these fissures, but then she remembered that Walimai had pointed out exactly where to climb. She rested a moment, then started off, up and down, from rock to rock, driven by some unknown force, with a kind of instinctive certainty.

She did not have to go far. Fairly near, in a cleft among large rocks, she found the nest, and in it the three crystal eggs. They were smaller, with more sparkle, than the ones in her vision. Wondrous.

Taking a thousand precautions to keep from slipping into one of the deep fissures where she would have broken every bone in her body, Nadia crawled to the nest. Her fingers closed over the gleaming perfection of one crystal egg, but she could not pick it up. Surprised, she tried a different one. She could not move it, either, nor the third. How was it possible that objects the size of a toucan's egg should weigh so much? What was happening?

She examined them closely, turning them over and over. She could see that they were not glued or screwed down; just the opposite, they seemed almost to be floating on their cushion of twigs and feathers. Nadia sat down on a nearby rock, confused by why that was, unable to believe that this whole adventure, all the effort it had taken to get here, was for nothing. She had found the superhuman strength to climb like a lizard up the internal walls of the *tepui,* but now that she was finally at the top, she didn't have the strength to budge the treasure she had come to find.

Nadia hesitated quite some time, upset and with no idea of how to solve this puzzle. Suddenly it came to her that the eggs belonged to someone. Maybe the Beasts had put them there, but they might also belong to some fabled creature, a bird, or a reptile like the dragons. If that were the case, the mother could appear at any moment, and when she found an intruder near her nest she would launch an attack with justifiable fury. She couldn't stay there, she decided, but neither did she intend to give up the eggs. Walimai had said that she could not return with empty hands. What else had the shaman told her? That she had to be back before nightfall. And then she remembered what the witch man had taught her the day before: the law of giving and receiving. For everything you take, you have to give something in return.

She looked herself over. She didn't have anything to give. All she had was her T-shirt, her shorts, and the basket strapped to her back. As she checked her body, she saw for the first time the scratches, bruises, and cuts inflicted by the rocks as she had climbed the mountain. Her blood, in which the vital energy that had allowed her to reach this goal was concentrated, was probably the only valuable she possessed. She stepped closer, holding her injured body so her blood would drip onto the nest. A few red drops splashed on the soft feathers. As she bent over, she felt the talisman on her chest and realized in a flash that this was the price she would have to pay for the eggs. No, she thought. To sacrifice it meant giving up the prodigious powers of protection she attributed to the carved bone, the shaman's gift. She had never had anything as magical as that amulet. It was much more important to her than the eggs, whose purpose she could not even guess. No, she couldn't give up her talisman, she decided.

Nadia closed her eyes, completely spent, as the sun filtering through the clouds began to change color. For an instant, the hallucination of the *ayahuasca* dream she had experienced during Mokarita's funeral returned, and she was once again the eagle soaring through a white sky, gliding on the wind, light and powerful. From above, she saw the eggs glittering in the nest, just as in the vision, and she experienced the same conviction she had then: Those eggs would save the People of the Mist. At last she sighed and opened her eyes. She removed the talisman from her neck and placed it in the nest. Then she reached out and touched one of them; this time she lifted it with no effort at all. The other two were equally easy to take. She placed all three carefully in her basket and was ready to climb down the way she had come up. There was still sunlight in the clouds; she realized that the descent would have to be very quick if she was to be back before nightfall, as Walimai had warned her.

CHAPTER SIXTEEN

The Water of Health

As Nadia was climbing to the top of the *tepui*, Alexander was wiggling down a narrow passage into the womb of the earth, a closed, hot, dark, throbbing world like his worst nightmares. If he at least had a flashlight! He had to grope his way, sometimes on hands and knees, sometimes scooting forward on his belly in total shadow. His eyes could not adjust because the darkness was absolute. He held out a hand, felt along the rock to estimate the direction and width of the tunnel, then moved forward inch by inch, slithering like a snake. The farther he went, the narrower the tunnel seemed to grow, and he feared he would not be able to turn around to go back. The supply of air was choking and foul; it was like being buried. His jaguar attributes would not be any help; here he needed a different totemic animal, maybe a mole or a mouse or a worm.

He stopped more than once with the intention of turning back before it was too late, but each time he kept going, spurred by memories of his mother. With every minute that went by, his chest grew tighter and his terror more intense. Again he heard the mute galloping of his heart that he had heard in the labyrinth with Walimai. His crazed mind ran through the list of dangers that lay in store, the worst of all being buried alive in the entrails of this mountain. How long was this tunnel? Would he make it to the end or meet defeat along the way? Would there be enough oxygen or would he suffocate?

Alexander simply collapsed facedown, bone weary, moaning. His muscles were tense, blood was pounding at his temples, every nerve was raw with pain. He couldn't think, he felt as if his head was going to burst from lack of air. He had never been so afraid, not even during the long night of his initiation among the Indians. He tried to remember what he had felt when he was hanging from a rope on El Capitán, but it wasn't comparable. Then he was at the top of a mountain, now he was deep inside one. There he had been with his father; here he was absolutely alone. He gave in to his despair, trembling, beyond exhaustion. For an eternity, darkness penetrated his brain and he lost his purpose, voicelessly summoning death, defeated. And then as his spirit faded into the shadows, his father's voice cut through the fog in his brain, first as a nearly imperceptible whisper, then more clearly. What had his father told him so many times when he was teaching him to climb? *Be calm, Alexander. Seek your center, that's where your strength is. Breathe. When you inhale, you are charged with energy, when you exhale, you rid your body of tension; relax. Don't think. Obey your instinct.* This was what he himself had counseled Nadia as they were climbing to the Eye of the World, how had he forgotten?

He concentrated on breathing: inhale energy, ignore the lack of oxygen; exhale terror; relax, reject the negative thoughts paralyzing him. "I can do it, I can do it . . . ," he repeated. Gradually he returned to his body. He visualized his toes and relaxed them one by one, then his legs, his knees, his hips, his back, his arms, down to the tips of his fingers, his neck, his jaw, his eyelids. Now that he could breathe more easily, he stopped sobbing. He located his center, a red, vibrant place at the level of his navel. He listened to his heartbeats. He felt a tickling on his skin, then warmth through his veins, and, finally, strength returning to his senses and his brain.

Alexander uttered a cry of relief. After a few seconds, the sound bounced against something and came back to his ears. He remembered that this was the principle of bats' sonar, what allowed them to find their way in the dark. He repeated the cry, hoping it would indicate distance and direction, and that way he could hear with his heart, as Nadia had so often told him. He had found the way to navigate in blackness.

The remainder of the journey through the tunnel passed in a state of semiconsciousness in which his body moved on its own, as if it knew the way. From time to time Alex connected briefly with his logical brain and with a spark of intelligence deduced that the air filled with unknown gases must be affecting his mind. Later he would think he had lived a dream.

When it seemed that the narrow passageway would never end, Alexander heard the sound of water, like a river, and a mouthful of warm air reached his gasping lungs. That renewed his strength. He pushed forward, and at a turn of the tunnel noted that his eyes could make out something in the darkness: a light, at first very faint, slowly growing stronger. He pulled himself on, hopeful because there was light and air. He was in a cave that must somehow be connected with the outside because it was weakly illuminated. A strange odor met his nostrils, persistent, slightly nauseating, like vinegar and rotten flowers. This cave had the same formations of glittering minerals he had seen in the labyrinth. The clean facets of these structures were like mirrors, reflecting and multiplying the faint light that penetrated from outside. He was at the edge of a small lake fed by a stream of white water that reminded him of skim milk. Coming from the tomb where he had been, that white lake and river were the most beautiful things he had ever seen. Could this be the fountain of eternal youth? The odor was sickening; he thought it must be from some gas emitted from the depths of the

Earth, maybe a toxic gas that dulled your brain.

A whispery, caressing voice caught his attention. Surprised, he saw something on the far shore of the little lake, maybe twenty feet away, and when his pupils adjusted to the new light of the cave, he glimpsed a human figure. He could not see it clearly, but the form and voice belonged to a girl. Impossible, he said, sirens don't exist. I'm going nuts. It's the gas, the smell. But the girl seemed real enough: her long hair swished, her skin radiated light, her gestures were human, her voice was seductive. Alex wanted to dive into the white water and drink till his thirst was satisfied and to wash off the dirt that covered him from head to foot, as well as the blood from the scrapes on his elbows and knees. The temptation to go to the beautiful creature calling to him, and to give himself to that pleasure, was unbearable. At the moment he started toward the apparition, he saw that she looked exactly like Cecilia Burns: the same chestnut hair, the same blue eyes, the same languid movements. Some part of his brain warned him that the siren was a mirage, a creation of his mind, like the filmy jellyfish floating in the pale air of the cavern. He remembered what he had heard about the mythology of the Indians, the stories Walimai had told them about the origins of the universe and the River of Milk that contained all the seeds of life but also decay and death. No, this was not the miraculous water that would restore his mother to health, he decided; this was a trick of his mind to distract him from his mission. There was no time to lose, every minute was precious. He tied his T-shirt over his nose, battling the penetrating, dizzying fragrance. He turned toward a narrow ledge that ran along the edge of the lake and followed the stream out of sight.

Alexander took that path, leaving the lake and the miraculous apparition of the girl behind. He was amazed that the pale light persisted; at least now he was not dragging himself along in the dark. The aroma was growing fainter, and before long it vanished. He walked as fast as he could, bent over, trying not to bang his head against the ceiling of the cavern, and concentrating on keeping his balance on the narrow overhang, fearing that if he fell into the river below he might be dragged away by the current. He regretted that he did not have time to investigate that white liquid that resembled milk but had the smell of salad dressing.

The long path was covered with a slippery moss seething with thousands of tiny creatures: larvae, insects, and worms, and large blue toads, their skins so transparent he could see their palpitating internal organs. They flicked their long, snakelike tongues toward his legs. Alex longed for his boots, because he had to kick them away with his bare feet and their soft, cool, slimy bodies made his stomach turn.

About two hundred yards further on, the layer of moss and the toads disappeared, and the path was wider. Relieved, he could look around, and that was when he noticed for the first time that the walls were splashed with beautiful colors. As he looked closer, he identified the source: precious stones and rich veins of ore. He opened his Swiss Army knife and dug into the rock, finding that the stones came loose rather easily. What were they? He recognized some colors, like the intense green of emeralds and the pure red of rubies. He was in the middle of a fabulous treasure: this was the true El Dorado that adventurers had sought for so many years.

He had only to scrape the walls with his knife to harvest a fortune. If he filled the gourd Walimai had given him with those precious stones, he would go home to California a millionaire; he could pay for the best treatments for his mother's illness, buy a new house for his parents, finance his sisters' educations. And for him? He could buy a racing car that would freak out his friends and leave Cecilia with her jaw hanging open. These jewels were the solution for his life: He could devote himself to music, climbing, anything he wanted, and never have to worry about earning a living . . . No! What was he thinking? Those precious stones were not only for him, they would help the Indians. With that incredible wealth he would have the power to fulfill the mission Iyomi had assigned him: to negotiate with the *nahab*. He would become the protector of the tribe and their forests and waterfalls; with his grandmother's pen and his money, they would transform the Eye of the World into the largest nature preserve in the world. In only a few hours, he could fill the gourd and change the fate of the People of the Mist and that of his own family.

Alex began to pry around a green stone with the tip of his knife, breaking off little pieces of the rock. Minutes later the stone was in his hand and he could take a better look. It did not have the brilliance of the cut emeralds in rings, but there was no doubt it was the same color. It was as he started to put it into the gourd that he remembered the purpose of this mission to the bowels of the Earth: to fill the gourd with the water of health. No. It would not be jewels that bought his mother's health; he needed something that would work magic. With a sigh, he put the green stone in the pocket of his shorts and moved on, concerned that he had wasted precious minutes and did not know how much farther he had to go to reach the miraculous fountain.

Almost immediately, the path ended before a massive pile of stones. Alex tested them, sure that there was a way to continue; it wasn't possible that his journey would end so abruptly. If Walimai had sent him on this trek into the depths of the mountain, it was because the fountain existed; it was merely a matter of finding it. But what if he had taken a wrong turn? Maybe he had gone astray at some fork in the tunnel. Maybe he was supposed to cross the milky lake, maybe the girl was not a temptation to distract him but his guide to the water of health. Doubts began to bounce around like screams in his brain. He pressed his temples, trying to calm himself, and he repeated the deep breathing he had practiced in the tunnel when he heard his father's remote voice guiding him. "I must go to my center, where there is calm and strength," he murmured. He disciplined himself not to contemplate possible mistakes he had made but to concentrate on the obstacle that lay in his way. Last winter, his mother had asked him to move a great stack of firewood from the patio to the back of the garage. When he claimed that Hercules himself couldn't do the job, his mother had showed him how: one log at a time.

He began removing rocks, first pebbles, then medium-size stones, which came loose easily, and finally the very largest. It was slow and difficult work, but eventually he broke through. A puff of hot vapor hit his face, as if he had opened the door of an oven, forcing him to step back. He waited, wondering what to do next, as the air streamed out. He didn't know anything about mining, but he had read that gases often build up inside mines and he supposed that was what was happening. If that was the case, he was out of luck. He noticed that the flow slowed down after a few minutes, as if it had been under pressure, and then it stopped. He waited, and then he put his head through the opening.

On the other side was a cavern with a deep pit in the center giving off clouds of smoke and reddish light. He could hear small explosions, as if something thick were boiling and erupting in bubbles. He did not have to be any closer to know it was molten lava, the last activity of an age-old volcano. He was at the heart of the crater. He considered the possibility that the vapors were toxic, but since they didn't smell bad, he decided to take a chance and go into the cavern. He wriggled through the opening and found himself standing on warm stone. He took one step, and then another, determined to explore the area. The heat was more intense than a sauna and within minutes he was bathed in sweat, but there was enough air to breathe. He took off his T-shirt again and tied it around his mouth and nose. Tears streamed from his eyes. He was aware that he had to move with extreme caution if he was not to slip into the lava pit.

The cave was large and irregularly shaped, glowing in the quivering, reddish light of the fire rumbling below. To his right was another chamber; he peered into it. It was even darker because little of the light from the first room reached it. In that cavern, the temperature was more bearable, fresh air must be seeping in through some fissure. Alex was near the limits of his endurance, dripping sweat and very thirsty, convinced that he was not strong enough to retrace the route he had traveled. Where was the fountain?

His thoughts were interrupted by a gust of wind, and then immediately a frightening vibration that reverberated as if he were inside a large metal drum. Instinctively, he covered his ears, but the disturbance was not a noise, it was a riveting energy force, and there was no way to defend against it. He turned, looking for the source. And then he saw it. A gigantic bat whose outstretched wings must have measured fifteen feet from tip to tip. Its ratlike body was twice the size of his dog, Poncho, and long fangs flashed in the gaping mouth of its large head. It was not black but totally white, an albino bat.

Terrified, Alex realized that this animal, like the Beasts, was a survivor from an ancient era when thousands and thousands of years ago the first humans had looked up from the ground to gaze with wonder at the stars. The bat's blindness was no advantage for Alex, that vibration had been its sonar: The vampire knew exactly what and where the intruder was. The wind gust was repeated: with wings flapping, the bat was preparing to attack. Was this the Indians' Rahakanariwa, the feared blood-sucking bird?

Alex's mind began to whir. He knew that the possibilities of escaping were nearly nil; he could not go back to the other cavern and start running across that treacherous floor without risking a fall into the lava pit. Instinctively his hand went to the Swiss Army knife at his waist, even though he knew it was a ridiculous weapon compared with the size of his enemy. His fingers brushed against the flute on his belt and without thinking twice he untied it and placed it to his lips. He whispered the name of his grandfather Joseph, asking for his help in this moment of mortal danger, and then began to play.

The first notes rang like crystal—cool and pure in that dark place. The enormous vampire, extraordinarily sensitive to sounds, tucked in its wings and seemed to shrink in size. It had probably lived for centuries in the solitude and silence of its subterranean world and those sounds must have been like an explosion in its brain; it must have felt as if it were riddled with millions of piercing darts. It screeched again on a wavelength inaudible to human ears, although clearly with pain. The vampire's signal mingled with the music and its sonar could not interpret it.

As Alex played his flute, the huge white bat moved backward, gradually retreating, until it was motionless in one corner, like a winged white bear, its fangs and claws visible but neutralized. Once more, the youth marveled at the power of that flute, which had accompanied him at every crucial moment of his adventure.

When the animal moved, Alex saw a tiny thread of water trickling down the wall of the cavern, and he knew he had come to the end of the trail: this was the fountain of eternal youth. It was not as legend described, a flowing spring in the midst of a garden. It was barely a few humble drops slipping down the face of the rock.

Alexander moved with caution, one step at a time, never dropping a note, approaching the monstrous vampire bat, trying to think with his heart and not his head. This was such an extraordinary experience that he could not trust in reason or logic alone; the moment had come to call on the same resources that had helped him when climbing and playing music, intuition. He tried to imagine how the animal was feeling and concluded that it must be as terrified as he was. This was the first time it had encountered a human being; it had never heard sounds like those from the flute and the noise must almost drown its sonar; that was why it was hypnotized. He remembered that he had to collect the water in his gourd and get back before nightfall. He had absolutely no way to calculate how many hours he had been in this subterranean world, but the one thing he wanted was to get out of there as quickly as possible.

As he played a single note on the flute, using one hand, he held out the gourd with the other, passing within inches of the vampire bat, but the instant the first drops fell into the gourd, the trickle stopped altogether. Alex's frustration was beyond words; he felt like beating the rock with his fists. The only thing that stopped him was the horrible creature poised like a guard at his side.

And then, at the point of turning away, he remembered Walimai's words about the unchanging law of nature: to give the equivalent of what you received. He reviewed his limited belongings: the compass, the Swiss Army knife, and the flute. He could leave the first two, which were not of much help at the moment, but he could not give up the magic flute, his instrument of power, he had inherited from his famous grandfather. Without that, he was lost. He lay the compass and knife on the ground and waited. Nothing. Not a single drop squeezed from the rock.

Then he realized that this water of health was the most valuable thing in the world to him, the only thing that could save his mother's life. He would have to leave his most valuable possession in exchange. He placed the flute on the ground as the last notes reverberated among the cave walls. The slow trickle immediately started again. He waited the seemingly endless moments it took to fill the gourd, always with one eye on the vampire bat at his side. It was so close that Alex could smell its fetid breath and count its teeth and feel boundless compassion for the profound solitude that enveloped it, but he did not allow that to distract him from the task at hand. Once the gourd was overflowing, he began moving away, slowly, in order not to provoke the monster. He went back to the first cavern, where he heard the gurgle of the molten lava in the entrails of the earth, and slipped back through the opening. He wondered about replacing the stones to close the hole, but he didn't have enough time, and it seemed to him that the bat was too big to get through and follow him.

He was faster returning than coming,

because now he knew the way. He was not tempted to stop and dig out precious stones, and when he passed the milky lake where he had seen the mirage of Cecilia, he did not even pause but held his nose to defend against the fragrance that addled his brain. The greatest difficulty came when he had to crawl back into the narrow tunnel through which he'd come, holding the gourd upright to keep from spilling its contents. He had a cover, a square of leather tied with a cord, but it wasn't waterproof and he didn't want to lose a drop of the miraculous water of health. This time the tunnel, though oppressive and dark, was not as horrible since he knew that at the end, he would reach light and air.

Struck by the last rays of the sun, the feather mattress of clouds at the mouth of the *tepui* was turning every shade of red from russet to pink gold. The six moons of light were beginning to fade from the strange heavens of the *tepui* when Nadia and Alexander returned. Walimai was waiting with Borobá in the amphitheater of the city of gold, facing the council of the Beasts. As soon as the monkey saw his mistress, he raced to her with obvious relief and wound his arms around her neck. The two young people were limp with fatigue; their bodies were covered with cuts and scratches and bruises but they had the treasures they had gone to seek. The ancient witch man showed no sign of surprise; he welcomed them with the same serenity with which he performed every act of his life, and notified them that it was time to leave. There was no time to rest; that night they would have to pass through the inside of the mountain and emerge in the Eye of the World.

"I had to leave my talisman," Nadia told her friend sadly.

"And I left my flute," Alex added.

"You can get another," the girl said. "You make the music, not the flute."

"Just like the powers of the talisman are within you," he consoled her.

Walimai examined the three eggs with care and sniffed the water in the gourd. He nodded with great seriousness. Then he untied one of the small leather pouches hanging from his healer's staff and gave it to Alex with instructions to grind the leaves and stir them with the water to cure his mother. Alex hung the pouch around his neck as tears came to his eyes. Walimai shook his quartz cylinder above Alex's head for a good while, blew on his chest, temples, and back, and touched his arms and legs with his staff.

"If you were not *nahab*, you would be my successor. You were born with the soul of a shaman. You have the power to heal. Use it well."

"Does that mean that I can cure my mother with this water and these leaves?"

"Maybe yes and maybe no . . ."

Alex realized that his hopes had no logical base; he should trust the modern treatments of the hospital in Texas and not a gourdful of water and a few dried leaves given him by a naked old man in the middle of the Amazon, but on this journey he had learned to open his mind to mysteries. Supernatural powers did exist, and other dimensions of reality, like this *tepui* filled with creatures from prehistoric times. True, nearly everything could be explained rationally, including the Beasts; however, Alex preferred just to hope for a miracle.

The council of the gods had accepted the

warnings of the foreigners and the wise Walimai. They would not go out to kill the *nahab*; that was a futile task, since they were as numerous as the ants and others would always come in their place. The Beasts would stay inside their sacred mountain where they were safe, at least for now.

Nadia and Alex said good-bye to the giant sloths with a heavy heart. In the best of cases, if everything turned out well, the labyrinthine passage to the *tepui* would not be discovered and helicopters would not descend there from the sky. With luck, another century might pass before human curiosity reached this last refuge of prehistoric times. But if not, they hoped that at least the scientific community would defend those extraordinary creatures before the greed of adventurers destroyed them. One way or other, they knew that they themselves would not see the Beasts again.

As it grew dark, their way lighted by Walimai's resin torch, Alex and Nadia climbed the steps that led to the labyrinth. They went straight through the intricate system of tunnels, which the shaman knew to perfection.

Not once did they come to a dead end, and they never had to turn back or retrace their steps, because the map was etched in the shaman's mind. Alex gave up on the idea of committing the turns to memory, because even had he been able to remember them, or set them down on paper, without points of reference it would be impossible to find where he was now.

They came to the marvelous cavern where they had seen the first dragon and once again marveled at the colors of the glittering precious stones and crystals and ores. It was like the true cave of Ali Baba, with all the fabulous treasure the most ambitious mind could imagine. Alex remembered the green stone he had put in his pocket, and he took it out to compare. In the pale splendor of the cave, the stone was no longer green, but yellow, and he realized that the color of the stones in the cave of his quest was the result of the light, and that possibly they had as little value as the fool's gold of El Dorado. He had done well to reject the temptation to fill the gourd with them instead of the water of health. He kept the false emerald as a souvenir; he would take it to his mother as a gift.

The winged dragon was in its corner, just where they had seen it before, but now a smaller one was with it, this one mostly red, perhaps its mate. They were not disturbed by the presence of the three humans, nor when the wife-spirit of Walimai flew over to greet them, fluttering around them like a fairy without wings.

On this occasion, just as on the pilgrimage into the depths of the Earth, the return seemed shorter and easier to Alex; he knew what it was like and was not expecting surprises. And there were none, so after passing through the last tunnel, they found themselves in a cave a few feet from the exit. There Walimai told them to sit down. He opened one of his mysterious little pouches and produced some leaves that looked like tobacco. He explained briefly that they must be "cleansed" to erase the memory of what they had seen. Alex did not want to forget the Beasts or his journey deep into the Earth, and Nadia did not want to give up what she had learned. Walimai assured them they would remember all that; he would merely erase the route from their minds so they could not return to the sacred mountain.

Walimai rolled the leaves, sealed them with saliva, and lighted them like a cigarette. He took a puff and then forcefully blew the smoke into the young people's mouths, first Alex and then Nadia. It was not a pleasant experience, the stinking, hot, biting smoke went right to their heads; the effect was like breathing pepper. They felt a sharp stinging, an uncontrollable desire to sneeze, and very soon they felt dizzy. Alex's first experience with tobacco came to mind, when his grandmother Kate had bundled them into a car and they had smoked until he was as sick as a dog. This time the symptoms were similar, except that everything was whirling around him.

Then Walimai extinguished the torch. There were no pale rays from the sun to light the cave, as they had several days before when they were just starting. The blackness was total. Each of the young people reached for the other's hand, and Borobá whimpered with fright, arms tight around his mistress's waist. They saw monsters lurking in the dark and heard hair-raising screams, but they weren't afraid. With what little sense they had left, they knew that those horrifying visions were the effect of the smoke they had breathed and that in any case, as long as the witch man was with them, they were safe. They made themselves comfortable on the ground, arms around each other, and within minutes had lost consciousness.

They could not estimate how long they slept. They awakened gradually, hearing the voice of Walimai calling their names as they reached out to find each other. The cave was not totally dark; the faintest light allowed them to see general outlines. The shaman pointed to the narrow tunnel that was the way out and, still a little dizzy, they followed it. They emerged in the forest of the ferns. The sun was rising in the Eye of the World.

CHAPTER SEVENTEEN

The Cannibal-Bird

THAT DAY THE TRAVELERS began the march back to Tapirawa-teri. As they came within sight of it, they saw the gleam of helicopters through the trees, and knew that the civilization of the *nahab* had finally reached the village. Walimai decided to stay in the forest; all his life he had kept his distance from the foreigners, and this was not the moment to change his habits. The shaman, like the People of the Mist, had the talent of making himself nearly invisible, and for years he had prowled around the camps and towns of the *nahab*, observing them without their suspecting he existed. The only ones who knew him were Nadia and Padre Valdomero, his friend from the time the priest had lived with the Indians. The witch man had met the "girl the color of honey" in several of his visions and was convinced that she was an envoy of the spirits. He thought of her as one of his people, which is why he allowed her to call him by name when they were alone.

Alex felt a thrill of happiness when he saw the helicopters in the distance: He was not forever lost in the planet of the Beasts, he could return to the known world. He imagined that the helicopters had flown over the Eye of the World for several days, looking for them. His grandmother must have raised a monumental uproar when he disappeared, and forced Captain Ariosto to comb the vast region from the air. Possibly they had seen the smoke of Mokarita's funeral pyre and had discovered the village that way.

Walimai advised the two young people to hide in the trees and watch what was going on in the village. Alex wanted to give him some remembrance in exchange for the miraculous cure for his mother, so he presented the Indian with his Swiss Army knife. Walimai took the red metal object and felt its weight and its strangeness, without the least notion of what it was for. Alex opened out the knives, tweezers, scissors, corkscrew, and screwdriver, one by one, until it was transformed into a gleaming, bristling hedgehog. He showed the shaman how to use each tool, and how to open and close them.

Walimai thanked him for his kindness, but he had lived more than a century without metal and, frankly, he felt a little old to learn the tricks of the *nahab*. He did not want to be discourteous, however, and he hung the marvel around his neck, where it joined a necklace of teeth and other amulets. Then he reminded Nadia that the screech of the owl would summon him, and that they would stay in touch that way. The girl gave him the basket with the three crystal eggs because she thought they would be safer in the hands of the ancient. She did not want to show up with them in front of the foreigners; they belonged to the People of the Mist. The trio said their good-byes, and in less than a second, Walimai faded into the vegetation, like an illusion.

Cautiously, Nadia and Alex approached the place where the "birds of noise and wind," as the Indians called them, had landed. They hid among the trees where they could watch without being seen, although they were too

far to hear clearly. In the center of Tapirawa-
teri, besides the birds of noise and wind, there
were three tents, a large awning, and even a gas
cookstove. A wire had been strung with gifts
to attract the Indians: knives, pots, hatchets,
and other steel and aluminum articles glinting
in the sun. They saw several armed soldiers, in
an attitude of alert, but no sign of Indians. The
People of the Mist had disappeared, as they
always did at the first hint of danger. That strat-
egy had served the tribe well; in contrast, other
Indians who had dealt with the *nahab* had
been exterminated or assimilated. Those who
had been incorporated into civilization had
become beggars; they had lost their dignity as
warriors, and their lands. That was why Chief
Mokarita had never allowed his people to
approach the *nahab* or take their gifts; he sus-
tained that in exchange for a machete or a hat,
the tribe would forget its origins, its language,
and its gods.

Nadia and Alex wondered what the soldiers
had in mind. If they were part of the plan to
eliminate the Indians of the Eye of the World,
it would be better not to go near. They
remembered every word of the conversation

they had heard in Santa María de la Lluvia between Captain Ariosto and Mauro Carías, and they knew that their lives were in danger if they dared to interfere with their plans.

It began to rain, as it did two or three times a day, brief and violent unexpected downpours that soaked everything for a while and stopped as suddenly as they had begun, leaving the world fresh and clean. The two friends had been observing the camp for almost an hour from their refuge among the trees when a party of three arrived in the village. They obviously had gone out to explore the area and now were running back, soaked to the bone. Even from a distance they were instantly recognizable: Kate, César Santos, and the photographer Timothy Bruce. Nadia and Alex could scarcely restrain a whoop of relief; that meant that Professor Leblanc and Dr. Omayra Torres were also nearby. With them present in the village, Captain Ariosto and Mauro Carías could not count on bullets to get rid of the Indians—or them.

The two friends left their hiding place and approached Tapariwa-teri with caution, but, after only a few yards, they were sighted by the guards and immediately surrounded. Kate's shout of joy when she saw her grandson was comparable only to that of César Santos's when he saw his daughter. They both ran to meet their loved ones, who were ready to drop, covered with scratches and scrapes, filthy, their clothes in tatters. Alexander also looked strangely different with his Indian haircut, which exposed a circle of scalp with the long, scab-covered cut. Santos swept Nadia up in his muscular arms and hugged her so hard that he nearly broke the ribs of Borobá, who was captured in the embrace. Kate, in contrast, was able to contain the wave of affection and relief she felt; as soon as her grandson was within reach, she slapped him in the face.

"That was for what you've put us through, Alexander. The next time you get out of my sight, I'll kill you," she said. In answer, Alex hugged her.

The others showed up immediately: Mauro Carías, Captain Ariosto, Dr. Omayra Torres, and the ineffable Professor Leblanc, who was covered with bee stings. Karakawe, as unsociable as ever, showed no sign of surprise at seeing the young people.

"How did you get here?" asked Captain Ariosto. "Without a helicopter, it's impossible."

Alex gave a quick summary of their adventure with the People of the Mist, without going into details or explaining where they had made the climb. Nor did he mention his journey with Nadia to the sacred *tepui*. That way he didn't think he was giving away any secret; the *nahab* already knew of the existence of the tribe. There were obvious signs that the village had been deserted by the Indians only hours before: cassava was piled in baskets, coals were still warm in the small fires, meat from the last hunt was covered with flies in the hut of the bachelors, and a few domestic pets were wandering around. The soldiers had chopped up the peaceful boas with their machetes and left the mutilated bodies rotting in the sun.

"Where are the Indians?" asked Mauro Carías.

"Far away," Nadia replied.

"I don't think they'll go very far with their women and children and old folk. They can't disappear without leaving a trace."

"They're invisible."

"Let's be serious, child!" he exclaimed.

"I always am."

"Are you going to tell me that these people can fly like witches?"

"They don't fly, but they run really fast," she clarified.

"Can you speak the language of these Indians, sweetie?"

"My name is Nadia Santos."

"All right, Nadia Santos. Can you talk with them or not?" Carías insisted impatiently.

"Yes."

Dr. Omayra Torres stepped in to explain the urgent need to vaccinate the tribe. Their village had been discovered; it was inevitable that sometime soon they would have contact with outsiders.

"As you know, Nadia, without wanting to we can infect them with diseases that are deadly for them. Whole tribes have perished in two or three months' time because of a common cold. Measles are an even graver danger. I have the vaccine, I can immunize these poor Indians and they will be protected. Can you help me?" the doctor begged.

"I will try," the girl promised.

"How can you communicate with the tribe?"

"I don't know yet, I have to think about it."

Alexander transferred the water of health to a bottle with a waterproof cap and carefully placed it in his knapsack. His grandmother saw him and wanted to know what he was doing.

"It's water to cure my mother," he said. "I found the fountain of eternal youth, what people have been looking for, Kate, for centuries. My mother will get well."

For the first time since he could remember, his grandmother initiated a show of affection. He felt her thin, sinewy arms around him and smelled her pipe-tobacco scent as her thick, self-cut hair and her dry, leather-tough skin brushed his face; he heard her hoarse voice saying his name, and he suspected that maybe she loved him a little after all. The minute Kate realized what she was doing, she stepped back, pushing Alex toward the table where Nadia was waiting. The two hungry, tired adventurers fell upon the beans, rice, cassava bread, and nearly burned fish bristling with bones. Alex devoured all of it with a ferocious appetite before the amazed eyes of Kate, who knew how picky her grandson had always been about food.

After they ate, the friends went to the river to bathe. They knew they were surrounded by invisible Indians who were following every movement of the *nahab* from the undergrowth. As they were splashing in the water, they felt eyes on them as clearly as if hands were touching them. They concluded that the Indians were not coming close because of the presence of the strangers and the helicopters they had seen in the sky. They tried to move a little away from the camp, thinking that if they were alone, the People of the Mist would show themselves, but there was a lot of activity in the village and it was impossible to drift into the forest without attracting attention. Fortunately, the soldiers did not dare step outside the camp because the stories about the Beast and the way it had gutted one of their companions had terrorized them. No one had ever explored the Eye of the World before, and they had heard tales of the spirits and demons that roamed in that region. They were less afraid of the Indians; they had their weapons to rely on, and then they themselves had indigenous blood in their veins.

At nightfall, everyone except those on guard duty sat in groups around the bonfire to smoke and drink. The atmosphere was dreary and someone suggested a little music to lift everyone's spirits. Alex had to admit that he had lost Joseph Cold's famous flute, but he couldn't say where without telling about his adventure inside the *tepui*. His grandmother shot him a murderous look, but didn't say anything, sure that her grandson was hiding a lot from her. A soldier produced a harmonica and played a couple of popular tunes, but his good intentions dropped into a black hole. Fear had possessed them all.

Kate led Nadia and Alex aside to tell them what had happened in their absence, from the moment the Indians had taken them away. As soon as it was realized that they had vanished, a search was begun; everyone was provided with flashlights, and they spread out through the forest and called for them almost all night. Leblanc contributed to the general anguish with another of his helpful prophecies: They had been dragged off by Indians and at that very moment were being roasted and eaten. The professor seized the opportunity to enlighten them on the habit of the Caribbean Indians, who hacked chunks of flesh off live prisoners to eat. Of course, he admitted, they were not among the Caribs, who had been either civilized or exterminated more than a hundred years before, but you never knew how far their cultural influences might have spread. César Santos had been close to pounding the anthropologist into the ground.

By the afternoon of the next day, a helicopter had finally arrived to rescue them. The boat with the unfortunate Joel González had reached Santa María de la Lluvia without incident, and the nuns from the hospital took over. Matuwe, the Indian guide, found help, and he himself went with the helicopter to pick up Captain Ariosto. His sense of orientation was so extraordinary that, although he had never flown, he was able to locate their position in that vast green expanse of jungle and to indicate with precision the place where the *International Geographic* party was waiting. As soon as they landed, Kate insisted that the captain call for reinforcements and organize a systematic search for the missing young people.

César Santos interrupted the writer to add that she had threatened Captain Ariosto with the press, the American embassy, and even the CIA if he did not cooperate; that was how she had obtained the second helicopter, which brought more soldiers and also Mauro Carías. She did not intend to leave there without her grandson, she had assured them, if it meant searching the entire Amazon on foot.

"Did you really say that, Kate?" asked Alex, amused.

"Not because of you, Alexander. It was a matter of principle," she growled.

That night, Nadia, Kate, and Omayra Torres stayed in one tent, Ludovic Leblanc and Timothy Bruce in another; Mauro Carías had his own, and the rest of the men hung their hammocks in the trees. Guards were posted at the four corners of the camp and oil lanterns were kept burning. Although no one said it aloud, they thought that would keep the Beast at bay. The lights made them an easy target for the Indians, but up until then, the tribes had never attacked in the dark because they were afraid of the nocturnal demons that escaped from human nightmares.

Nadia, who was a light sleeper, slept for a few hours and was wakened after midnight by Kate's snoring. After she checked and saw that the doctor, too, was fast asleep, she ordered Borobá to stay where he was and silently slipped out of the tent. She had studied the People of the Mist very closely, resolved to master their ability to move about unseen, and had discovered that it was more than a matter of camouflaging the body; it took a strong determination to dismiss the physical being. Concentration was required to reach the mental state of invisibility in which it was possible to stand three feet away from another person without being seen. She knew when she had achieved that state because her body felt very light, then seemed to dissolve into thin air. She had to hold to her goal without being distracted and not allow her nerves to betray her, the only way to remain hidden from others. As she left the tent, she had to pass a short distance from the guards patrolling the camp, but she did that without fear, protected by the extraordinary mental field she had created around herself.

As soon as she felt she was safe in the forest, which was faintly lighted by the moon, she imitated the screech of the owl twice, and waited. A little later, she sensed the silent presence of Walimai at her side. She asked the witch man to speak with the People of the Mist and convince them to come to the camp and be vaccinated. They could not hide forever in the shadows of the trees, she said, and if they planned to build a new village, they would be discovered by the "birds of noise and wind." She promised him that she would keep track of the Rahakanariwa, and that Jaguar would negotiate with the *nahab*. She said that her friend had a powerful grandmother, but did not try to explain the value of writing and publishing; she didn't think the shaman would understand what she was talking about since he didn't know what writing was and had never seen a printed page. She limited herself to saying that the grandmother had a lot of magic in the world of the *nahab*, although it was of little use in the Eye of the World.

Alexander had tied his hammock outside, a

little apart from the others. He had hoped that during the night the Indians would communicate with him, but he dropped off to sleep like a stone. He dreamed of the black jaguar. The meeting with his totemic animal was so clear and precise that the next day he wasn't sure whether he had dreamed it or if it had really happened. In the dream, he got out of his hammock and carefully walked away from the camp without being seen by the guards. As he entered the forest, outside the reach of the light from the fire or the oil lanterns, he saw the black feline stretched along the thick branch of an enormous chestnut tree, its tail switching, it eyes glittering in the night like dazzling topazes, just as it had appeared in the vision after he had drunk Walimai's magic potion. With its teeth and claws he could gut a caiman, with such powerful muscles he could run like the wind, with his strength and courage he could confront any enemy. He was a magnificent animal, king of the beasts, son of the Sun Father, prince of South American mythology. In the dream, Alex stopped a few steps from the jaguar, and, as in his first meeting in Mauro Carías's courtyard, he heard the cavernous voice speaking his name: Alexander . . . Alexander . . . The voice vibrated in his brain like a gigantic bronze gong, repeating his name again and again. What did the dream mean? What message was the jaguar trying to send him?

When he awoke, people were already moving around in the camp. The night's vivid dream upset him. He was sure it contained a message, but he couldn't decipher it. The one word the jaguar had spoken in his appearances to him had been his name: Alexander. Nothing more. His grandmother brought him a cup of coffee with condensed milk, something he had not tried before but that now seemed like a delicious breakfast. On impulse, he told her his dream.

"Defender of men," said his grandmother.

"What?"

"That's what your name means. Alexander is a Greek name and means 'defender.'"

"Why did they name me that, Kate?"

"Because of me. Your parents wanted to call you Joseph, like your grandfather, but I insisted on naming you Alexander, like the great warrior of ancient times. We tossed a coin, and I won. That's why you're called what you are," Kate explained.

"What made you think I should have that name?"

"There are many victims in this world, Alexander, and many noble causes to defend. A good warrior name helps in the fight for justice."

"You're in for a big disappointment, Kate. I'm no hero."

"We shall see," she said, passing him the cup of coffee.

The sensation of being observed by hundreds of eyes had everyone in the camp nervous. In recent years, several government employees who were sent to help the Indians had been murdered by the very tribes they were intended to protect. Sometimes the first contact was cordial, with gifts and food being exchanged, but suddenly the Indians would seize their weapons and attack by surprise. Indians are unpredictable and violent, according to Captain Ariosto, who was totally in agreement with Leblanc's theories, and that was why you could not lower your guard, you had to be on constant alert. Nadia tried to argue that the People of the Mist were different, but no one paid any attention to her.

Dr. Omayra Torres explained that for the last ten years her medical work had been principally among peaceful tribes; she knew nothing about the Indians Nadia called the People of the Mist. In any case, she expected to have more luck than in the past, and this time vaccinate them before they were infected. She admitted that on several previous occasions the vaccine had arrived too late. She gave the injections, but within a few days they fell ill anyway and died by the hundreds.

By then, Ludovic Leblanc had completely lost patience. His mission had been fruitless; he would have to return empty-handed, with no evidence of the famous Beast of the Amazon. What would he tell the editors of *International Geographic*? That a soldier had died in mysterious circumstances, badly slashed; that they had been exposed to a terrible smell; and that he had taken an involuntary wallow in the excrement of an unknown animal? Frankly, that was not very convincing proof of the existence of the Beast. Nor did he have anything to add about the Indians of the region, because he hadn't had so much as a glimpse of them. It had all been a wretched waste of his time. He could not wait to return to his university, where he was treated like a hero and was safe from bee stings and other discomforts. He felt that his relations with this group left a lot to be desired, and with Karakawe? A disaster. The Indian he had hired as his personal assistant had stopped the banana-leaf fanning the minute they left Santa María de la Lluvia, and instead of serving him, devoted himself to making the anthropologist's life even more unpleasant. Leblanc accused him of putting a live scorpion in his knapsack and a dead slug in his coffee, and of purposely having led him to where he was stung by the bees. The other members of the expedition tolerated the professor because he was such a character and because they could make fun of him to his face without his catching on. Leblanc took himself so seriously he could not imagine that others didn't.

Mauro Carías sent soldiers out to explore in various directions. The scouts left unwillingly and came back very quickly without any news of the tribe. They also searched the area by helicopter, even though Kate assured them that the noise would frighten the Indians. The writer suggested patience. Sooner or later, the tribe would come back to their village. Like Leblanc, she was more interested in the Beast than in the Indians because she had an article to write.

"Do you know something about the Beast you haven't told me, Alexander?" she asked her grandson.

"Maybe yes and maybe no," he replied, lacking the nerve to look her in the eye.

"What kind of answer is that?"

About midday, there was an alert: A figure had come out of the forest and was timidly approaching the camp. Mauro Carías made friendly signals, and ordered the soldiers to stand back and not spook her. The photographer Timothy Bruce handed his camera to Kate and picked up a video camera; the first contact with a tribe was a unique occasion. Nadia and Alex immediately recognized the visitor. She was Iyomi, chief of the chiefs of Tapirawa-teri. She came alone, naked, incredibly ancient, all wrinkled and toothless, leaning her weight on a twisted pole that served as a staff and with the circle of yellow feathers pulled down to her ears. Step by step she came, to the stupefaction of the *nahab*. Mauro Carías called Karakawe and Matuwe to ask if they knew the tribe this woman belonged to, but neither did. Nadia moved forward.

"I can speak with her," she said.

"Tell her we mean her no harm; we are friends of her people and they should come to us without their weapons because we have many gifts for her and all the others," said Mauro Carías.

Nadia translated freely, without mention of the part about the weapons, which she did not think was a very good idea considering the numbers of arms the soldiers had.

"We do not want the gifts of the *nahab*, we want them to leave the Eye of the World," Iyomi replied firmly.

"It's no use, they won't leave," the girl explained to the ancient woman.

"Then my warriors will kill them."

"More will come, many more, and all your warriors will die."

"My warriors are strong; these *nahab* do not

381

have bows or arrows, they are slow, clumsy, and they have soft skulls; besides they frighten as easily as children."

"War is not the solution, Chief of Chiefs. We must negotiate," Nadia urged.

"What the hell is the old crone saying?" asked Carías, impatient because the girl had not been translating the exchange.

"She says that her people have not eaten in several days and she is very hungry," Nadia invented on the fly.

"Tell her we will give them all the food they wish."

"They are afraid of the weapons," she added, although in truth the Indians had never seen a pistol or a rifle, and could not suspect their deadly power.

Mauro Carías ordered his men to put down their arms as a sign of goodwill, but Leblanc, frightened, intervened to remind them that the Indians often attacked treacherously. With that in mind, the soldiers laid down the sub-machine guns but kept the pistols in their holsters.

Iyomi accepted a large bowl of meat and corn from the hands of Dr. Omayra Torres, and started back the way she'd come. Captain Ariosto tried to follow her, but in less than a minute she had turned to smoke in the vegetation.

They waited the rest of the day, staring at the undergrowth, without seeing anyone, while they put up with the warnings of Leblanc, who expected a contingent of cannibals to burst out of the jungle at any moment. The professor, armed to the teeth and surrounded by soldiers, had been petrified ever since his first glimpse of the naked great-granny in her crown of yellow feathers. The hours went by without incident, except for a moment of tension caused when Dr. Omayra Torres surprised Karakawe snooping through her boxes of supplies. It was not the first time that had happened. Mauro Carías came in and told the Indian that if he saw him near the medicines again, Captain Ariosto would immediately arrest him.

That afternoon, just when everyone thought the old woman was not coming back, the entire tribe of the People of the Mist materialized in front of the camp. First they saw the women and children, insubstantial, dim, and mysterious. Several seconds passed before they saw the men, who in fact had been there longer and were standing in a semicircle. They surged out of nothingness, mute and proud, headed by Tahama, painted for war with the red of the *onoto*, the black of charcoal, the white of lime, and the green of plants, adorned with feathers, teeth, claws, and seeds, and with all their weapons in their hands. They were right in the camp, but they blended so well with their surroundings that the *nahab* had to blink their eyes to see them clearly. They were airy, ethereal; they seemed barely sketched upon the background, but there was no doubt that they were also fierce.

For long minutes, the two bands observed each other in silence, on one side the transparent Indians and on the other the dumbfounded foreigners. Finally Mauro Carías shook himself out of his trance and took action, instructing the soldiers to serve food and hand out gifts. Heavy-hearted, Alex and Nadia watched the women and children accept the trinkets intended to draw them into the camp. They knew that those innocent gifts signaled the end of the tribe. Tahama and his warriors stood alert, weapons still in hand. The most dangerous were the thick clubs, which they could swing in a matter of seconds; aiming an arrow would take longer, giving the soldiers time to shoot.

"Explain to them about the vaccine, sweetie," Mauro Carías directed.

"Nadia. My name is Nadia Santos," she repeated.

"It's for their good, Nadia, to protect them," Dr. Omayra Torres added. "They will be afraid of the needles, but actually, it's not as bad as a mosquito bite. Maybe the men would like to be first, to set an example for the women and children."

"Why don't you set the example?" Nadia asked Mauro Carías.

The perfect smile that never left the tanned entrepreneur's face faded at the girl's challenge, and an expression of absolute terror flitted across his face. Alex noted Carías's extreme reaction. He knew people who were afraid of getting a shot, but Carías looked as if he had seen Dracula.

Nadia translated, and after long discussion, in

which the name of the Rahakanariwa came up often, Iyomi agreed to think about it and to consult with the tribe. They were in the midst of these conversations about the vaccine when suddenly Iyomi murmured some order—imperceptible to the foreigners—and the People of the Mist vanished as quickly as they had appeared. They returned to the forest like shadows, without so much as the sound of a footfall or a single word or one baby's cry. The rest of the night, Ariosto's soldiers stood guard, expecting an attack at any moment.

Nadia awakened at midnight when she heard Omayra Torres leaving the tent. She supposed the doctor was going outside to relieve herself in the bushes, but she had a hunch that she should follow her. Kate was snoring away, deep asleep as usual, and had no inkling of her tent-mate's activities. Silent as a cat, using her newly learned talent to be invisible, Nadia moved forward and hid behind a huge fern. The doctor was silhouetted against the pale moon-light. A minute later, a second figure approached and to Nadia's surprise took the doctor in his arms and kissed her.

"I'm afraid," the doctor said.

"Nothing to fear, my love. Everything will work out fine. In a couple of days, we'll be finished here and on our way back to civilization. You know how much I need you . . ."

"Do you really love me?"

"Of course I love you. I adore you, and I will make you very happy. You will have everything you desire."

Nadia made her way back to the tent, lay down on her mat, and pretended to be asleep.

The man with Dr. Omayra Torres was Mauro Carías.

The next morning, the People of the Mist returned. The women brought baskets of fruit and the meat of a large tapir to repay the gifts they had received the day before. The attitude of the warriors seemed more relaxed, and although they did not put down their clubs, they exhibited the same curiosity as the women and children. They watched from a distance, and though they didn't go near the extraordinary birds of noise and wind, they felt the clothing and weapons of the *nahab*, pawed through their belongings, went into their tents, posed for their cameras, decked themselves in plastic necklaces, and tested the machetes and knives with wonder.

Dr. Omayra Torres thought the climate was right for undertaking her project. She asked Nadia to explain once again to the Indians the urgent need to protect against epidemics, which she did, but they were not convinced. The only reason for Captain Ariosto's not forcing them at gunpoint was the presence of Kate and Timothy Bruce. He could not use intimidation before the press, he had to keep up appearances. There was no choice but to wait patiently through the eternal discussions between the girl and the tribe. The absurdity of shooting them to death to keep them from dying from some disease never crossed the captain's mind.

Nadia reminded the Indians that she had been named by Iyomi to appease the Rahakanariwa, which had the habit of punishing humans with terrible epidemics; therefore they should do what she said. She offered to be the first to submit to the shot, but that was offensive to Tahama and his warriors. They would be the first, they said finally. With a sigh of satisfaction, she translated the decision of the People of the Mist.

Dr. Omayra Torres had a table set up in the shade, and laid out her syringes and vials while Mauro Carías tried to organize the tribe in a line to assure that no one would miss being vaccinated.

In the meantime, Nadia took Alex aside to tell him what she had seen the night before. Neither of them knew what to make of that scene, but they felt vaguely betrayed. How was it possible for the sweet Omayra Torres to have a relationship with Mauro Carías, the man who carried his heart in a totebag? They concluded that there was no doubt that Mauro Carías had seduced the good doctor. Didn't everyone say he had great success with women? Nadia and Alex could not see anything the least bit attractive about the man, but they supposed that his manners and his money could deceive others. The news would fall like a bomb among the doctor's admirers, César Santos, Timothy Bruce, and even Ludovic Leblanc.

"I don't like this one bit," said Alex.

"Are you jealous, too?" Nadia joked.

"No!" he replied, indignant. "But I feel something here in my heart, something like a terrible weight."

"Does it have to do with the vision we shared in the city of gold? You remember? When we drank Walimai's potion and we all dreamed the same thing, even the Beasts."

"Right. That dream was like one I had before I came on this trip: a huge vulture kidnapped my mother and flew away with her. I interpreted that to be the cancer threatening her life; I thought the vulture represented death. In the *tepui*, we dreamed that the Rahakanariwa broke out of its cage where it was prisoner and that the Indians were tied to the trees, remember?"

"Yes, and that the *nahab* were wearing masks. What do masks mean, Jaguar?"

"Secrets. Lies. Betrayal."

"Why do you think that Mauro Carías is so interested in seeing the Indians vaccinated?"

The question hung in the air like an arrow stopped in midflight. The two friends looked at each other in horror. In a flash of insight, they realized the terrible trap they had all fallen into: the Rahakanariwa was the epidemic! The death that threatened the tribe was not a mythological bird but something much more concrete and immediate. They ran to the center of the village, where Dr. Omayra Torres was just touching the needle of her syringe to Tahama's arm. Without thinking, Alex threw himself like a battering ram against the warrior, sending him sprawling to the ground. He jumped back up and raised his club to crush the youth like a cockroach, but a cry from Nadia froze his arm in the air.

"No! No! This is the Rahakanariwa!" the girl screamed, pointing to the vials of vaccine.

César Santos thought his daughter had gone mad, and tried to hold her but she pulled away and ran to join Alex, yelling and pounding her fists on Mauro Carías, who had stepped in front of her. As quickly as she could, she tried to explain to the Indians that she was wrong, that the vaccine would not save them, just the opposite, it would kill them, because the Rahakanariwa was in the syringe.

CHAPTER EIGHTEEN

Bloodstains

DR. OMAYRA TORRES did not lose her calm. She said this was all some fantasy of the young people and that the heat had made them a little crazed, and she demanded that Captain Ariosto take them away. She tried to resume her interrupted task, despite the fact that the mood of the tribe had changed completely. At that moment, with Captain Ariosto ready to impose order by force and as the soldiers were wrestling with Nadia and Alex, Karakawe, who had not spoken more than a dozen words the whole trip, came forward.

"Just a minute!" he cried.

To everyone's surprise, this man who had scarcely opened his mouth for days announced that he was an officer of the Department for the Protection of Indigenous Peoples, and explained that his assignment was to find out why the Amazon tribes were dying en masse, especially those who lived near fields of gold and diamonds. For some time, he had suspected Mauro Carías, the man who had benefited most from exploitation in the region.

"Captain Ariosto, seize those vaccines!" Karakawe ordered. "I will have them examined in the laboratory. If I am right, these vials do not contain vaccine but deadly doses of the measles virus."

Captain Ariosto's response was to aim his pistol and shoot Karakawe in the chest. The officer fell dead on the spot. Mauro Carías pushed Dr. Omayra Torres aside, pulled out his weapon, and as César Santos was running to shield the woman with his body, emptied his gun at the vials lined up on the table, shattering them to bits. The liquid drained into the ground.

Events happened with such sudden violence that afterward no one could describe them with precision; everyone had a different version. Timothy Bruce's camcorder registered part of the events and the rest were captured in the camera Kate was holding.

When they saw the destroyed vials, the Indians believed that the Rahakanariwa had

...d its prison and would come back in the ...m of the cannibal-bird to devour them. Before anyone could stop him, Tahama let out a bloodcurdling yell and brought his club crashing down on the head of Mauro Carías, who dropped to the ground like a sack of meal. Captain Ariosto turned his weapon on Tahama, but Alex clipped him from behind and Nadia's monkey, Borobá, jumped into his face. The captain's bullets went astray, giving Tahama time to retreat, protected by his warriors, who had armed their bows.

In the few seconds it took the soldiers to get organized and unholster their pistols, the tribe scattered. The women and children raced away like squirrels, disappearing into the undergrowth, and the men got off several arrows before they, too, fled. The soldiers fired blindly, while Alex struggled with Ariosto on the ground, helped by Nadia and Borobá. The captain cracked the youth in the jaw with the butt of his pistol, leaving him half-stunned, then beat off the girl and the monkey. Kate ran to help her grandson, dragging him out of the center of the melee. In all the yelling and confusion, no one heard Ariosto's commands.

seemed to be in a state of shock, with a scream stuck in her chest and her eyes glued on the dead Indians and the soldiers moaning on the ground. Dr. Omayra Torres, blind to what was going on around her, tears streaming, was holding Mauro Carías's head in her lap. She kept kissing him and begging him not to die, not to leave her, as his blood soaked into her clothing. "We were going to be married . . . ," she repeated like a litany.

"The doctor is Mauro Carías's accomplice. She was the one he meant when he said that someone they could trust was traveling with the expedition. You remember? And we were accusing Karakawe," Alex whispered his new understanding to Nadia, but she was so paralyzed with fright that she didn't hear him.

Alex realized that the entrepreneur's plan to exterminate the Indians with a measles epidemic had required the collaboration of Dr. Torres. For several years, the natives had been dying off, the victims of measles and other diseases despite the authorities' efforts to protect them. Once an epidemic broke out, there was nothing to be done, because the Indians had no defenses; they had lived in isolation for

s of years and their immune systems
not withstand the viruses carried by the
hites. A common cold could kill them
within a few days, to say nothing of more serious illnesses. Physicians who were studying the
problem could not understand why none of
the preventive measures were having results.
Who could imagine that Omayra Torres, the
person entrusted to vaccinate the Indians, was
the one injecting them with death so her lover
could appropriate their lands?

This woman had eliminated several tribes
without raising a single suspicion, and that was
what she had intended for the People of the
Mist. What had Carías promised that would
cause her to commit a crime of such magnitude? Was it simply out of love for him, and
not for money? Whatever her reason, whether
love or greed, the result was the same:
Hundreds of men, women, and children were
murdered. If not for Nadia Santos, who had
seen Omayra and Mauro Carías kissing, the
designs of that pair would never have been discovered. And they could thank the timely
intervention of Karakawe—who had paid
with his life—that the plan had failed.

Now Alexander understood the role Mauro Carías had in mind for the members of the *International Geographic* expedition. A couple of weeks after being inoculated with the measles virus, an epidemic would break out among the tribe and the contagion would rapidly spread to other villages. Then the befogged Professor Ludovic Leblanc would testify to the world press that he had been present when the first contact was made with the People of the Mist. No one could be blamed; the necessary precautions had been taken to protect the village. The anthropologist, backed by the reporting of Kate and the photographs of Timothy Bruce, could prove that all the members of the tribe had been vaccinated. In the eyes of the world, the epidemic would be an inevitable misfortune; no one would suspect otherwise, and in that way Mauro Carías would be guaranteed that there would be no government investigation. It was a clean and efficient method of extermination that left no trail of blood, unlike the bullets and bombs used for years against native peoples in order to "clean out" the Amazon territory and open the way for miners, traffickers, settlers, and adventurers.

eard Karakawe's accusation, Captain Ariosto had lost his head and impulsively killed him to protect Carías and himself. He had acted with the confidence bestowed by his uniform. In that remote, nearly unpopulated region, too distant to be reached by the long arm of the law, no one disputed his word. That gave him a dangerous power. He was a crude, unscrupulous man who had spent years in border posts; he was accustomed to violence. As if the weapon at his belt and his position in the military were not enough, he had the protection of Mauro Carías. The entrepreneur, in turn, had connections in the highest ranks of the government; he was a member of the ruling class, he had a great deal of money and prestige, and no one asked him for an accounting. The association between Ariosto and Carías had been beneficial for both. The captain estimated that in less than two years he would be able to hang up his uniform and go live in Miami, a millionaire. But now Mauro Carías was lying there with his head split open and could not protect him any longer. This was the end of the ride. He would have to justify the murder of Karakawe to government officials, as well as the deaths of the Indians lying there in the middle of the camp.

Kate, with the baby still in her arms, understood that her life and those of the other expedition members, including her grandson and Nadia, were in grave danger; Ariosto's first priority would be to prevent having the events at Tapirawa-teri revealed. It was not simply a matter here of pouring gasoline over the bodies, setting fire to them, and declaring they had "disappeared." The captain's plan had backfired; the presence of *International Geographic* had shifted from being an advantage to being a serious problem. He had to get rid of the witnesses, but he would have to do it very carefully; he couldn't shoot them without really putting his foot in it. Unfortunately for the foreigners, they were a long way from civilization and that would make it easier for the captain to cover his tracks.

Kate was sure that if the captain decided to kill them, the soldiers would not lift a finger to stop him, nor would they dare report their superior. The jungle would swallow up the evidence of the crimes. They couldn't just cross their arms and wait for the fatal shot, they would have to *do* something. They had nothing to lose, the situation could not be any worse. Ariosto was heartless, and nervous besides; they could all suffer Karakawe's fate. Kate didn't have a plan, but she thought that the first thing she should do was create a distraction in the enemy ranks.

"Captain, I think it's urgent that we send these men to a hospital," she offered, pointing to Carías and the wounded soldiers.

"Shut up, old woman!" he barked back.

A few minutes later, nevertheless, Ariosto had Mauro Carías and the three soldiers loaded onto one of the helicopters. He ordered Omayra Torres to try to remove the arrows from the wounded men before putting them onboard, but the doctor ignored him completely; all her attention was for her dying lover. Kate and César Santos took on the task of attempting to improvise bandages for the soldiers to stop their bleeding.

While the military men went about getting the wounded into the helicopter and trying in vain to contact Santa María de la Lluvia by radio, Kate, in a low voice, communicated her fears regarding their situation to Professor Leblanc. The anthropologist had reached the same conclusion: they were in greater danger in Ariosto's hands than with the Indians or the Beast.

"If only we could escape into the trees," Kate whispered.

For once, the man surprised her by keeping a cool head. Kate was used to the professor's fits and his insolence, but seeing him calm and collected, she yielded authority almost automatically.

"That would be madness," Leblanc replied firmly. "The only way to get out of here is by helicopter. Ariosto is the key. Luckily he is ignorant, and vain; that works in our favor. We must pretend we do not suspect him, and conquer him with cunning."

"How?" asked the writer, skeptical.

"By manipulating him. He is frightened, so we will offer him the opportunity to save his skin, and in the bargain come out of this a hero," said Leblanc.

"Never!" exclaimed Kate.

"Don't be foolish, Cold. That is what we will offer him, it doesn't mean that is what we will give him. Once we are safely out of this country, Ludovic Leblanc will be the first to denounce the atrocities being committed against these poor Indians."

"I see that you have changed your opinion about the Indians," Kate growled.

The professor did not dignify her with an answer. He rose up to the full extent of his small stature, tugged at the tails of his mud- and blood-spattered shirt, and walked up to Captain Ariosto.

"And how, my esteemed Captain, shall we return to Santa María de la Lluvia? We will not all fit in the second helicopter," he said, pointing to the soldiers and the group under the tree.

"Keep your nose out of this! I'm giving the orders here!" bawled Ariosto.

"But of course! It is a great relief to have you in charge, Captain. If not, we would be in a most difficult situation," Leblanc commented smoothly.

Ariosto, thrown off guard, listened.

"Were it not for your heroism, we would all have perished at the hands of the Indians," the professor added.

Ariosto, slightly calmer, counted the people

and concluded that Leblanc was right; he then decided to send half his contingent of soldiers in the first chopper. That left him with only five men and the expedition party, but as they were not armed, they represented no danger. The helicopter took off, raising clouds of red dust as it lifted from the ground. It flew off over the green canopy of the jungle, fading into the sky.

Nadia had been following developments but was still clinging to her father and Borobá. She regretted having left Walimai's talisman in the nest of the crystal eggs, because without its protection she felt lost. Abruptly, she started crying like an owl. César Santos was afraid that his daughter had been through more than she could handle and was having a nervous breakdown. The bloodshed in the village was horrifying, and the moans of the wounded soldiers and the blood streaming from Mauro Carías's head had been a harrowing spectacle. The bodies of the Indians still lay where they had fallen; no one had made a move to pick them up. The guide concluded that his daughter was disoriented from the brutality of recent events;

there was no other explanation for the screeches coming from her. In contrast, Alexander had to mask a smile of pride when he heard his friend: Nadia was casting about for the last possible lifeline.

"Hand over the film!" Captain Ariosto ordered Timothy Bruce.

For the photographer, that was the same as giving up his life. He was a fanatic when it came to his negatives; he had never in his career handed one over, ever; they were all carefully cataloged in his studio in London.

"I think it an excellent idea, Captain Ariosto, that you take measures to ensure that those valuable negatives are not lost," Leblanc intervened. "They are the proof of what happened here, how that Indian attacked Señor Carías, how the valiant soldiers fell before the arrows, how you yourself were obliged to shoot Karakawe."

"The pest was meddling in things that did not concern him!" exclaimed the captain.

"But of course. He was a madman. He tried to prevent Dr. Torres from performing her duty. His accusations were insane," said Leblanc, and cleverly added, "I regret that the vials with the vaccine were destroyed in the heat of the fighting. Now we shall never know what they contained, and we have no proof that Karakawe was lying."

Something happened around Ariosto's mouth that in other circumstances might have been taken for a smile. He put his pistol back in his holster, ignored the matter of the film for the moment, and for the first time spoke without shouting. Perhaps these foreigners did not suspect anything; they were much dumber even than he had thought, he muttered to himself.

Kate followed the dialogue between the anthropologist and the captain openmouthed. She had never imagined that the self-important Leblanc was capable of such cool-headed thinking.

"Please, Nadia, be quiet," César Santos pleaded as Nadia repeated her screech-owl cry for the tenth time.

"I suppose we will be spending the night here. Do you want us to prepare a bite for the evening meal, Captain?" Leblanc offered pleasantly.

Ariosto gave them permission to cook

whatever they could find and to move around the camp, but he ordered them to stay within a radius of a hundred yards, where he could see them. He commanded the soldiers to collect the dead Indians and put them all in one place. The next day they would bury them or burn them. The nighttime hours would give him the opportunity to make a decision regarding the foreigners. Santos and his daughter could disappear and no one would question it, but the others would take more care. Ludovic Leblanc was a celebrity, and the old woman and her grandson were Americans. In his experience, when something happened to an American, there was always an investigation; those arrogant gringos thought the world belonged to them.

Although it had been Professor Leblanc's suggestion, it was César Santos and Timothy Bruce who prepared the meal because the anthropologist was incapable of boiling water for an egg. Kate excused herself by saying that the only thing she knew how to make were meatballs, and she didn't have those ingredients. Besides, she was completely occupied with trying to feed the baby spoonfuls of a solution of water and condensed milk. Meanwhile, Nadia sat down to keep scanning the underbrush, repeating her owl call from time to time. At a quiet command from her, Borobá jumped from her arms and loped off into the forest. A half hour later, Captain Ariosto remembered the issue of film, and forced Timothy Bruce to hand it over, using the excuse Leblanc had given him: in his hands, it would be safe. The English photographer protested in vain. He even tried a bribe, but the captain was firm.

They ate in shifts while the soldiers stood guard, and then Ariosto assigned tents for the expedition party; they would be somewhat more protected there in case of attack, as he said, although the real reason was that he could control them better that way. Nadia and Kate and the baby occupied one of the tents, and Ludovic Leblanc, César Santos, and Timothy Bruce the other. The captain did not forget that Alex had knocked him down, and had taken a blind dislike of him. It was the fault of those two kids, especially the damned American, that he was in such a predicament, anyway. Mauro Carías's skull was crushed, the Indians had escaped, and his plans to be a millionaire and live in Miami were in serious jeopardy. Alex represented a danger to him; he had to be punished. He decided to separate him from the others, and ordered him tied to a tree at the edge of the camp, far from the tents of the other members of the group and far from the oil lanterns. Kate furiously protested the treatment her grandson was receiving, but the captain shut her up.

"Maybe it's best this way, Kate. Alex may find a way to escape," Nadia whispered.

"Ariosto is planning to kill him during the night, I'm sure," the writer replied, trembling with anger.

"Borobá went to get help," said Nadia.

"You actually think that little monkey can save us?" she snorted.

"Borobá is very smart."

"Child, you are sick in the head!" Alex's grandmother exclaimed.

Several hours went by. No one in the camp could sleep except the baby, exhausted from crying. Kate had made him a place to sleep on a bundle of clothing, wondering what she was going to do with the poor little creature; the last thing she wanted in her life was to be responsible for an orphan. The writer was watchful, convinced that at any moment Ariosto would murder her grandson first and then the rest of them—or perhaps the reverse, first them, and then take his revenge on Alex with some slow, horrible death. The man was extremely dangerous. Timothy Bruce and César Santos also had their ears to the canvas of their tent, trying to make out the movements of the soldiers outside. Professor Ludovic Leblanc, in contrast, had gone outside, using the excuse of relieving himself, and was standing talking with Captain Ariosto. The anthropologist, aware that every hour that went by increased the risk for them, wanted to distract the captain; he suggested a game of cards to Ariosto, and invited him to share a bottle of vodka provided by Kate.

"Don't try to get me drunk, Professor," Ariosto warned, but filled his glass.

"How could you think that, Captain! A little vodka won't faze a man like you. It's going to be a long night; we might as well enjoy ourselves," Leblanc replied.

CHAPTER NINETEEN

Protection

🐒

As OFTEN HAPPENS on the altiplano, the temperature dropped when the sun went down. The soldiers, used to the heat of the lowlands, shivered in clothes still soaked from the afternoon showers. None were asleep; by the captain's orders, they all were guarding the camp. They were alert, weapons held two-handed across their chests. Now they were afraid not only of the demons in the jungle, or the possible appearance of the Beast, but they had the Indians to fear—they might come back at any minute to avenge their dead. The soldiers had the advantage of firearms, but the natives knew the terrain and had the mystical ability to materialize out of nowhere, like wandering souls. If it weren't for the bodies laid out by a tree, they would think they weren't human, and that bullets couldn't harm them. The soldiers were eager for morning, when they could get out of there as early as possible. Time passed very slowly in the darkness, and the sounds of the forest around them were terrifying.

Kate, sitting cross-legged beside the sleeping baby in the women's tent, was thinking how she might help her grandson, and how to leave the Eye of the World alive. A little light from the campfire showed through the canvas of the tent, enough for the writer to see the silhouette of Nadia wrapped in her father's jacket.

"I'm going out now—" the girl whispered.

"You can't!" her companion said, cutting her off.

"No one will see me, I can make myself invisible."

Kate took the girl in her arms, sure she was delirious.

"Nadia, listen to me . . . You are not invisible. No one is invisible, that's only a fantasy. You can't leave here."

"Yes, I can. Don't make any noise, please. Take care of the baby till I get back. Later we'll return him to his tribe," Nadia murmured. She was so sure, and her voice so calm, that Kate did not dare stop her.

First Nadia put herself in the mental state of invisibility, as she had learned from the Indians; she reduced herself to nothingness, to pure transparent spirit. Then silently she lifted the flap of the tent and slipped outside, aided by the shadows. Stealthy as a weasel, she passed within a few yards of the table where Professor Leblanc and Captain Ariosto were playing cards, past the armed guards patrolling the camp, and past the tree where Alex was tied, without anyone's seeing her. She moved away from the flickering circle of light from the lanterns and the campfire and disappeared among the trees. Soon the screech of an owl interrupted the croaking of the frogs.

Like the soldiers, Alex was shivering with cold. His legs were asleep and his hands were swollen from the too-tight bonds around his wrists. His jaw hurt; he could feel the stretched skin, he must have a huge lump. He ran his tongue over his broken tooth, and felt the puffy gums where the captain's pistol had struck. He tried not to think about the dark hours ahead or about the possibility of being killed. Why had Ariosto separated him from the others? What was he planning to do with him? He wished he were the black jaguar, that he had the strength, the fierceness, the agility of the big cat, that he could turn into pure muscle and tooth and claw and confront Ariosto. He thought about the bottle with the water of health in his knapsack, and how he had to leave the Eye of the World alive and take it to his mother. His memory of his family was hazy, like a badly focused photograph in which his mother's face was barely a pale blob.

He was beginning to nod, overcome with strain, when suddenly he felt little hands. He jerked upright. In the dark, he could identify Borobá, sniffing his neck, hugging him, whimpering slowly in his ear. "Borobá, Borobá," Alex murmured, so moved that his eyes filled with tears. It was just a monkey no bigger than a squirrel, but its presence wakened a wave of hope. He was deeply comforted by the animal's caresses. Then he became aware of another presence at his side, a silent, invisible presence veiled in the shadows of the tree. At first he thought it was Nadia, but then realized it was Walimai. The tiny ancient was close beside him; he could smell his odor of smoke, but however much he tried, he couldn't see him. The shaman laid one of his hands on Alex's chest, as if feeling for his heartbeat. The weight and warmth of that friendly hand transmitted courage to the youth; he felt calmer; he stopped trembling and could think clearly. "The knife, the Swiss Army knife," he murmured. He heard the click of the metal being opened, and soon the blade slipped across his bonds. He didn't move. It was dark, and Walimai had never used a knife; he could easily saw into his wrists, but within minutes the Indian had cut through the ties and taken his arm to lead him into the jungle.

In the camp, Captain Ariosto had finished the card games and emptied the vodka bottle. Ludovic could think of nothing more to distract him, and there were still many hours before dawn. The alcohol had not stunned the captain, as Leblanc had hoped; he really did have guts of steel. He suggested that they try the radio, to see if they could reach the barracks in Santa María de la Lluvia, and for quite a while they twiddled the dials, in the midst of deafening static, but it was impossible to reach the operator. Ariosto was preoccupied; he didn't like being away from the barracks, he needed to get back as quickly as possible in order to control the versions the soldiers might tell about what had happened in Tapirawa-teri. What were their stories? He needed to send a report to his superiors in the army and meet with the press before the gossip spread. Omayra Torres had left muttering about the measles virus. If she started talking, he was ruined. What a stupid woman! the captain fretted.

Ariosto ordered the anthropologist to go back to his tent, and he took a turn about the camp to check that everything was as it should be. Then he went to the tree where he had tied the American boy, ready to have a little fun at his expense. At that instant, the smell struck him like a club, so strong that the impact threw him backward to the ground. He tried to reach his pistol, but he couldn't move. He felt a wave of nausea, and his heart bursting in his chest, and then nothing. He sank into unconsciousness. He never saw the Beast only three steps away, spraying him directly with the lethal stench of its scent glands.

The asphyxiating odor of the Beast floated through the rest of the camp, first felling the soldiers, and then those inside the tents. In less than two minutes, no one was left standing. For a couple of hours, a terrifying silence lay over Tapirawa-teri, and in the nearby jungle, where even the birds and animals had fled, frightened by the foul smell. The two Beasts that had attacked in tandem retired at their habitual lumbering pace, but their odor persisted most of the night. No one in the camp was aware of anything that happened during those hours, because they did not regain consciousness until the next morning. Later they saw the tracks and were able to reach some conclusions.

Alex, following Walimai, with Borobá on his shoulders, pushed through the vegetation, keeping very low until the quivering lights from the camp disappeared from view. The shaman moved through the jungle as if it were broad daylight, perhaps following his wife-angel, whom Alex couldn't see. They snaked among the trees for quite some time, and finally came to the place where the ancient

418

had left Nadia waiting. They had communicated through the owl calls most of the afternoon and night, until she was able to slip out of camp and join him. Nadia and Alex embraced when they saw each other, and Borobá clung to his mistress uttering little shrieks of happiness.

Walimai confirmed what they already knew: The tribe was watching the camp, but they had learned to fear the magic of the *nahab* and would not dare challenge them. The warriors were so close they had heard the baby's crying, as well as the call from their dead who had not been given a dignified funeral. The spirits of the murdered men and the woman were still joined with their bodies, said Walimai; they could not let go without a proper ceremony, and without being avenged. Alex explained that the Indians' one hope was to attack by night, because during the day the *nahab* could use the bird of noise and wind to search the Eye of the World until they found them.

"If they attack now, some will die, but otherwise the entire tribe will be exterminated," said Alex. He was ready to lead them and fight at their side; that was why he had been initiated: he, too, was a warrior.

"Chief for war: Tahama. Chief for negotiating with the *nahab*: you," Walimai replied.

"It's too late to negotiate. Ariosto is a murderer."

"You said that some *nahab* are evil and other *nahab* are friends. Where are the friends?" the witch man persisted.

"My grandmother and some of the men in the camp are friends. Captain Ariosto and his soldiers are enemies. We cannot negotiate with them."

"Your grandmother and your friends must negotiate with the enemy *nahab*."

"The friends do not have weapons."

"They have no magic?"

"In the Eye of the World, they do not have much magic. But there are other friends with much magic far away from here, in the cities, in other parts of the world," Alexander argued, frustrated by the limitations of language.

"Then you must go where those friends are," the ancient concluded.

"How? We are trapped here!"

Walimai would not answer any more questions. He sat crouched on his haunches, staring into the night, accompanied by his wife; she had adopted her most transparent form and neither of the two young people could see her. Alex and Nadia passed the hours awake, very close together, trying to keep each other warm, and not speaking because there was little to say. They were thinking of the fate awaiting Kate, César Santos, and the other members of their group. They were thinking of how the People of the Mist were condemned. They were thinking of the centuries-old sloths and the city of gold. They were thinking of the water of health and the crystal eggs. And them? What would become of them, trapped as they were in the jungle?

A gust of terrible odor came to them suddenly, diluted by distance but perfectly recognizable. They jumped to their feet but Walimai did not move, as if he had been expecting it.

"It's the Beasts!" Nadia cried.

"Maybe yes and maybe no," replied the impassive shaman.

The rest of the night was very long. Shortly before dawn the cold was intense, and Nadia and Alex, huddled with Borobá, shivered while the ancient witch man, totally motionless, his eyes lost in the shadows, waited. With the first signs of dawn, the monkeys and birds awakened and Walimai gave the sign to leave. They followed him through the trees, again for some time, until as the sunlight began to pierce the foliage they came to the camp. The bonfire and lanterns had gone out; there were no signs of life and the foul odor still lingered on the air, as if a hundred skunks had sprayed the camp at the same time. Covering their noses, they entered the outer edge of what until only recently had been the peaceful village of Tapirawa-teri. The tents, the table, the kitchen . . . everything . . . lay scattered across the ground; the remains of food were tossed everywhere, but no monkey or bird was scrabbling through the debris or the garbage because none dared brave the hideous stench of the Beasts. Even Borobá hung back, shrieking and jumping up and down. Walimai showed the same indifference to the smell that he had to the cold the night before. The young people had no choice but to follow where he led.

There was no one, no trace of the members of the expedition, nor of the soldiers, nor of

Captain Ariosto, nor of the bodies of the murdered Indians. Weapons, luggage, even Timothy Bruce's cameras were there. They also found a large bloodstain darkening the earth near the tree where Alex had been tied. After a brief inspection, which seemed to leave him very satisfied, Walimai was ready to leave. Alex and Nadia dropped in line behind him without asking any questions, so nauseated by the odor they could barely stagger. As they got some distance away and filled their lungs with the cool morning air, their spirits revived but their temples were pounding and their stomachs were churning. Borobá joined them shortly, and the group plunged into the jungle.

Several days before, on seeing the birds of noise and wind circling in the sky, the inhabitants of Tapirawa-teri had fled from their village, abandoning the spare possessions and domesticated animals that inhibited their ability to hide. Screened by vegetation, they traveled to a safe place and there crafted temporary dwellings in the branches of the trees. The parties of soldiers sent by Ariosto passed by very close without seeing them; but the foreigners' every movement was observed by Tahama's warriors, who blended into the scenery.

Iyomi and Tahama had argued a long time about the *nahab* and the advantage of approaching them as Jaguar and Eagle had advised. It was Iyomi's opinion that her people could not hide forever in the trees, like monkeys. The time had come to visit the *nahab* and accept their gifts and their vaccines; it was inevitable. Tahama thought it was better to die fighting, but Iyomi was chief of chiefs, and finally her judgment prevailed. She had decided to be the first to approach, which was why she came to the camp alone, adorned with the proud crown of yellow feathers to demonstrate to the foreigners who was in charge. Seeing Jaguar and Eagle—who had returned from the sacred mountain—among them was reassuring to her. They were friends and they could translate; that way the poor creatures dressed in stinking cloth would not feel lost in her presence. The *nahab* welcomed her; no doubt they were impressed with her regal bearing and her many wrinkles, proof of how long she had lived and of the knowledge she had acquired. Despite the meal they offered, the ancient chief found herself obliged to demand that they leave the Eye of the World, because they were a nuisance there. That was her last word; she was not prepared to negotiate. She retired majestically with her bowl of meat and corn, certain of having terrorized the *nahab* with the weight of her supreme dignity.

In view of the success of Iyomi's visit, the rest of the tribe worked up their courage and followed her example. They returned to the site of their village, overrun now by foreigners who obviously did not know the most elementary rule of prudence and courtesy: You did not ever visit a *shabono* without being invited. There the Indians saw the great shiny birds, the tents, and the strange *nahab* about whom they had heard such horrifying stories. Those strangers with their rude behavior deserved a good clubbing, but by Iyomi's order the Indians were to exercise patience with them. They accepted their food and their gifts, so as not to offend them, then left to hunt and harvest honey and fruits so they could repay the gifts received, as was proper.

The next day, once Iyomi was sure that Jaguar and Eagle were still there, she authorized the tribe to present themselves once more to the *nahab* and be vaccinated. Neither she nor anyone else could explain what happened then. They could not understand why the young foreign friends, who had insisted so strongly on the need for vaccination, suddenly tried to prevent it. They heard an unknown sound, like brief thunder. They saw that when the vials burst, the Rahakanariwa leaped free and in his invisible form attacked the Indians, who fell dead without being touched by arrows or clubs. In the violence of the battle, the others escaped however they could, in disarray and confusion. They didn't know who were friends and who were enemies.

Finally Walimai came to give them an explanation. He said that young Eagle and Jaguar were friends, and that they must help them, but that all the others might be enemies. He said that the Rahakanariwa was loose and could take on any form; it would take very powerful conjuring to send him back to the kingdom of the spirits. He said they needed to call on the gods. Then the two gigantic sloths, which had not returned to the sacred *tepui* but were ambling around the Eye of the World, were summoned and during the night led to the ruined village. They would never have gone near an Indian dwelling on their own account; they hadn't done that in thousands and thousands of years. Walimai had to convince them that it was no longer the village of the People of the Mist because it had been profaned by the presence of the *nahab* and by the killing that had taken place on its soil. Tapirawa-teri would have to be rebuilt in a different part of the Eye of the World, far from there, where human souls and the spirits of the ancestors would feel at ease, and where evil did not contaminate the noble earth. The Beasts were given the chore of spraying the camp of the *nahab*, immobilizing friends and foe alike.

Tahama's warriors had to wait many hours for the smell to disperse enough for them to approach. First they collected the bodies of the Indians and took them to be prepared for a proper funeral; then they came back for the others and dragged them away, including the corpse of Captain Ariosto, slashed by the awesome claws of the gods.

One by one, the *nahab* were waking up. They found themselves in a clearing in the jungle, lying on the ground and so dazed that they did not remember their names. And even less how they had got where they were. Kate was the first to react. She had no idea where she was, or what had happened to the camp, the helicopter, the captain, or—most of all—to her grandson. She remembered the baby, and looked around the surrounding area but couldn't find him. She shook the others, who were slowly coming to. All of them had terrible pains in their heads and joints, and were vomiting and coughing and crying. They felt as if they'd been beaten, but could find no marks of violence.

The last to open his eyes was Professor Leblanc, who was so deeply affected by the experience he couldn't stand up. Kate reflected that a good cup of coffee laced with a shot of vodka would do them all good, but they had nothing of any kind to drink. Their clothing, their hair, their skin reeked from the stench of the Beast; they had to drag themselves to a nearby stream and soak for a good while. The five soldiers were lost without their weapons or their captain, so when César Santos assumed command, they obeyed without hesitation. Timothy Bruce, who was very upset at having been so near the Beast and not having got a photograph, wanted to go back to camp and look for his cameras, but he didn't know which direction to walk in and no one seemed inclined to go with him. That phlegmatic Englishman who had accompanied Kate through wars, cataclysms, and many adventures, seldom lost his bored air, but recent events had made him grouchy. Kate and César Santos could think of nothing but her grandson and his daughter. Where were they?

The guide inspected the site thoroughly and found broken branches, feathers, seeds, and other signs of the People of the Mist. He concluded that the Indians had brought them there, which had actually saved their lives, since otherwise they would have died of asphyxiation or attack by the Beast. And if that was so, he couldn't explain why the Indians hadn't seized the opportunity to kill them and get revenge for their dead. Had he been in any condition to think, Professor Leblanc would have been forced once again to revise his thesis about these tribes, but the poor anthropologist was flat on his back, moaning and half dead from nausea and an aching head.

Everyone was sure that the People of the Mist would return, and that was exactly what happened: Suddenly the entire tribe emerged from the bush. Their incredible ability to move in absolute silence and materialize in seconds allowed them to surround the foreigners before they knew what was happening. The soldiers responsible for the death of the Indians were trembling like babies. Tahama walked toward them, staring straight at them, but did not touch them. Maybe he thought that such low forms of life did not merit a clubbing from a warrior as noble as himself.

Iyomi stepped forward and delivered a long speech in her native tongue, which no one understood, then seized Kate's shirt lapels and, pushing her face as close as she could, began shouting something. The only thing the writer could think to do was to take the old woman with the ring of yellow feathers by the shoulders and shout back in English. There they

were, the two grandmothers trading incomprehensible insults, until Iyomi got tired,
turned away and took a seat beneath a tree.
The other Indians also sat down, talking
among themselves, sharing the fruit, nuts, and
mushrooms they had found among the roots.
Tahama and several other warriors were being
vigilant but not aggressive. Kate recognized
the baby she had taken care of in a young
woman's arms and was pleased that the child
had survived the fatal stench of the Beast and
was back at the breast of one of its own.

By midafternoon, Walimai and Alex and
Nadia appeared. Kate and César Santos ran
over to meet them, and hugged them hard,
since they'd been afraid they might never see
them again. With Nadia there, communication
improved; she could translate and was able to
clear up a few points. The foreigners learned
that the Indians did not as yet relate the death
of their companions with the soldiers'
firearms, since they had never seen weapons.
All they wanted was to rebuild their village at
another site, consume ashes of their dead, and
recapture the peace they had always known.
They wanted to send the Rahakanariwa back

to his place among the demons and banish the *nahab* from the Eye of the World.

Professor Leblanc, somewhat recovered but still not in top form, took over. He had lost his Aussie hat with the feathers and, like everyone else, he was filthy and his clothing reeked. Nadia translated, cheating a little, so the Indians would not believe that all *nahab* were as arrogant as this little man.

"Have no fear. I promise that I personally shall protect the People of the Mist. The world listens when Ludovic Leblanc speaks," the professor assured them.

He added that he would publish his impressions on what he had seen—not only in an article in *International Geographic*, but also in a book. Thanks to him, he said, the Eye of the World would be declared an Indian reservation and protected from any form of exploitation. They would see who Ludovic Leblanc was!

The People of the Mist did not understand a word of that diatribe, but Nadia summed it up by saying this was a *nahab* friend. Kate added that she and Timothy Bruce would help Leblanc in his proposals, with which they, too, were included in the category of *nahab* friends. Finally, after endless negotiations about who were friends and who were enemies, the Indians agreed that the next day they would lead all of them back to the helicopter. By then they expected the stink from the Beasts to have dissipated.

Iyomi, always practical, ordered the warriors to go hunt while the women made a fire and braided hammocks for the night.

"I'm going to ask you again, Alexander. What do you know about the Beast?" Kate said to her grandson.

"It isn't one Beast, Kate, there are several. They look like gigantic sloths; they're very ancient animals, maybe from the Stone Age, or earlier."

"You've seen them?"

"If I hadn't seen them, I wouldn't be able to describe them, would I? I saw eleven of them, but I think there are one or two more wandering around here. They seem to have a really slow metabolism, and they live for many years, possibly centuries. They learn, they have a good memory, and—you're not going to believe this—they talk."

"Now you're pulling my leg!" his grand-mother exclaimed.

"It's true. Let's say they're not very eloquent, but they speak the same language as the People of the Mist."

Alexander proceeded to inform her that in exchange for the Indians' protection, the Beasts preserved their history for them.

"Once you told me that the Indians didn't need writing because they have good memories. The Beasts are the tribe's living memory," he added.

"Where did you see them, Alexander?"

"I can't tell you, it's a secret."

"I suppose they live in the same place where you found the water of health," his grand-mother ventured.

"Maybe yes and maybe no," her grandson replied.

"I need to see those Beasts and photograph them, Alexander."

"What for? An article in a magazine? That would be the end of them, Kate. People would come hunt them and cage them in zoos or study them in laboratories."

"I have to write something, that's why they hired me . . ."

"Write that the Beast is a legend, pure superstition. I can tell you that no one is going to see them for a long, long time. They'll be forgotten. It's more interesting to write about the People of the Mist. That tribe hasn't changed for thousands of years, and it can disappear at any moment. Tell how they were going to be injected with the measles virus, as other tribes have been. You can make them famous and save them from extinction, Kate. You can become the protector of the People of the Mist, and if you play your cards right, you can get Leblanc to be your ally. Your pen can bring a little justice to life here. You can denounce villains like Carías and Ariosto, and question the role of the military, and bring Omayra Torres to trial. You have to do something, or soon other evil people will be committing crimes in this part of the world with the same impunity as always."

"I see that you have matured a lot in these weeks, Alexander," Kate admitted with admiration.

"Can you call me Jaguar, Grandmother?"

"You mean, like the car?"

"Yes."

"Everyone to his own taste. I'll call you whatever you like, as long as you don't call me Grandmother," she replied.

"That's great, Kate."

"Roger, Jaguar."

That night, the *nahab* shared a meager meal of roast monkey with the Indians. With the arrival of the birds of noise and wind to Tapirawa-teri, the tribe had lost its garden, its plantains and its cassava, and since they didn't want to light a fire and attract enemies, they had gone hungry for several days. While Kate tried to exchange information with Iyomi and the other women, Professor Leblanc, fascinated, questioned Tahama about their customs and war arts. Nadia, who was called on to translate, realized that Tahama had a wicked sense of humor and was telling the professor a series of fantasies. He told him, among other things, that he was the third husband of Iyomi and that he had never had sons, which demolished Leblanc's theory about the genetic superiority of alpha males. In a near-at-hand future, the stories Tahama told would be the basis for another book by the famous Professor Ludovic Leblanc.

The next day, the People of the Mist, with Iyomi and Walimai in the lead, and Tahama and his warriors bringing up the rear, led the *nahab* back to Tapirawa-teri. A hundred yards from the village, they saw the corpse of Captain Ariosto, which the Indians had left wedged between two large branches of a tree to be picked clean by animals and birds, treatment for those who did not deserve a funeral ceremony. The body was so mangled by the claws of the Beast that the soldiers did not have the stomach to take it down and carry it with them to Santa María de la Lluvia. They decided they would come back later and recover the bones for a Christian burial.

"The justice of the Beast," Kate murmured.

César Santos directed Timothy Bruce and Alexander Cold to collect the soldiers' weapons, which were scattered around the camp, to prevent another outbreak of violence in case someone got nervous. It was not likely that would occur, however, because the smell of the Beasts lingered enough that they were all subdued. Santos saw to it that the supplies were loaded into the helicopter, except for the tents, which were buried because he didn't think it was possible to get rid of the smell. Timothy Bruce recovered his cameras and several rolls of film from among the debris, although Captain Ariosto had exposed the film he had commandeered. Alex found his knapsack, and inside, unharmed, the bottle containing the water of health.

The expedition party was in a hurry to get back to Santa María de la Lluvia, but they did not have a pilot, since one helicopter had come with Captain Ariosto at the controls and the other pilot had taken back the wounded. Santos had never flown one of these machines, but he was sure that if he could fly his broken-down airplane, he could manage this. The moment had come to say good-bye to the People of the Mist, which included exchanging gifts, the custom among the Indians. The *nahab* gave up belts, machetes, knives, and cooking utensils, while the Indians produced feathers, seeds, orchids, and necklaces of animal teeth. Alex gave his compass to Tahama, who put it around his neck as adornment, and the warrior gave the American boy a handful of darts dipped in curare and a three-meter-long blowgun, which Alex could barely find room for in the cramped helicopter. Iyomi again grabbed Kate and shouted something at the top of her lungs, and the writer responded with the same passion in English. At the last instant, as the *nahab* were hurrying to climb into the bird of noise and wind, Walimai handed Nadia a small basket.

CHAPTER TWENTY

Separate Ways

THE FLIGHT BACK TO Santa María de la Lluvia was a nightmare because it took César Santos more than an hour to get the hang of the controls and stabilize the helicopter. During that first hour, no one thought they would reach civilization alive, and even Kate, who was as cool as a deep-sea fish, had bid her grandson farewell with a firm handshake.

"Good-bye, Jaguar. I'm afraid this is as far as we go. I'm sorry your life had to be so short," she told him.

The soldiers were praying aloud and drinking liquor to calm their nerves, while Timothy Bruce showed his deep concern by lifting his left eyebrow, the thing he did when he was about to explode. The only persons who were truly calm were Nadia, who had lost her fear of heights and trusted in her father's firm hand, and Ludovic Leblanc, who was so airsick he had no sense of their danger.

Hours later, after a landing as gripping as the takeoff, the members of the expedition could finally find some relative calm in the miserable hotel in Santa María de la Lluvia. The next day they would go back to Manaus, where they would take planes to their countries. They would make that trip down the Río Negro, the same way they had come, because César Santos's plane refused to leave the ground despite the new engine. Joel González, Timothy Bruce's assistant, whose condition was much improved, would be going with them. The nuns had improvised a plaster cast that immobilized him from neck to hips, and they predicted that his ribs would heal without consequences, although possibly the poor soul would never recover from his nightmares. He dreamed every night that he was in the coils of an anaconda.

The nuns also assured them that the three soldiers' wounds would mend. Fortunately for them, the arrows had not been poisoned. On the other hand, Mauro Carías's future looked dim. Tahama's blow had damaged his brain, and in the best scenario he would be confined to a wheelchair for the rest of his life, fed through a tube, his mind in the clouds. He had already been transported to Caracas in his own airplane, accompanied by Omayra Torres, who would not leave him for an instant. The woman had no idea that Ariosto had died and could not protect her any longer; nor did she suspect that as soon as the foreigners told the story of the fake vaccine she would have to face the authorities. Her nerves were shattered. She kept repeating that it was all her fault, that God had punished Mauro and her for the measles virus. No one understood what she was talking about, but Padre Valdomero, who went to offer spiritual counsel to the wounded man, paid attention and took note of her words. The priest, like Karakawe, had suspected for a long time that Mauro Carías had some plan to exploit the Indians' lands, but had not discovered what it was. The doctor's apparent ravings gave him the key.

While Captain Ariosto was in command of the barracks, the entrepreneur had done whatever he wanted in the territory. The missionary had been powerless to unmask those men, although for years he had reported his suspicions to the Church. His warnings had been ignored because he lacked proof, and also because some considered him half crazy. Mauro Carías had made a point of spreading the rumor that the priest had talked nonsense ever since being kidnapped by the Indians. Padre Valdomero had once traveled to the Vatican to denounce abuses against the native peoples, but his superiors in the Church had reminded him that his mission was to carry the word of Christ to the Amazon, not to get involved in politics. He had returned defeated, asking himself how he could try to save souls for heaven without first saving lives on earth. And beyond that, he wasn't certain about the propriety of Christianizing the Indians, who had their own form of spirituality. They had lived in harmony with nature for thousands of years, like Adam and Eve in Paradise. Why, Padre Valdomero wondered, was it necessary to teach them the concept of sin?

When he learned that the *International Geographic* party was back in Santa María de la Lluvia, and that Captain Ariosto had died, the missionary called at the hotel. The soldiers' versions of what had happened on the altiplano were contradictory; some threw the blame on the Indians, others on the Beast, and there was one who pointed a finger at members of the expedition. Whatever the case, without Ariosto in the picture, there was at last a small opportunity to see justice done. Soon another military man would be in charge of the troops, and there was no guarantee that he would be any more honorable than Ariosto. He, too, might succumb to bribes and crime, as happened all too often in the Amazon.

Padre Valdomero turned over the information he had gathered to Professor Ludovic Leblanc and Kate. The idea that Mauro Carías had generated epidemics with the help of Dr. Omayra Torres and protection from an officer of the army was a crime so horrible that no one would believe it without proof.

"The news that they are massacring Indians in that way would enrage world opinion. It's a shame we can't prove it," said the writer.

"I think we can," César Santos interjected, taking from a jacket pocket one of the vials of the supposed vaccine.

He explained that Karakawe had managed to slip it from the doctor's luggage shortly before he had been murdered by Ariosto.

"Alexander and Nadia surprised him looking through the boxes of vaccines, and though he threatened to hurt them if they told, they reported it to me anyway. We thought that Karakawe had been sent by Carías; we never dreamed he was a government agent," Kate said.

"I knew that Karakawe was working for the Department for the Protection of Indigenous Peoples, and that was why I suggested Professor Leblanc hire him as his personal assistant. That was a way for him to go on the expedition without raising suspicion," César Santos explained.

"So you used me, Santos," the professor protested.

"You wanted someone to fan you with a banana leaf and Karakawe wanted to go on the expedition. No one was the loser, Professor." The guide smiled, and added that Karakawe had been investigating Mauro Carías for many months and had a thick file regarding the man's dark dealings, especially the way he was exploiting the lands of the Indians. Surely he suspected the relationship between Mauro Carías and Dr. Omayra Torres, and that was why he had decided to follow where she led.

"Karakawe was my friend, but he was a quiet man and never said more than what was absolutely necessary. He never told me he suspected Omayra," said Santos. "I imagine he was looking for the clue that would explain the mass deaths of the Indians, and that was why he stole one of the vials of vaccine and gave it to me to keep in a safe place."

"With this, we should be able to prove their sinister history in spreading epidemics," said Kate, holding the small bottle against the light.

"I have something for you, too, Kate," and Timothy smiled as he showed her the rolls of film in his hand.

"What's this?" she asked, intrigued.

"These, old girl, are images of Ariosto murdering Karakawe at point-blank range, of Mauro Carías destroying the vials, and of the Indians being shot. Thanks to the good offices of Professor Leblanc, who distracted the captain for half an hour, I found the time and opportunity to switch rolls before those chappies destroyed them. I gave Ariosto the film from the first part of the trip and saved these," Timothy Bruce reported.

Kate had a reaction unusual for her. She threw her arms around Santos and Bruce in turn, and gave both a kiss on the cheek.

"Blessings on you, lads!" she exclaimed, overjoyed.

"If this contains the virus, as we believe, Mauro Carías and that woman are guilty of genocide and will have to pay for it," murmured Padre Valdomero, holding the small vial in his fingertips, his arm extended as if he feared the poison would jump out in his face.

It was he who suggested that they establish a foundation for the purpose of protecting the Eye of the World, and especially the People of the Mist. With Kate's eloquent pen and the international prestige of Ludovic Leblanc, he was sure they would succeed, he explained enthusiastically. They would need financial backing, it was true, but among them they would succeed: they would go to churches, political parties, international organizations, governments . . . They would knock on every door until they found the necessary funds.

They had to save the tribes, the missionary insisted, and the others were in agreement with him.

"You, Professor, will be the president of the foundation," Kate offered.

"Moi?" asked Leblanc, genuinely surprised and enchanted.

"Who better than you? When Ludovic Leblanc speaks, the world listens . . . ," said Kate, imitating the anthropologist's pompous tone, and they all burst out laughing—except for Leblanc, naturally.

Alexander and Nadia were sitting on the dock of Santa María de la Lluvia, where some weeks before they had held their first conversation and begun their friendship. As on that occasion, night had fallen, with its croaking frogs and screeching howler monkeys, but this time there was no moon. The sky was dark and dotted with stars. Alexander had never seen a sky like that; he had never imagined there were so many thousands of stars. The young people felt as if they had lived a lot of life since they met; they both had grown and changed in those few weeks. They sat without talking, staring at the sky, brooding over the fact that soon they would go their separate ways, until Nadia remembered the little basket she was bringing to her friend, the same basket Walimai had given her as they left. Alex took it with reverence and opened the top; inside shone the three eggs from the sacred mountain.

"Keep them, Jaguar. They are very valuable; they are the largest diamonds in the world," Nadia whispered to him.

"These are diamonds?" Alex asked, frightened, afraid to touch them.

"Yes. They belong to the People of the Mist. According to what I saw in my vision, these eggs can save the Indians and the rain forest where they have always lived."

"Why are you giving them to me?"

"Because you were named chief to negotiate with the *nahab*. The diamonds will help you do that," she explained.

"Oh, Nadia! I'm just a fifteen-year-old. I don't have any power in the world; I can't negotiate with anybody, even less be responsible for this fortune."

"When you get to your country, give them

to your grandmother. She will know what to do with them. She seems to be a very powerful woman, and she will help the Indians," the girl assured him.

"They look like glass. How do you know they're diamonds?" he asked.

"I showed them to my father. He knew immediately. But no one else must learn about them until you are in a safe place, or they'll be stolen. You understand, Jaguar?"

"I understand. Has Professor Leblanc seen them?"

"No, only you, my papa, and me. If the professor knew, he would go running to tell the whole world," she declared.

"Your papa is a very honest man. Anyone else would have kept the diamonds."

"Would you?"

"No!"

"Well, neither would my papa. He didn't want to touch them. He said they carry bad luck, that people kill for those stones."

"And how am I going to get them through U.S. Customs?" asked Alex, hefting the weight of the magnificent stones.

"In your pocket. If anyone sees them, they'll

450

think they're Amazon tourist souvenirs. No one would suspect that diamonds of this size exist, certainly not in the pocket of a kid with half his head shaved." Nadia laughed and ran her hand over the bald crown of Alex's head.

For a long time they were silent, looking at the water below their feet, and the shadowy vegetation around them, sad because in a very few hours they would have to say good-bye. They felt that nothing as extraordinary as the adventure they had shared could ever again happen in their lives. Nothing could compare to the Beasts, the city of gold, Alexander's voyage to the depths of the Earth and Nadia's climb to the nest of the marvelous eggs.

"My grandmother has been assigned to write another article for *International Geographic*. She has to go to the Kingdom of the Golden Dragon," Alex commented.

"That sounds as interesting as the Eye of the World. Where is it?" she asked.

"In the mountains of the Himalayas. I would like to go with her, but . . ."

Alex realized that another trip would be nearly impossible. He had to get back into his normal life. He had been gone for several weeks. It was time to go back to class or he would lose the school year. He also wanted to see his family and hug his dog, Poncho. He especially wanted to deliver the water of health and Walimai's herbs to his mother. He was sure that with them, in addition to the chemotherapy, she would get better. Having to leave Nadia, however, really hurt. He wished that dawn would never come, that he could stay forever with his friend, beneath the stars. No one in the world knew him so well; no one was as close to his heart as this honey-colored girl whom he had met, as if by magic, at the ends of the Earth. What would she be like in the future? Would she grow up wise and wild in the jungle, thousands of miles from him?

"Will I see you again?" Alex sighed.

"Of course!" she said, hugging Borobá with feigned happiness, so that Alex wouldn't see her tears.

"We'll write, won't we?"

"Let's say the mail around here isn't the very best . . ."

"It doesn't matter. Even if letters take a long time, I'm going to write to you. For me, the greatest thing that happened on this trip was meeting you. I will never, ever forget you; you will always be my best friend," Alexander promised, his voice quivering.

"And you will be my best friend, too—as long as we see each other with our hearts," Nadia replied.

"Until we meet again, Eagle . . ."

"Until then, Jaguar . . ."

ALEX AND NADIA'S ADVENTURES
CONTINUE IN

Kingdom of the Golden Dragon

❖

THE BUDDHIST MONK named Tensing and his disciple, Prince Dil Bahadur, had been climbing in the high peaks north of the Himalayas for many days, a region of eternal ice where no one but a few lamas had ever ventured. Neither of the two was counting the hours, because time did not interest them. The calendar is a human invention; time does not exist on the spiritual level, the master had taught his student.

For them it was the crossing that was important; the prince was making it for the first time. The monk remembered having done it in a previous life, but those memories were rather blurred. They were following the markings on an ancient parchment, orienting themselves by the stars in a terrain where even

1

in summer conditions were very harsh. The temperature of several degrees below zero was endurable only two months during the year, when ominous storms were not lashing the mountains.

Even beneath the sunny, cloudless skies, the cold was intense. They were wearing rough wool tunics, and cloaks made from yak hide. Leather boots from the same animal covered their feet, with the long hair turned in and the outside weather-proofed with yak butter. The travelers placed each foot with care; one misstep on the ice and they could tumble hundreds of yards into the deep chasms that sliced through the mountains as if cleft by God's hatchet.

Luminous snowy peaks stood out against a sky of deep blue. The travelers moved at a slow pace, because at those heights there was very little oxygen. They rested frequently, so their lungs would become accustomed to the altitude. Their chests ached, as did their ears and their heads. They were suffering from nausea and fatigue, but neither of the two mentioned such bodily weakness, saving their breath in order to get the maximum benefit from each mouthful of air.

They were searching for rare plants found only in the Valley of the Yetis, plants essential in preparing medicinal lotions and balms. If they survived the dangers of this journey, they would consider themselves initiated, for their characters would be tempered like steel. Their will and courage would be put to the test many times during that climb. The disciple would need both will and courage to carry out the task that awaited him in life, which was why he had been given the name Dil Bahadur, "brave heart" in the language of the Forbidden Kingdom. The pilgrimage to the Valley of the Yetis was one of the last steps in the harsh training the prince had been undergoing for twelve years.

The youth did not know the true reason for their trek, which was much more important than the gathering of curative plants or his initiation as a lama, or superior being. His master could not reveal it to him, just as he could not speak to him of many other things. Tensing's role was to guide the prince during each stage of his long apprenticeship; he was charged with strengthening the young man's body and his character and cultivating his mind, testing the quality of his spirit again and again. Dil Bahadur would discover the reason for the journey to the Valley of the Yetis later, when he found himself before the fabled statue of the Golden Dragon.

On their backs, Tensing and Dil Bahadur were carrying bundles that contained the blankets, grain, and yak butter they would need to survive. Rolled around their waists were coils of yak-hair rope, which they used in climbing, and in one hand each grasped a long, strong walking staff, which they used for support, for defending themselves in case of attack, and for setting up their improvised tent at night. In places where experience had taught them that fresh snow often covered deep openings, they also used their staffs to test the depth and firmness of a surface before stepping onto it. Frequently they were forced to make long detours around fissures that couldn't be jumped over. Sometimes, to avoid going out of their way for hours, they laid one of the staffs across the crevasse, and only when they were sure it was firmly seated on either side did they dare step onto it and then leap to the other side—never more than one step, because the risk of plummeting into empty space was too big. They made such leaps without thinking, with their minds clear, trusting in physical skill, instinct, and luck, because if they stopped to weigh each move it would be impossible to make it. When the opening was wider than the length of the staff, they looped a rope around an overhanging rock, then one of them tied the other end of the rope around his waist, took a running start, and leaped, swinging back and forth like a pendulum until he reached the other side. The young disciple, who had great stamina and courage in the face of danger, always hesitated at the moment they were forced to use those methods.

The pair had come to such a chasm, and the lama was looking for the best place to cross. The youth briefly closed his eyes, sending a prayer skyward.

"Do you fear dying, Dil Bahadur?" Tensing inquired, smiling.

"No, honorable master. The moment of my death was written in my fate before my birth.

5

I shall die when my work is finished in this reincarnation and my spirit is ready to fly, but I do fear breaking all my bones down there, and living," the youth replied, pointing to the impressive precipice yawning at their feet.

"That could, perhaps, present a problem," the lama conceded with good humor. "If you open your mind and heart, it will seem easier," he added.

"What would you do if I were to fall?"

"Should that occur, I would possibly have to think about it. For the moment, my thoughts are turned to other things."

"May I know what, master?"

"The beauty of the panorama," the lama replied, indicating the endless chain of mountains, the immaculate white of the snow, the brilliant sky.

"It is like the landscape of the moon," the youth observed.

"Possibly . . . What part of the moon have you visited, Dil Bahadur?" the lama asked, hiding another smile.

"I have not traveled that far as yet, master, but I imagine it like this."

"On the moon, the sky is black and there

are no mountains like these. There is no snow, either; everything is rock and ash-colored dust."

"Perhaps someday I shall be able to make an astral voyage to the moon, like my honorable master," the disciple conceded.

"Perhaps . . ."

After the lama positioned his staff, both took off their tunics and cloaks, which kept them from moving freely, and made four bundles of their belongings. The lama was built like an athlete. His shoulders and arms were pure muscle, his neck was as broad as a normal man's thigh, and his legs as thick as tree trunks. That formidable warrior's body contrasted markedly with his serene face, gentle eyes, and delicate—almost feminine—and always-smiling mouth. Tensing took the bundles one by one, built up momentum by rotating his arm like the vanes of a windmill, and tossed the bundles to the other side of the chasm.

"The fear is not real, Dil Bahadur; it is only in your mind, like all other things. Our thoughts form what we believe to be reality," he said.

"At this moment, my mind is creating a very

7

deep crevasse, master," the prince murmured.

"And my mind is creating a very strong bridge," the lama replied.

He waved to the youth, who stood waiting in the snow, then took one step above the void, planting his right foot at the middle of the wood staff and a fraction of a second later throwing himself forward, reaching the other side with his left foot. Dil Bahadur imitated him with less grace and speed, but gave no sign of nervousness. The master noticed that his student's skin was gleaming with sweat. They quickly dressed and resumed walking.

"Is it much farther?" Dil Bahadur wanted to know.

"Possibly."

"Would it be imprudent, master, to request that you not always answer 'possibly'?"

"Perhaps it would." Tensing smiled, and after a pause added that, according to the instructions on the parchment, they were to continue north. The most difficult portion of their path lay ahead.

"Have you seen the Yetis, master?"

"They are like dragons, they shoot fire from their ears and they have four pairs of arms."

8

"Amazing!" the youth exclaimed.

"How many times have I told you not to believe everything you hear? Seek truth for yourself," the lama laughed.

"Master, we are not studying the teachings of Buddha, we are simply talking." The disciple sighed, annoyed.

"I have not seen the Yetis in this life, but I remember them from a previous one. We share common ancestors, and several thousand years ago they had a civilization almost as developed as our own, but now they are very primitive and of limited intelligence."

"What happened?"

"They are very aggressive. They killed each other and destroyed everything they had, including the land. The survivors fled to the peaks of the Himalayas and there their race began to decline. Now they are like animals," the lama explained.

"Are there many of them?"

"Everything is relative. They will seem to be many if they attack us and few if they are friendly. In any case, they do not live very long lives but they reproduce easily; therefore I suppose there will be a number of them in the

9

valley. They live in an inaccessible region where no one can find them, but sometimes one of them ventures out in search of food and gets lost. That is possibly the source of the tracks attributed to the Abominable Snowman, as he is called," the lama put forward.

"Their footprints are enormous. They must be giants. Will they still be very aggressive?"

"You ask many questions for which there are no answers, Dil Bahadur," the master replied.

Tensing led his disciple through the mountain peaks, leaping chasms, scaling vertical faces, slipping along narrow paths cut into the rock. Occasionally they came across old hanging bridges, but they were in very poor condition and could be used only with great care. When there was wind or sleet, they looked for shelter and waited. Once a day they ate their *tsampa*, a mixture of toasted barley flour, dried herbs, yak butter, and salt. They found abundant water beneath the crust of ice. Young Dil Bahadur often had the impression that they were walking in circles, because the landscape looked the same, but he said nothing about his doubts: it would be discourteous to his master.

As evening fell, they looked for a sheltered place to spend the night. Sometimes it was nothing but a rift in which they could find comfort protected from the wind, other nights they might find a cave, but occasionally they had no choice but to sleep out in the open, barely shielded by their yak cloaks. Once they set up their austere camp, they sat facing the setting sun, legs crossed, and chanted the essential mantra of Buddha, repeating over and over *Om mani padme hum*—Hail, precious jewel in the heart of the lotus. The echo would repeat their prayer, multiplying it to infinity among the high peaks of the Himalayas.

During the day's march they gathered sticks and dried grasses, which they carried in their pouches for building the nightly fire and for cooking their food. After the evening meal, they meditated for an hour. During that time the cold left them stiff as ice statues, but they scarcely felt it. They were used to such immobility, which brought them calm and peace. In their Buddhist practices, master and student sat in absolute relaxation, but remained alert. They rid themselves of all the distractions and worries of the world, though they never forgot the suffering that existed everywhere.

After scaling mountains for several days and climbing the frozen heights, they came to Chenthan Dzong, the fortified monastery of the ancient lamas who had invented the form of hand-to-hand combat called Tao-shu. In the nineteenth century, the monastery had been destroyed by an earthquake and had to be abandoned. It was built of stone, brick, and wood, with more than a hundred rooms that seemed glued to the edge of an impressive cliff. For centuries the monastery had housed monks whose lives were dedicated to spiritual quest and to perfecting the martial arts.

The Tao-shu monks had originally been physicians with an exceptional knowledge of anatomy. In their practice they had identified vulnerable points of the body that were numbed or paralyzed when pressed, and they combined that knowledge with techniques of wrestling known in Asia. Their objective was to reach spiritual perfection through control of their own strength and emotions. Although they were invincible in hand-to-hand combat, they did not use the Tao-shu for violent ends, only as a physical and mental exercise. Similarly, they did not teach their art to just anyone, only to certain chosen men and women. Tensing had learned Tao-shu from those monks, and he had taught it to his disciple Dil Bahadur.

The earthquake, snow, ice, and the passage of time had eroded most of the building, but two wings were still standing, although they were in ruins. The travelers had reached the monastery by climbing a precipice so difficult and remote that no one had attempted it for more than half a century.

"Soon they will come to the monastery by air," Tensing observed.

"Do you believe, master, that they will discover the Valley of the Yetis from airplanes?" the prince inquired.

"Possibly."

"Imagine how much effort could have been saved. Before long we could have flown here."

"I hope that it will not be so. If they trap the Yetis, they will turn them into circus animals, or slaves," the lama said.

They went into Chenthan Dzong to rest

and to spend the night in its shelter. Threadbare tapestries with religious images still hung on some of the walls, and they found cooking vessels and weapons the warrior monks who survived the earthquake had not been able to take with them. There were several representations of Buddha in varying postures, including an enormous statue of the Enlightened One lying prone on the ground. The gilt had cracked away, but the remainder of the statue was intact. Ice and blowing snow covered nearly everything, lending the ruins a particularly beautiful aspect, as if it were a crystal palace. Behind the building, an avalanche had created the only level surface in the area, a kind of courtyard about the size of a basketball court.

"Could an airplane land here, master?" asked Dil Bahadur, unable to disguise his fascination with the few modern apparatuses he knew.

"I know nothing of these things, Dil Bahadur. I have never seen an airplane land, but it seems to me that this space is very small, and besides, the mountains act like a funnel, drawing strong air currents."

In the kitchen they found pots and other

iron implements, candles, charcoal, sticks for making a fire, and some grains preserved by the cold. There were also vessels for holding oil and a container of honey, which the prince had never seen. Tensing gave him a taste, and for the first time in his life the prince felt something sweet on his tongue. The surprise and the pleasure nearly knocked him off his feet. They built a fire for cooking and lighted candles before the statues, as a sign of respect. That night they would eat well and they would sleep beneath a roof: the occasion merited a special brief ceremony of thanks.

They were meditating in silence when they heard a low moan echoing through the ruins of the monastery. They opened their eyes just as a rare white tiger padded into the ruined room, a half-ton of muscle and white fur, the fiercest animal known to the world.

Telepathically, the prince received his master's command, and tried to obey, although his instinctive reaction had been to call on Tao-shu and leap up to defend himself. If he could get close enough to reach behind the cat's ears, he could paralyze it; he sat motionless, however, trying to breathe calmly so the beast would not pick up the scent of fear. The huge feline slowly advanced toward the monks. Despite the imminent danger in which he found himself, the prince could not help but admire the animal's extraordinary beauty. Its fur was a pale ivory with dark markings, and its blue eyes were the color of some of the glaciers in the Himalayas. It was an adult male, enormous, powerful, a perfect specimen.

Sitting in the lotus position with legs crossed and hands upon their knees, Tensing and Dil Bahadur watched the tiger move toward them. They both knew that if it was hungry, there was little possibility of stopping it. Their hope was that the animal had eaten, although it was not very likely that game was abundant in these barren solitudes. Tensing possessed uncommon psychic powers because he was a *tulku*, the reincarnation of a High Lama of antiquity. He concentrated that power like a beam to penetrate the beast's mind.

They felt the breath of the great cat on their faces, an exhalation of warm, fetid air escaping from its jaws. Another terrible roar shook the air. The beast approached to within a few inches of the two, so close that they could feel the prick of its stiff whiskers. For several seconds, which seemed eternal, it circled around them, sniffing them and feinting with one enormous paw, but not menacing them. The master and his disciple sat absolutely motionless, leaving themselves open to warmth and compassion, displaying no fear or aggression, only empathy. Once the tiger's curiosity had been satisfied, it left with the same solemn dignity with which it had come.

"You see, Dil Bahadur, how sometimes calm is effective," was the lama's only comment. The prince was unable to answer because his voice had frozen in his breast.

Despite that unexpected visit, master and student decided to stay and spend the night in Chenthan Dzong, but they took the precaution of sleeping near a bonfire, and of keeping within reach a couple of lances they found among the weapons abandoned by the Taoshu monks. The tiger did not return, but the next morning, when they continued their march, they saw its paw marks on the gleaming snow, and far away they heard its roars echoing among the peaks.